ADDITIONAL PRAISE FOR
THE BARKERY & BISCUITS MYSTERIES

Bite the Biscuit

"Recipes for both dogs and people add enjoyment in this clever cozy that will taste just right to fans of both foodie and pet mysteries."

—*Booklist*

"Kicking off a cozy new series, prolific Johnston blends mystery and romantic intrigue."

Kirkus Reviews

"An enjoyable myste  *Book Reviews*

To Catch a Treat

"A mystery to delight dog lovers."

—*Booklist*

"A tale filled with fun, mystery and excitement."

—*Suspense Magazine*

"This sophomore outing is as delightful as its predecessor."

—*Library Journal*

Bad to the Bone

"Veteran Johnston has her formula down."

—*Kirkus Reviews*

"This cozy will appeal to fans of Susan Conant's Dog Lovers' series and is also reminiscent of Joanne Fluke's Hannah Swensen novels."

—*Booklist*

"Dog lovers (not to mention lovers of great mysteries) will be thrilled to see this third book in the fantastic series."

—*Suspense Magazine*

— A BARKERY & BISCUITS MYSTERY —

FOR A GOOD PAWS

LINDA O. JOHNSTON

MIDNIGHT INK
WOODBURY, MINNESOTA

FIRST EDITION
First Printing, 2019

Book format by Samantha Penn
Cover design by Ellen Lawson / Shannon McKuhen
Cover illustration by Christina Hess

Midnight Ink, an imprint of Llewellyn Worldwide Ltd.

Library of Congress Cataloging-in-Publication Data
Names: Johnston, Linda O., author.
Title: For a good paws / Linda O. Johnston.
Description: First edition. | Woodbury, Minnesota : Midnight Ink, [2019] |
    Series: A barkery & biscuits mystery ; #5
Identifiers: LCCN 2018059339 (print) | LCCN 2018060790 (ebook) | ISBN
    9780738755946 (ebook) | ISBN 9780738752440 (alk. paper)
Subjects: | GSAFD: Mystery fiction.
Classification: LCC PS3610.O387 (ebook) | LCC PS3610.O387 F67 2019 (print) |
    DDC 813/.6—dc23
LC record available at https://lccn.loc.gov/2018059339

Midnight Ink
Llewellyn Worldwide Ltd.
2143 Wooddale Drive
Woodbury, MN 55125-2989
www.midnightinkbooks.com

Printed in the United States of America

3361408141411448

As with the other books in this series and just about everything that I write, *For a Good Paws* is dedicated to people who love their pets. And to those pets, who are so important to their human family members.

For a Good Paws is also dedicated to you, my readers, who enjoy mysteries, including those involving pets and food.

And, yes, for those of you who read other things I've written, you know I always dedicate each book to my dear husband Fred.

ONE

"GOOD MORNING, CARRIE!" MY assistant Dinah Greeley's voice sounded even more exuberant than usual as I turned to see her close the kitchen door behind her.

"Good morning, Dinah. Happy birthday!" Was her special day the reason she seemed so jazzed? I assumed so.

"Thanks," she said.

"Hope you don't mind working on your day of celebration."

"I love it," she replied. "And I'm really looking forward to tonight."

"Me too." I'd already invited her to a celebratory dinner at the Knobcone Heights Resort that evening, along with my other assistants and a few more people.

Now I tossed her a big smile that matched her own but didn't stop kneading the dough for some of my favorite carob-flavored dog biscuits, next on the agenda for me to bake.

I was standing on the Barkery and Biscuits side of the kitchen's long, stainless-steel counter, which was divided by center shelves that separated the Barkery half of the room from the Icing on the Cake side. The kitchen was connected at the front end to both of my bakeries. Since one shop sold healthy dog treats, which I created, and the other side sold sweets for people, I kept what we baked as separate as the stores.

At six a.m., the kitchen already smelled delightful from the people treats. And, as always, I listened for any sounds from my beloved dog Biscuit, who was loose in the still-closed Barkery. But she stayed silent.

"By the way, sorry I'm a little late." Dinah headed to the supply cabinet at the back of the kitchen and put her purse on the bottom shelf.

"That's forgivable on your birthday," I said. "I've got cookies baking already for Icing, but I'd love for you to start on the red velvet cupcakes." They were among our most popular products for people, and I wanted to make sure we had plenty to start the day.

"Sure." As per standard protocol, Dinah grabbed one of our long, clean aprons from a hook on the wall and put it on over her *Barkery and Biscuits* T-shirt and jeans. Then she spent some time washing her hands at the large sink against the wall near the door to the Barkery. Only then did she grab ingredients from the fridge and kitchen shelves. Finally, she faced me across the counter.

What did that huge-eyed, enormous grin still on her round face mean? Was she *that* happy it was her birthday?

Maybe so, but I suspected it was something more.

Dinah's slight pudginess always suggested how much she enjoyed sampling our baked goods. She was a pretty young lady, and I was delighted that she continued to work for me. I'd inherited her over a year ago when I bought Icing from my dear friend, Brenda Anesco, who had to move down the mountain from Knobcone Heights to care for her ailing mother. Brenda had been very supportive of my turning half of her former shop into my Barkery.

Although I had other assistants, Dinah was now my only full-time one. She did take two days off a week, although she occasionally worked overtime and stepped in for others on Monday and Tuesday. Today was Wednesday.

In a few minutes, Dinah was kneading dough, too, though our respective ingredients were quite different. She didn't say anything more at first, but something in the way she kept aiming giant smiles at her busy hands made me ask, "So what's going on, Dinah? Are you smiling that way because you're happy it's your birthday?"

"That's part of the reason," she responded without explaining further.

My curiosity had snapped into high gear, however. Knowing Dinah and what appeared to make her happy, I hazarded a guess. "Have you been doing any research lately?"

In addition to being a wonderful assistant here in my shops, Dinah enjoyed writing. She'd had a few articles published online, as well as a short story or two, but I knew she'd been working on some longer fiction as well.

"I sure have." This time her vast, toothy smile was aimed toward me. "And there's been an amazing twist in what I've been checking out."

Aha. I'd guessed it—sort of. But with Dinah, my guess hadn't been difficult to come by. "What's the twist?"

"Well ..." The pace of her kneading increased, as if she was revving up to say something highly significant.

To her, it undoubtedly was.

"That doesn't sound very amazing," I prompted.

"Oh, but—well, Carrie, this morning while I was getting dressed I turned my TV on, and the most astonishing coincidence occurred—kind of."

"What's that?" I again prompted, as she seemed to hesitate. Was she trying to torment me into pushing her, or was her mind circling around whatever that new coincidence was?

"Amazing!" she said again. But this time she continued. "There was a teaser on KnobTV news that said Mike Holpurn was being paroled." Her blue eyes were huge again as she studied my face for a reaction.

"Who's Mike Holpurn?" I had to ask. The name didn't sound familiar.

She shook her head slightly, as if in exasperation, but then sighed and said, "I forgot you're a relative newbie to Knobcone Heights. I only moved here after graduating from college—but ever since I got here, I've been researching the town's history, or part of it at least."

"So Mike Holpurn is a historical figure?" One who was being paroled, evidently … but why had he been incarcerated, and where? I had no doubt that Dinah knew the particulars.

"Kind of." Dinah had pulled out a rolling pin, as I had, and was now flattening her dough, too. "Here's the story that I've found so far."

She proceeded to explain that Mike Holpurn had been a contractor for a home-building company in this area. But he'd been sent to prison around ten years ago after entering into a plea bargain—for apparently murdering former Knobcone Heights Mayor Flora Morgan Schulzer.

"I've been researching it because it's so fascinating," Dinah finished. "I'm considering turning a fictionalized version of it into a novel—and the fact that the guy got parole? Wow! How can I resist? Especially since I may even be able to interview him!"

I'd vaguely heard of the mayor and her murder, which occurred about five years before I'd moved to Knobcone Heights. Dinah's desire to interview the apparent perpetrator didn't sound like a good idea to me. I liked my able assistant—a lot.

Plus, I'd found myself in danger now and then lately, when I'd snooped into several murders that had occurred in our otherwise quiet town. I didn't want anything to happen to Dinah.

"You can, and should, resist," I told her. "I doubt someone in that situation would want to talk about it. And—is he getting out because someone else is now a suspect?"

"I don't know," Dinah said. "That's one of the things I need to learn."

"You don't *need* to," I said. "And—"

Just then, the door from our parking lot opened again and another of my assistants, Janelle Blaystone, walked in. She and my brother Neal were an item, and since Neal lived at my house with me but hadn't come home last night, I suspected Janelle had left him at her house early this morning as she headed to work.

"Hi," she called out immediately. "Happy birthday, Dinah."

"Hi, Janelle." Dinah shot her a smile and raised her eyebrows as she looked back at me.

I gathered that she wanted our conversation to end. Which was fine with me. For now.

But if Dinah really was going to try to research that long-ago murder in person, with a paroled convict who was now loose . . . well, we would discuss it again.

She could be sure of that.

All three of us talked briefly for a while about Dinah's birthday, what was already baking in the oven, what treats I'd been working on most recently, and what Dinah had just started on.

We also talked about the time for the party, the anticipated weather this August day, and what kinds of crowds we could anticipate in each of our shops . . .

Neither Dinah nor I mentioned the news item that had excited her so much, but I could still see the anticipation in her eyes when she looked at me . . . and, occasionally, at her wristwatch. Was she anticipating her party that much? More likely, she was trying to figure out a time to return to talking about what really interested her at the moment. And as far as I could tell, time was passing at its usual rate.

I soon ceded my place in the kitchen to Janelle, so that I could stick the dog treats I'd been working on in the appropriate oven to bake. Then I moved my newly baked people cookies out of another oven to cool before they were put into the display case in Icing.

Next, I needed to check on Biscuit.

"I'll be back in a few minutes," I told my assistants. My other two helpers, Vicky and Frida, weren't scheduled to work that day, though they would join us at the resort in the evening. All but Dinah were part-timers, and with Vicky's able assistance I was able to schedule and keep track of who would be around when.

After removing my apron and hanging it up, I washed my hands again and left the kitchen, heading into the Barkery.

Barkery and Biscuits was my favorite of the two shops. It was my own creation, just like the recipes for the treats I sold there. When I opened the door, I was immediately greeted by my adorable golden toy poodle/terrier mix, Biscuit. She sped to me across the blue tile floor, which had a beige decoration in the center that looked like— yes—a dog biscuit. When she reached me she stood on her hind legs, her paws on the legs of my jeans as she greeted me.

"You weren't by yourself very long," I reminded her, even while smiling at the excitement of her greeting. I knelt and hugged her, then stood again and patted her head. Checking the clock on the wall, I saw we still had a half hour before opening time, so I hugged her once more. "It's not time yet for you to go into your enclosure," I told her.

Leaving her loose, I took a couple of sanitary wipes from the counter behind the glass-fronted display cases and cleaned my hands, then went around to the front of these refrigerated cases to assess again the treats we already had there. I would wash my hands more carefully when it was time to actually move any of my products.

Earlier, I'd removed the items that, although edible, were getting too old to sell. I placed them in boxes I'd take to either Knobcone

Veterinary Clinic, where I still worked as a vet tech, or to Mountaintop Rescue, our local shelter. I had a shift scheduled at the vet clinic that afternoon.

Thinking about it reminded me of my discussion with Dinah, since my boss at the clinic, Dr. Arvus—Arvie—Kline was a longtime resident of Knobcone Heights. I wondered what he might be able to tell me about the murder of that mayor a while back...

Yes, my curiosity had been piqued. I felt certain I'd hear enough about the situation from Dinah if I gave her the slightest encouragement. Which I would do, as long as it didn't affect her ability to concentrate on her work at the bakery—or at least, no more than it already had. And this would also give me more opportunity to discourage her from doing anything dangerous.

For now, I peeked out my shop's front window. Daylight had arrived and there were cars on Summit Avenue in front of the stores, but I didn't see any people walking by. That was fine. I hoped, though, that some would appear once we were ready to open.

"Okay," I finally told Biscuit. "You stay here." It was time to remove my first batch of dog treats of the day from the oven and bring out the cookies I'd baked for Icing. After I was done with that, it would be time to walk Biscuit before putting her into her open-topped enclosure at the far side of the Barkery.

First thing, back in the kitchen, was to wash my hands again. Or maybe that was the second thing, since I immediately began eavesdropping on the conversation Dinah and Janelle were having.

No, it wasn't about the murdered mayor or the apparent parole of the person incarcerated for killing her. Nor was it about Dinah's birthday. They were discussing, appropriately, some recipes for sugar cookies, a standard of Icing.

"Hey, Carrie," Janelle said. "I was wondering if you'd be interested in trying a new version of sugar cookies. I saw this recipe online on a site that's devoted to healthy sweets."

"An oxymoron," I said right away, but I listened to her suggestions for changing the recipe we used. When she was done, I said, "Well, feel free to bake us a batch, but I'm reluctant to change something that's been selling well. And I don't think our Icing customers are too concerned about healthfulness. Although..."

"Although we could maybe start a section of Icing that we'd call something like our 'Healthier Alternatives,'" Dinah piped up.

"I don't think so," I said. "That would suggest that our other products are unhealthy. If they turn out well, and we like them enough to sell some, let's just give them another name.

In a few minutes, my assistants and I brought the morning's first newly baked items into the appropriate shops and placed them in the display cases. A little while later, we brought out the new cookies, too. Yes, we liked them. I decided to just call them "lighter" sugar cookies. If they sold well, we would make more.

Full daylight shone through the windows, and our clocks told us it was quarter to seven.

"Okay, sweetheart," I said to Biscuit. "Let's go for a short walk." Which we did. When we returned, it was opening time.

Several people, a couple with dogs, had followed us back to the Barkery, while a few more had headed for Icing. I placed Biscuit into her enclosure and opened both shop doors.

Our day had begun.

I helped serve our customers, gave out a few samples to canine customers in the Barkery, and felt happy that the day seemed to be going great. The first to get free goodies that morning included canine customers who came to my shop often, such as Dog, a

Doberman owned by my neighbor, Bob, and Morocco, a fuzzy Chihuahua who, as always, arrived in the arms of her owner, Lonnie. Lonnie was clearly generous with treats. I made sure everyone had a sample or two before choosing what to buy.

As much as I preferred hanging out in the Barkery, I always divided my time between the two shops. So, leaving the Barkery in Dinah's capable hands, I headed over to Icing on the Cake. Yes, Dinah seemed to be concentrating on her work, despite her birthday and her obsession with researching the news about the paroled killer.

I didn't see any of our regulars in Icing that morning but also gave out free samples there, including some of our new cookies, which seemed to be a hit. Janelle gave some samples out as well. Icing was her primary focus that day. Like Dinah, Janelle had a secondary career—I often saw her studying our patrons as if she were determining how they'd look in a portrait. Pretty Janelle, with her big blue eyes, was a distinguished photographer as well as a wonderful assistant in my shops ... and a really sweet girlfriend to my brother.

Not to mention, a former murder suspect I'd helped clear. Just like I'd cleared several others—myself included.

I helped pack up cookies and cupcakes as people bought them, then rang up their orders at the register. I spent a half hour or so at Icing, chatting with customers and enjoying it, as always.

Then it was time to return to the Barkery.

Dinah seemed to have things well under control, even though the shop was delightfully crowded. As I entered, a guy came in with two golden cocker spaniels on leashes—he was someone I didn't recall seeing before. And even if I didn't remember him, I'd have remembered his dogs.

"Hi," I said, greeting him. "Welcome to Barkery and Biscuits."

"Thanks," he said. "Nice shop."

"I think so," I said with a grin. I introduced myself as the owner of both the Barkery and Icing, and gave his dogs—Duke and Prince—some introductory treats. He introduced himself as Henry.

He bought a nice selection of biscuits and other treats for his dogs, which made me happy. The dogs seemed happy, too, and even on their leashes they traded nose sniffs with Biscuit in her enclosure.

"Thanks a lot," Henry said as they got ready to leave.

"Thank you," I countered. "Come back anytime."

"We will," he said, and then they left.

As the morning progressed, things slowed a bit, which was okay with me. In addition to having a shift to do at the vet clinic that afternoon, I had an urge to go get a quick cup of coffee at Cuppa-Joe's, my favorite hangout in Knobcone Heights—mostly because its owners, whom I called the Joes, were like substitute parents to me.

I needed a dose of their presence, just because.

And so around eleven that morning, I checked with both Janelle and Dinah. They were fine with my leaving for an hour or so. I put my beloved Biscuit on her leash and we headed out the door.

The summer air was warm, which was not surprising, but fortunately it wasn't too hot. I allowed Biscuit to take her time as she sniffed the sidewalk along Summit Street, and also in the town square across the street from the stores. My dog enjoyed the park area, with its grass and knobcone pine trees, and as usual I figured she'd like to spend more time there. Instead, we kept walking.

Cuppa-Joe's wasn't far away, just on the other side of the square along Peak Road. It consisted of a one-story sprawling building, with a couple of patios outside and in the center. With Biscuit along I generally preferred finding a spot on a patio, although ever since the Joes adopted their adorable dog Sweetie, who also hung out at the shop a lot, it wasn't always necessary.

Sure enough, when I walked inside the large main room that smelled like—what else?—coffee, with Biscuit beside me, I saw Sweetie, who kind of resembled my pup, lying in her usual corner beneath a table. Joe and Irma Nash, a.k.a. the Joes, sat at that table.

They weren't alone. Several people sat with them, and a few others stood around them. Interesting. Their place was often busy, but I didn't recall ever seeing the Joes so engaged in conversation with so many customers.

Some tables in the room were available, but I didn't choose one. Instead, I approached the Joes. Not that I anticipated a place would open up for me there, but I wanted to at least say hi.

Irma saw me coming, and she stood up and gestured invitingly. I smiled, and Biscuit and I kept walking in that direction while avoiding tables, chairs, and other people. In the meantime, Irma had apparently said something to one of the guys with them, since by the time I got there he had stood up, stolen an empty chair from a nearby table, and put it down for me.

I knew it was for me because Joe had stood up, too, and held out his arms for a hug before telling me to have a seat.

Both Joes were in their sixties. They'd seemed to adopt me as one of their kids when I'd first arrived in Knobcone Heights. Joe looked his age, with receding gray hair and lots of wrinkles on his face that I chalked up to the fact that he was nearly always smiling. Irma, on the other hand, resembled a lovely senior model, with perfect makeup and stylishly cut and highlighted brown hair. Today, both wore casual jeans with slightly more formal shirts tucked into them. Joe's shirt was gray, and Irma's was a frilly peach.

"Hi." I raised my voice to be heard over the loud rumble of conversations throughout the room. "Good to see both of you. All of you," I amended. A few people around the table were occasionally customers at my shops, too. But I was of course happiest to see my dear buddies the Joes.

"You too, dear." Irma, sitting beside me, reached over and squeezed my hand. When people began talking again around us, I quickly realized that her gesture was simultaneously one of affection and a request for me to be quiet.

What was that about?

I found out quickly.

"Does he have any family around here?" asked Mr. Harbin, a tall guy with thin shoulders. I didn't know his first name, but I remembered that his dog was named Remus. Harbin had brought him into the vet clinic a couple of months ago with injuries from a car accident. I believed the dog was okay. But I wondered who Harbin was talking about.

I figured it out nearly immediately. Someone else at the table, a woman I hadn't met, gave a shudder. "You don't really think he'll come back to Knobcone Heights, do you?"

"Where else would he go?" Harbin asked. "He lived and worked here before. Unless he's got family someplace else, I bet we'll be seeing him around. Maybe a lot."

I glanced at Irma, and she turned her head to look at me.

"Are we talking about—"

"Mike Holpurn," she finished. "The man who's about to be paroled."

TWO

So word was spreading in this town. Not that I was surprised. Dinah had seen it mentioned on TV that morning, and she wouldn't have been alone.

But all the hoopla about it concerned me even more.

"Can anyone tell me about this Mike Holpurn and what happened with him?" I asked, breaking into another conversation that had erupted beside me about whatever family or other contacts Holpurn might still have in this area. I was interested in that topic—but first I wanted to hear more about what occurred back then.

Since Holpurn had confessed to the murder of the mayor as part of his plea bargain, he had to be guilty. But why had he done it?

And why, after admitting it, was he being paroled after only ten years?

Would his parole, and possible return to this area, cause any problems in town? Any danger?

Maybe I was worrying too much—but I'd gotten involved in solving local murders lately, too many of them. I had no interest in having any more deaths occur around me … especially if a convicted murderer showed up.

I hadn't spoken loudly, but suddenly all attention around the table seemed focused on me: from the Joes and Mr. Harbin, four other men, and a couple of women.

"You mean you don't know?" asked the woman sitting catty-corner to me. She didn't look familiar so I assumed she didn't have a pet, or at least not one that would have brought her to my Barkery or vet clinic. And I didn't recall seeing her at Icing, either. She appeared around the Joes' age.

I shook my head. "I've lived here for about five years, and I gather that whatever happened involving Holpurn occurred a while before that."

"Yeah, about five or six years before," Harbin said. "It was one very nasty situation."

"It sure was," said another guy, standing behind Irma at my side.

But I still wasn't learning anything. I looked at Joe, then Irma. "I'd like to hear about that nasty situation," I said. "I gather the mayor he killed was a woman." The current mayor of Knobcone Heights was also a woman, Sybill Gabbon, and I knew her a bit because she'd recently adopted a couple of dogs from Mountaintop Rescue, at one of the adoption events we'd held in the Barkery.

"That's right," Irma said—and that was when the server Kit, whom I genuinely liked, happened to come over at the wrong time to take my order. In her mid-twenties, she had cute, curly blond hair and pink cheeks, and as usual she wore a knit shirt with a coffee cup logo on the pocket, a yellow one today.

Fortunately, Kit apparently recognized that it wasn't a great time to do more than find out what I wanted. "Coffee and cream today?" she asked—which was currently my usual.

"Yes, please," I said.

Kit quickly surveyed the others around the table. All either had cups or glasses in front of them or in their hands. "Anyone else?" she asked nevertheless.

Everyone was fine, and Kit hurried off.

I looked back at Irma expectantly, hoping she got the message and would describe what had happened in the past with Holpurn. It wouldn't necessarily explain what was going on in the present, with his parole, but it would start to answer my questions.

But it was Joe who started talking next. "Here's the situation as I recall it." His expression, as he looked at the others around us, didn't encourage anyone to interrupt him with their recollections, at least not yet.

He proceeded to talk about Mayor Flora Morgan Schulzer, who'd been the first female mayor of Knobcone Heights. "She was a nice lady," Joe said.

"She sure was," Irma broke in, and Joe didn't shush her even with a look. "She used to come here a lot and even hold official meetings and parties here now and then."

"Best I recall," Joe continued as Irma finished, "she was having the mayor's residence renovated. It's a nice-looking mansion with historical significance around here, but it needed some upgrades. Maybe it needs more now, but—anyway, the city hired our biggest and presumably best local construction company, Knobcone Construction, to do the work." He paused. "Mike Holpurn was one of its employees. He was in management, as I recall, but he also did some of the construction work."

The rest of the story flowed from him, and I didn't think I was the only one staring at Joe raptly. Apparently the mayor had gotten appropriate approvals to have the renovations done at the city's expense. They'd put the job out for bid, and the esteemed local construction company had provided the best quote. The work was started, and the mayor and her husband moved into a city-funded condo while it was being worked on.

"But Mayor Flora was apparently a stickler for things to be done as she mandated," Joe said. "That was the case regarding city business. I remember some of the controversies in the news back then, from the time she assumed the office. And her precision and criticism apparently carried over to her residential project."

Not many people got to see how things were going, Joe said, but apparently there were issues regarding the updating of some of the rooms, including the kitchen, living room, and master bedroom, that the mayor criticized harshly after insisting she be allowed to observe what was going on.

My coffee arrived then, and I thanked Kit while Joe pointed at his own nearly empty cup. Kit nodded, and some of the others around us also requested refills of their drinks.

While orders were being given, I pondered what Joe had said so far, and my mind raced ahead to where this was probably going: The mayor had disparaged what the contractor—represented at the site by Holpurn—was doing. Obviously, Holpurn wouldn't be happy about it, whether or not she was correct. Maybe he'd even criticized her back. That wouldn't be surprising, I thought. Again, whether or not the mayor was in the wrong.

But to murder her for it?

My thoughts were definitely engaged as I waited to learn more. For surely there had to be more to it.

But there wasn't. Or at least not in the story Joe told. Critical Mayor Flora had visited the site often, spent some time there, and let the world know of her displeasure, plus other things she wished to have fixed.

Management at the construction company—higher-ups to Mike Holpurn—had criticized her in response, which didn't cause her to back down in the least. Apparently just the opposite. But some rumors had circulated, too, about what she thought of the workers.

Then one day, when the mayor visited the site, she didn't return to her office on time. Her staff started looking for her ... and finally located her. Her body was found in the torn-apart master bedroom of the residence being remodeled. She had been skewered by a large screwdriver.

"There was a lot of horror around here then," Joe said, and Irma nodded vehemently. "The police investigated, and everyone at the company was considered a suspect for a while."

"Everyone the mayor knew was a suspect," Irma insisted. This turned out to be a good time for Kit and other servers to bring a coffee pot and additional containers to refresh the rest of the drinks, including mine. Plus, I ordered a tuna salad wrap that I ate quickly, since I had a shift at the veterinary clinic that afternoon and otherwise wouldn't have time for lunch.

The conversation wound down, though I realized that the usual loud hum of discussion in the rest of the coffee shop had stopped, as others also were listening to Joe's description.

He didn't know what had led Mike Holpurn to finally admit his guilt and enter a plea. His prison sentence was for much longer than ten years, as Joe recalled. It was for life.

But that had apparently changed.

I didn't think I was going to learn much more as the discussion morphed into speculation about Holpurn's motive for killing and for entering into a plea bargain. Nor could I tell myself exactly why I cared. Just for Dinah's research? No.

But the fact that a situation like this, complete with a murder, captured my attention really bothered me. I hadn't intended to turn into an amateur sleuth. It had just sort of happened to me.

Well, at least this time I didn't need to try to find the killer. He'd already been found and sent to prison. The fact that he was now paroled was interesting, but it really wasn't my concern.

Even so, I hung around for a few more minutes, reaching down to pet Biscuit more frequently since she seemed to be getting restless. Was it just from hanging out there, or did she have something she needed to do?

Either way, I used her as my excuse. I pulled my wallet from my small purse and extracted money for my coffee, wrap, and a generous tip, then placed it on the table and rose.

"Bye, everyone," I called. Then, to the Joes, I added, "I'll want to hear if anyone reaches a conclusion about ... well, any of this. Biscuit and I will be back soon."

"I hope so," Irma responded, blowing me a kiss.

"You'd better," Joe grumped, then smiled.

Biscuit and I headed around tables to the coffee shop's door, then hurried across the town square back to my shops. Stopping, of course, now and then as Biscuit insisted.

The park within the town square wasn't very crowded, despite it still being summer vacation for local kids, but Summit Avenue was crowded with cars and the sidewalks along both sides were busy. We nevertheless made good time getting to the Barkery, which had quite a few patrons now, many with dogs. Some of the people peered into our display cases, and others sat at the few tables eating treats from Icing and feeding their dogs treats from the Barkery.

I quickly shut Biscuit into her enclosure and approached the counter, where Dinah was busy serving customers and taking care of their purchases. "Hi," I said. "Has it been this busy since I left?"

She glanced at me, holding a white bag of dog treats. "Pretty much." Then she turned back to the customer facing her over the counter and handed the bag to her. "Here you are. I hope Jojim likes it all." She leaned over and looked at the terrier mix that sat on the floor beside the T-shirt-and-jeans-clad lady.

"I'm sure he will. You were so sweet and generous with the samples." The lady looked at me, apparently recognizing that I was in charge, and I just smiled.

"So glad he got to try some," I said, in essence patting my assistant on the back for what she'd done.

And it had clearly been good. This lady's order seemed extensive.

Soon she had placed her chipped credit card into the reader to pay, and then, after Dinah gave her a receipt, she left, Jojim leashed at her side.

A few more people with dogs had been peering into the glass display case. Fortunately we still had a good supply of treats. I went behind the counter to bring out a few samples, and as I passed behind Dinah I had to tell her, "No time to talk about it now, but it seemed like everyone at Cuppa's was talking about … the subject of your research this morning."

Her round face lit up as she grinned in surprise. "Really? Wow, I'll want to hear all about it."

"Not much to say," I told her, "but we'll talk later."

I doubted I'd have much time to discuss it, though, before I had to leave again, this time for my shift at Knobcone Veterinary Clinic. Well, I'd be with Dinah in the evening—but I didn't really want to talk about a murder at her birthday party.

We'd figure out sometime to talk soon, though. I felt sure of it. Dinah wasn't one to give up on anything regarding research.

For now, though, I headed into Icing to see how Janelle was doing there. That shop was busy, too, which made me happy. Since it was August, there weren't any holidays around the corner to make people feel obligated to load up on cupcakes or cookies or other treats, like with Christmas or Halloween. Therefore these folks must be here because they liked our products—enough to brave the crowds on a normal weekday. Or because they were all planning to come to Dinah's party at the resort tonight … not likely. I'd invited several people, of course, and Dinah might have invited others as well, but I hadn't issued an open invitation to the world.

I helped Janelle for a while. She reminded me that the new, "lighter" sugar cookies were a hit, and I agreed that we should make them often.

When only a few people remained in line to buy Icing treats I told Janelle, "I need to head out for my shift at the clinic. Do you feel you have things under control?"

"I sure do. You go ahead."

I gave her a quick hug, then went back into the Barkery, where things were now a bit quieter than in Icing. I told Dinah, as she finished up with a customer, where I was going.

"I figured," she said. "Have fun, and we'll see you later. Oh, and I really, really want to talk to you about what you heard at Cuppa's about the … research." She glanced toward the person facing her in line, and I was glad she hadn't been more specific.

"Sure," I said, but I wasn't sure at all about how we'd fit that in. I took Biscuit out of her enclosure again and leashed her for our next outing.

We drove this time, since I was running a little late—but even more so because I figured I'd be in a big hurry to get back after my shift. I wouldn't close the shops early, but I wanted to be sure I had plenty of time to finish up in the bakeries for the day and get to the resort to prepare for the party.

Also, I'd packed up some of our Barkery dog treat leftovers, which I'd take to Mountaintop Rescue before returning to the shops later, and it would take much too long for Biscuit and me to do all that by walking.

I drove my usual route: down Pacific Street, past the town square and Peak Road where Cuppa's was. Then came Hill Street, where the Knobcone Vet Clinic was located, and it didn't take us long to get there.

After we parked in the rear lot, as usual, and headed through the back door, Biscuit led me down the hall to the daycare area. It was a large room with a gleaming beige linoleum floor—easy enough to clean if any visitors had an accident. Along the walls were various-sized crates, used when any of those visitors didn't play well with others.

I was greeted immediately by Faye, who called "Hi, Carrie" from where she sat in the middle of the floor. She was surrounded by a bunch of her charges for that day—dogs of many sizes and colors. She was in her forties and very energetic, which she had to be to ensure the pets left in her care had fun. She had assistants, of course, but I only saw Al with her that day, and not Charlie. Of course, both those young guys only worked in the daycare part-time, since they were still in school deciding whether or not to become veterinarians. Al's shirt today was black, and like most shirts he wore, it said *Knobcone Vets Rock*.

I headed in their direction and unleashed Biscuit, who immediately began playing with her counterparts. "Thanks," I called to Faye and Al, pointing to Biscuit and waving to them as I left.

I strode down the otherwise empty inside hall to the room where I could change into my vet tech scrubs and lock my purse in my locker. Then I headed to the reception area to check in. Yolanda, one of the longest-term techs at the clinic despite only being my age, was in charge, which wasn't a surprise. She also was organized, which made her a good fit for the front desk assignment.

Right now, Yolanda sat behind the desk at one side of the room looking at her computer screen. Checking the schedule, I figured. She wore a blue uniform shirt like mine. As usual, her black hair was pulled back into a bun at her neck, which emphasized the sharpness of her face.

The rest of the waiting room was crowded, people in all the seats with dogs or cats beside them or in their laps, and Yolanda stared straight at me as I walked in. "Good," she said. "Dr. Kline could use your help right now."

"Fine," I told her—not that I expected her to give me a choice. She told me the exam room he was in, and I headed that way immediately.

Dr. Arvie Kline was a good buddy of mine, another pseudo parent for me in this town, and the most senior veterinarian at the clinic. I was delighted to be working with him first that day.

I walked into the exam room without knocking, since I figured he was expecting a vet tech to be assigned to him.

"Carrie!" he exclaimed immediately. "Good timing. I need your help holding Duke and Prince for their shots." Duke and Prince were golden cocker spaniels, and I'd seen them in my shops that morning.

I glanced up at their owner before I knelt to pick up the first dog to put on the table for Arvie to inoculate. I'd seen him in the Barkery, too. "Hi," I said and smiled. The man had introduced himself to me then. As I recalled, his name was Henry.

His return smile appeared ... well, unhappy. "You're the lady from the dog treat shop, right?"

"That's right." I picked up warm, fuzzy, and fortunately not too heavy Duke and placed him on the metal table in the center of the room as Arvie got the DHPP, which included distemper and three other diseases, and Bordetella—kennel cough—shots ready. "I hadn't seen you before so I assumed that this morning was your first time there. Here, too? Are you and your pups new to Knobcone Heights?"

Arvie, preparing to stick the needle into the dog I controlled, gave me a look I could only describe as weird. What was he trying to tell me?

I could guess the answer when the patients' parent replied, "Yes, as to the dogs. No as to me. I used to live here."

"That's right," Arvie said. "Henry, let me introduce you to our bakery shops' owner, Carrie Kennersly. And Carrie, let me introduce you to Henry Schulzer."

"Good to officially meet you," I said, holding on tighter as Duke struggled. But my mind was still at work.

Schulzer. Why did that name sound familiar?

And then I remembered. The one-time mayor of Knobcone Heights who'd been murdered. Hadn't her name been Flora Morgan Schulzer?

THREE

Both Duke and Prince were perfect gentlemen—er, gentledogs—as they received their shots. Almost. They wriggled a bit as I tried to hold them still, especially as they felt the needles go in. But no nips, no attempts to get away, just sweet spaniel acceptance.

I couldn't turn to look at Arvie as he gave the shots. I mostly stared at the shelves holding veterinary supplies along the exam room's back wall. As I moved the dogs onto the table and off, though, I glanced at Henry Schulzer. I'd noticed before that he was a tall, thin guy with loose facial skin and a slight, scruffy gray beard that matched his short hair. I caught his glance twice before looking away, and I managed to smile at him.

Was he the former mayor's widower? The name fit, and possibly his age did, too. I wanted to ask whether I was right, and if so, why did he happen to be in town now, when his wife's murderer was apparently being paroled? Could it be a coincidence? The news had been reported that morning, and who knew if Mike Holpurn would come back to Knobcone Heights anyway?

Did Schulzer know any of this?

And why was I suddenly obsessing over this situation? Dinah was the researcher, not me. I'd had my fill of nosing around murders.

The appointment was soon over. I said, as Henry began to leave with his dogs, "I hope to see you in the Barkery again soon. I'd say the same about this office, too, but that would mean one of your dogs has a health issue." I made myself grin. I was trying to be funny, after all—sort of.

It became clear that I wasn't going to get answers to any of my questions here, or maybe anywhere.

"Right," Henry said. "See ya."

Arvie, too, prepared to leave the room but after Henry and his dogs were gone, I looked at him with a "can we talk?" expression. He knew what it meant, so he closed the door.

"How are you doing, Carrie?" he asked with a curious look on his aging, intelligent, and totally aware face. But I knew there were a lot more questions behind the basic one.

"Okay, but…Do you know who that man is—or was?"

"If what you're asking is do I know that Henry is our former mayor's widower, the answer is yes." His light brown eyes appeared amused beneath his wispy silvery hair. He shoved his hands into the pockets of his white medical jacket. "That was a sad situation, around ten years ago, I think. He moved away with their kids shortly after the murder but returned a month or so ago. He brought his dogs in at that point for a brief physical, but I think he was just letting some of his former contacts know he was back. The mayor used to breed cockers who were sometimes our patients, and Duke and Prince are descendants of them. I gather that Henry also breeds occasionally, but he doesn't have any females now."

"Really? What does he do for a living? And where's his home?"

"I don't know the answer to either of those questions," Arvie said with a slight shrug of his narrow shoulders. "I gather, though, that his wife's life insurance was generous, plus he might have received some kind of stipend from the city. It's possible he doesn't need to work now. Of course, I don't know where he and his kids lived in the interim, or whether he might have worked then. And his home here? I gather he's not settled in to anyplace long-term. At least that was what was on the form he filled out when he brought his dogs here a few weeks ago."

The fact that Henry had apparently been in Knobcone Heights for a few weeks appeared to indicate that he hadn't returned simply because Mike Holpurn was being released. Of course, I had no idea how long the parole decision might have been pending, or who might have known about it besides the authorities.

Well, none of it should matter to me. Nor *did* it matter to me, except that my curiosity still kept pawing at my mind.

Oh. It occurred to me that Arvie might not know about Holpurn's release. "I doubt this is related," I told him, "but there was a news story on TV this morning that the mayor's killer is being, or has been, paroled."

"Really?" Arvie's eyes went wide. He clearly hadn't heard this yet. "Holpurn?"

"Yes," I said, and briefly explained how I'd heard it first from Dinah, and then in discussions at Cuppa's.

"Wow," Arvie said. "I wonder if Henry knows this."

I had no idea, of course—but somehow, I figured he did.

———

I stayed with Arvie to help with several more patients, but eventually I wound up in another exam room with one of the clinic's other veterinarians, Dr. Reed Storme.

The guy I was pretty much an item with.

Reed and I had been seeing each other socially for months, and we'd grown even closer when I'd helped to find the last murderer in town, a case in which Reed had been the primary suspect. We'd acknowledged, then, that we needed to talk sometime about our future, and we had, a bit. But we hadn't reached any conclusions.

Yet I was happy with things the way they were. We were seeing each other exclusively and often—and not only here at the clinic.

I helped him do an annual physical on a cat who was a longtime patient of the clinic. The cat seemed right at home, as did the owner, who asked questions about Arvie and Dr. Paul Jensin, as well as Dr. Angela Regles, who had recently retired.

And the cat? She checked out just fine. In fact, quite healthy for her thirteen years.

As I'd done with Arvie, I waited in the exam room with Reed while the patient and her owner left. I closed the door this time.

"Everything okay?" Reed asked. We didn't usually hang out one-on-one at the clinic, despite how much we did elsewhere.

"Sure," I said brightly. Then I added, "If you don't count some strange goings-on about town."

Reed had been standing beside the metal-topped table in the middle of the room. Now he approached me quickly and grabbed the tops of my arms gently.

He was one great-looking guy. His nearly black hair contrasted well with his white lab jacket, and though his face was fully shaved, a hint of dark beard showed under his skin. He had high cheekbones, and I'd always considered the planes and shadows of his perfect face similar to those of a movie hero.

"Dare I ask you to tell me about those goings-on?" he asked, looking down, straight into my eyes. "And if you tell me there's been another murder, I'll hang on to you till I'm sure you'll keep out of any investigation."

"That's not what you said last time," I reminded him with a grin. Reed had even encouraged me to get involved since he was the main suspect. Of course, he'd changed his mind as things turned somewhat dangerous, but that hadn't stopped me. And he did have me to thank for figuring out who really was guilty.

"That was then. Different circumstances. Or at least I assume so. No one has accused me of murder lately."

"That's a good thing." I stood on my toes and gave him a quick kiss on his sexy mouth.

He kissed me back ... for a nice, longer time.

"So what's going on?" he asked when we both broke away. After all, we were at work.

I told him quickly the little bit I knew—about Mike Holpurn's parole and Henry Schulzer's return. "More to come, I assume," I said. "And yes, there's a murder involved, but it was solved years ago, as well as occurred long before I moved here."

"Good. Then there's nothing for you to get involved with."

A knock sounded on the exam room's door, and with a regretful grin I backed away from him and opened it. Yolanda stood there, a guy with a shepherd mix behind her. "Oh, Dr. Storme, are you available now to check out a dog with some tooth issues?" She sounded all professional veterinary technician, but the look she leveled first on Reed and then on me was both amused and accusatory, as if she believed something risqué and inappropriate was going on.

"Absolutely," he said. "Can you stay to help?" he asked me.

"Unfortunately my shift is over and I need to return to the shops," I told him. "But will I see you tonight at the resort for Dinah's birthday celebration?" I'd already invited him.

"Count on it," Reed said, with a raise of his brows that suggested the possibility of multiple celebrations.

After hanging my scrubs in my locker, I went to the daycare area to get Biscuit. We had one stop to make before returning to the shops. I'd already left a nice-sized bag of leftover treats from the Barkery in the reception area for fellow vet tech Kayle, the guy now on duty as receptionist, to pass out to dogs waiting to be seen, but I'd brought another bag along, which I now retrieved from my car. Those were for Mountaintop Rescue.

Our town's only animal shelter was a couple of blocks east of the clinic, also on Hill Street, an easy walk. I encouraged Biscuit to hurry since I didn't have a lot of time before I needed to return to my bakeries, and I hoped to at least get the opportunity to say hi to Billi—Wilhelmina—Matlock, assuming she was there. Billi was one busy lady, even busier than me, with her three careers compared with my two. She ran the wonderful shelter, owned a successful day spa, and was a member of the Knobcone Heights City Council.

It didn't take Biscuit and me long to get to the pleasant, gold-colored stucco building. It was a couple of floors high, with windows decorated with attractive tile.

I opened the front door, and Biscuit and I walked into the main building. Behind it were other structures secured by fences, where the hopefully temporary resident animals were housed. But I wasn't going to visit them on this trip. I didn't have time—and I knew they were well cared for here.

The receptionist was Mimi, as usual. She was young and sweet and busty, and always wore a shirt with an appropriate message. Today's was a blue one that said, *Dogs leave paw prints on your heart.* She was alone in the reception room working on the computer—most likely checking on the current dogs and cats and their known backgrounds, or looking on various sites to see if any other shelters had room or excess animals needing temporary homes.

"Hi, Carrie," she said immediately. "And hi, Biscuit." Her tone changed to dog-love mode as she stood and looked down at my pup, and that made me smile.

Mimi was behind the chest-height wooden reception desk that kept visitors out till they were welcomed inside—which I always was. I placed the bag of treats I'd been carrying on top of the desk.

"Thanks," Mimi said with a grin. "I know a lot of residents here are going to be very happy this afternoon and evening."

"I hope so. Is Billi here?"

"Sure. I'll call her for you." But as she picked up the cell phone on her desk, Billi appeared at the top of the wooden stairway on the right-hand side of the reception area.

"Hi, Carrie," she called and hurried down the stairs toward me. Billi was a slender and fit woman—not surprising, since she not only owned but also worked out at the Robust Retreat, a highly posh day spa. This was one of her relaxed days, I assumed, since she often dressed in her city councilwoman mode but today wore a long-sleeved T-shirt over her jeans. When she reached me, we shared a hug, and Biscuit got one, too. Billi glanced at the bag on the counter. "You brought us some treats?"

"I sure did." I paused only momentarily. "Do you have a few minutes?"

The expression on her lovely face appeared slightly puzzled, though welcoming. "Come on upstairs."

I didn't intend to stay long but also didn't want to ask questions in front of Mimi. "Thanks," I said, and Biscuit and I followed her.

At the top of the stairs, she led me down the hall and into her office—and as always, I got a kick out of the sign on the door: *Councilwoman Wilhelmina Matlock, Boss of the City, Canines, and Cats.* I sat down quickly on one of the wooden chairs on the antique area rug, facing her highly professional-looking desk. Biscuit sat by my feet.

"So what's going on, Carrie?" she asked immediately.

"Let me ask first: Were you around here when Mayor Flora Morgan Schulzer was killed?"

"Murdered, you mean. And yes I was." Billi's pretty, deep brown eyes narrowed. "Surely you aren't getting involved with that murder. It was solved, even though the killer is apparently being paroled."

So she knew about it. "That's the point," I told her, and briefly described my day so far as it related to Mike Holpurn being in the news, Dinah seeing it, people at Cuppa's talking about it, Henry Schulzer showing up at the vet clinic when I was there ... and I felt exhausted as I finished. "I know that's too much information, but though I'm not involved at all with this, it seems to have taken over my life for today."

"There's nothing for you to worry about, Carrie." Billi stood and came around her desk to hug me as I stood, too. "And you need to let something else take over the rest of the day for you, like Dinah's birthday party." I'd invited Billi, too.

"Sounds good," I said ... but couldn't help asking, "Did you feel justice was done back then? I mean, if the man confessed to the murder, why is he getting out now?"

"We on City Council were informed of the impending release just yesterday," she said. "We were told that Holpurn has been an exemplary inmate and all sorts of crap like that, but no real reason was given as to why a confessed murderer is getting paroled so soon. I imagine we'll hear more about it—in the media, at least— even if we don't get any actual explanation."

"Then you do think something is wrong?"

Billi shrugged her shoulders beneath her T-shirt once again. "Something is different. But wrong? We don't know enough to believe that—although I suspect it. And since we don't know if Holpurn is returning to town, it might not be a big deal in Knobcone Heights

... even though it was our mayor who was killed all those years ago. I wasn't on City Council then, but from what I understood, yes, justice was served, and Holpurn was believed to be guilty even before he confessed. And—" The look she leveled on me appeared to be a glare at first, but then she softened it. "I'm not sure why you're feeling so involved with this, but it's over. It's in the past. It's not a murder like the ones you've helped to figure out. So please, Carrie—and I'm acting official now, as a City Council member—assume that all's well and don't get involved."

"Oh, I won't," I assured her. "I only found out about it because Dinah was doing some research for her writing and heard the news on TV. Sure, I find it interesting—but there's nothing for me to do even if I wanted to. Which I don't."

We said our farewells then, with Billi regarding me skeptically.

Biscuit and I left a few minutes later to walk back to the clinic for my car. I drove us to the parking lot behind my shops, and I was busy with the bakeries till our regular closing time.

But Dinah kept looking at me questioningly. She knew what I'd heard at Cuppa's, of course, but not that I learned that one of our customers at the Barkery earlier that day happened to have been married to the murdered mayor. I'd have to tell her eventually, since she would be fascinated by it and incorporate it into her research.

But for now, it was time to stay busy selling the day's baked goods, and then get ready for Dinah's birthday party that night.

FOUR

AFTER CLOSING THE SHOPS right on time that evening, I hurried home to change clothes and feed and walk Biscuit, who wasn't joining us for the party. Biscuit was never any trouble at the resort restaurant, but I didn't want to have to worry about where she was in what I anticipated would be a nice-sized crowd. And since I was the hostess, I wanted to concentrate on making sure everyone had fun. As a result, Biscuit was staying home.

Dinah left the shops a little early, as I'd encouraged her to do. I let her know she didn't have to get too dressed up—unless she really wanted to. This was her celebration, after all. "If you could get there around seven," I told her, "that would be great."

And me? I was aiming for six thirty, although I expected to arrive a little later than that.

I actually pulled into the resort parking lot at about six twenty-five. Yes, I'd hurried, and it was just as well I hadn't seen any cops on the road on the short ride over. I'd made it even shorter, though I'd remained careful.

The several long rows of parking were nearly filled, but I was lucky enough to pull up near someone leaving their spot, not far from the resort's main entrance. I smiled as I drove into the space. Surely this was a harbinger of a fun evening to come. My brother, who worked at the reception desk, would sometimes get me a parking validation, which was always great since parking in the lot was expensive. But I decided to not even ask him. I was, after all, a hostess that evening.

The resort consisted of several sprawling buildings, each two stories high. They all had sloping slate roofs over thick white walls, and lots of windows trimmed with dark wood. The outer buildings mostly consisted of hotel rooms, while the middle building was the largest and contained the resort's main features: a restaurant, a bar, a spa, and a walkway to the Knobcone Lake beach. I couldn't see the lake from the parking lot, but I knew we would have a great view of it from the restaurant, at least till it got dark. And then we'd see lights reflecting on the water.

I headed toward the reception desk and saw that fortunately, Neal wasn't busy. I often had to just wave and move on when visiting the resort. Tonight, I had some questions for him, so I was glad to be able to stop and talk.

The reception desk was on the right side of the lobby area, and Neal managed to keep it fairly neat. The lobby itself was large, with high slanted ceilings and multiple seating areas surrounding tall stone fireplaces. The wall nearest to me as I walked in was lined with offices, and along the opposite wall were the restaurant, bar, and spa, which overlooked the lake on the far side.

I'd seen the lobby filled with a lot more people than were there that evening, but it was still crowded and a bit noisy.

"Hi, bro," I said, and Neal looked up from the computer where he was working. As always when I saw my brother, I felt as if I was viewing a version of myself. We both have the Kennersly longish nose and blunt chin, as well as somewhat-sharp cheekbones. We both have blond hair. Neal keeps his hair short, and he usually has a shadow of a light beard on his cheeks and chin.

Me? At thirty-three, I'm four years older than him. I've added some pale highlights to the Kennersly blond hair and wear my waves mid-length to frame my face. And no shadow of a beard here.

"Hi, sis." Neal smiled at me, then added, "And before you ask, yes, your reservations in the dining room are in order. I checked. And they've even baked the birthday cake you wanted." He shook his head as if still surprised about this, but I'd explained that I wanted something different for Dinah than what we baked and sold in Icing. She could—and probably did—always taste our products, and since this was a special day, she was entitled to something surprising. So were the rest of us.

"Great," I said. "Thanks. I'll go wait there for the guests. Do you know if anyone has come yet?"

"Not sure. And—well, you invited me, remember. I'll be off the clock here in about fifteen minutes and will join you then."

"Great," I said again, then turned and made my way through people and seating areas to the back wall of the lobby, where the restaurant, spa, and other amenities were located.

I entered the restaurant through the arched doorway from the lobby and looked around. The side to my right was crowded, with nearly all the tables occupied and several servers walking between them, but to the left there was a large area that was nearly empty of people. The tables had been pushed together to make one long one, with pristine white tablecloths gleaming on top of it.

Two people sat there already—my assistants who hadn't been on duty today, Frida Grainger and Vicky Valdez. They both waved as I headed their direction.

35

"Good to see you both," I told them as I reached the table. They had taken seats toward the middle, which was good. Dinah's place would be at the head of the table, and I'd sit beside her.

"Good to see you too," Vicky said. "How was business today?" Vicky was the chief scheduler at both my shops. She'd lived in the San Bernardino Mountains all her life but only recently moved to Knobcone Heights. Her dark eyebrows, arched over her deep brown eyes, were visible over the top of her thick glasses. I regularly counted on her administrative skills and was glad she was scheduled to come in tomorrow.

"Pretty good," I told her. "Did you enjoy your day off—both of you?"

I glanced at Frida, whose particular talent was in cooking and baking. As always, her brown hair was pulled back into a ponytail, even though she was dressed in a frilly blouse, not the shirts she usually wore to work. Frida clearly enjoyed her own cooking, since she was a little plump. She'd graduated from the Art Institute of California and worked as a chef, but then married a man who was now an assistant manager at a supermarket in Knobcone Heights— a fortunate thing for me. She still did a lot of cooking and creation of non-treat recipes at home, and she seemed happy to be working at my shops—not only baking and creating, but also displaying our products in enticing ways.

"I'll bet you can guess what I did," Frida said, grinning at me.

"What's your new recipe?" I responded, smiling back.

She'd been working on new scone ideas for the shop, it turned out, and I quickly cheered. We had some good recipes already, but it never hurt to have new kinds of scones available.

Vicky reported that she'd been checking some things out on the computer and might be able to share some additional scheduling ideas with me as well.

I really liked my staff—and, as I thought about that, Janelle came into the restaurant with Neal. Reed entered right behind them.

So where was our guest of honor? I considered calling Dinah, but figured it was her day. If she wanted to make a grand late entrance, that would be just fine.

I also didn't know what time Billi or any of the other guests might arrive. My invitations had all been verbal and informal, and I figured Dinah's had been, too, so once she arrived, we might make up the entire group.

I was glad that Reed sat down on my other side. He even bent and gave me a quick kiss as he took his seat. I churned all over, and as usual my mind focused for an instant on when we'd have that real talk about our future.

But, heck, I was fine with how things were right now, even if nothing else happened. Maybe.

Despite what I'd told Dinah, I had dressed up a bit, in a deep blue shirt-dress and moderate heels. I was glad I had, since Reed wore a suit—and even my assistants were fairly well dressed. Neal looked neat, too, since he'd just gotten off his shift at the desk rather than hurrying in after one of the hikes he led. He was wearing a nice button-down shirt and slacks.

A server came over—one I'd not met before. She stopped to talk to Neal, so I figured she was the one he had talked to about tonight's menu and the celebratory cake. My favorite server here these days, Stu, was on the other side of the restaurant assisting customers.

"Carrie," Neal said from across the table. "I'd like you to meet our new maitre d', Ruth."

"Hi, Ruth," I called. So Ruth was in fact more than a server.

"Hi, Carrie," she replied, grinning. She looked mature enough that, even if she was new at the resort, she'd probably had some experience in serving people or working as a maitre d' somewhere else.

She wore a beige dress, and her hair was short and dark with silver highlights. She moved away from Neal toward me, and for a few minutes we discussed the menu she and Neal had planned. In addition to the special birthday cake, we'd be eating one of my favorite meals at the restaurant, chicken Kiev, although guests would have the option of ordering a meat-free vegetarian dish.

All sounded great. And it got even better when I spotted Dinah at the door. She saw us at the same time and, waving, headed in our direction. She had decided to dress up for her special occasion after all, and was wearing a bright blue blouse tucked into a black skirt, with stilettos that matched her top.

In this outfit, she appeared slimmer than usual. In fact, she looked quite pretty—and maybe that was partly the result of the glow on her face, which was lit up even more by her big smile.

"Thank you so much, Carrie," she said as she reached the table. I stood up and she immediately reached over to hug me. "This is so wonderful!"

I'd made sure my other assistants knew, when inviting them to the party, that this was a special occasion for my most senior and only full-time employee, so they shouldn't feel bad if I didn't do something similar for each of them. Yet in some ways the party was to celebrate the whole staff, since everyone was here.

Ruth still stood nearby, and I motioned to her. "May we have our wine now?" I asked as she came over.

"Of course. Do you know yet how many others will join you?"

"Unfortunately, no. But I'd like to get us started soon, if that works for you."

"Of course." She walked away and motioned to Stu, who was still on the other side of the restaurant but waiting on tables not far from us. Good. I knew he was an excellent server, and hoped he waited on us, too.

As I was looking that direction, I saw someone else come into the restaurant whom I recognized. I shouldn't have been surprised, of course, but I inhaled deeply as I watched Henry Schulzer enter, head to the area where the regular crowd was seated, and bend down to talk to a woman. Then he took a seat beside her.

"What's wrong, Carrie?" Dinah looked over at me. She was always observant, and I knew I'd had at least a small reaction.

I leaned toward her. "This isn't a good time to get into anything about—you know. About what you told me this morning. But as I indicated, I've learned a little more today. And—well, the guy who just came in was the deceased mayor's husband."

This time it was Dinah who drew in her breath. Again her face lit up as she turned to look at the newcomer. "Really?" She paused, a little frown erasing the smile. "Hey, he looks familiar. He's come into the Barkery a time or two with some adorable cocker spaniels, right?"

"That's right. His wife used to breed them. But look, let's wait till later, maybe tomorrow, for me to tell you the little bit I found out."

Dinah frowned a little. "You're right. But—well, this is my birthday. Maybe I should give in to my whim and go over and start asking him questions."

"I understand … but please don't. Let's enjoy your party, then you can go from there with your research. Okay?"

"Okay. You're right, Carrie. And you're such a dear for doing this for me."

Which was a great time for Stu and another server to bring over wine glasses and a bottle of the merlot Neal had picked out for us.

After I went through the procedure of checking it out and tasting it, they poured the wine and we all toasted Dinah. "May she work at my shops forever—while also writing lots of bestselling books," I said.

"Hear, hear," said everyone except Dinah, though like all of us she raised her glass in a toast.

The other side of the restaurant seemed to grow noisier and more crowded. I was so glad that Neal had reserved this area for us.

Our side salads were soon served, and I had a hard time eating as I talked to Reed, at my left, about our respective days and some of his more interesting patients at the clinic. I also talked to Dinah, at the head of the table on my right, who was answering questions from some of the others about where her research stood for her latest book. Not surprisingly, Dinah seemed a little reluctant to talk about her current research topic.

Thinking about this made me glance toward Henry. He was standing once again, apparently having a conversation with a man beside him. Two men … and I gathered that some of the increased noise in the area was because Silas Perring was one of them. The local TV news anchor must be attempting to interview Henry, given that his sidekick was aiming a camera on them.

Dinah must have followed my gaze, since she suddenly grabbed my arm. "Is that who I think it is with Henry Schulzer? I mean, my day started out with the media, and I think it's about to wrap up that way—in person. Excuse me." She rose, put her napkin on her chair, and started across the restaurant.

I glanced at Reed. "I think this could lead to something that spoils Dinah's birthday," I told him.

"Or not. Maybe it's a present of sorts." Reed knew how Dinah loved to do research for her writing.

"Well … I don't like it. She can certainly make her own choices, including ruining her party. But I can make my own choices, too. I'm going to find out what's going on over there. Care to join me?"

"Of course."

With that, we both excused ourselves, too, and hurried across the room after Dinah, who was staring raptly at the three men as she strode toward them.

FIVE

Yet even before Dinah reached Henry and the others, he stomped out of the restaurant—with Silas and the cameraman close behind him. And Dinah, Reed, and I not far behind.

Interestingly, Henry's dogs were in the lobby, their leashes held by a young lady. A relative?

Dinah had pulled a tablet computer out of her purse and placed it on a table near where the three men now stood, right beside one of the lobby's fireplaces—which of course remained unlit on this warm August evening. She typed something quickly, then looked up again as the men continued interacting. Reed stayed behind me.

"Hi," I said to the young woman holding the dogs' leashes. "I own the Barkery and Biscuits shop and I met Mr. Schulzer and his dogs there. Are you related to him?"

"No, I'm a dog walker and he has me take care of his dogs a lot."

"Then he brought them—and you—here tonight?"

The girl looked at me. "No, Henry's living at the resort with his dogs till he finds a place to rent. We work out a schedule for me to come here to help out."

Interesting. Henry had been in town for a few weeks, at least. The resort didn't seem the best place to stay long-term with dogs. Although...

"Leave me alone!" Henry's shout, aimed at Silas, interrupted my thoughts. Dinah had been off to one side, but instead of scaring her off, the shout intrigued her. She drew even closer, now holding her tablet in one hand.

Silas was the head anchor of KnobTV's evening news. He always was impeccably dressed on television, as he was right now. He was a little taller in real life than I'd anticipated, since he and the female newscasters appeared to be around the same height on camera. He had a cap of nicely styled black hair and large, arched brows over his dark eyes. Silas tended to be solemn in his reports, but I rather liked the guy, or at least his on-air persona, since he appeared to care about dogs.

I gathered now that he was also a tenacious reporter when tracking down a story.

"But we would really like your opinion about Mike Holpurn's parole. Were you aware it was going to happen?" Silas spoke into a microphone, which he then held out toward Henry.

"I don't want to talk about it. Now really, leave me alone."

"Well, could you tell me what you've been doing recently? It must have been so hard to lose your wife that way, all those years ago—and lose a good bit of your life, too, since she was Knobcone Heights' mayor. How have you been?"

I realized it was Dinah talking now. Not necessarily how a news reporter would conduct an interview, but it seemed to calm Henry a little.

He turned his back on Silas and the cameraman and faced only Dinah. He was the least dressed up of all of us, in his short-sleeved green T-shirt and jeans. His grayish beard, which I'd noticed before at the Barkery, seemed a little longer and scruffier, too. I imagined he hadn't anticipated being interviewed, especially on camera. On the other hand, maybe that was the image he liked best.

But, no. The way Henry was acting, he surely hadn't wanted to be confronted by Silas and a microphone.

"You're right," he said to Dinah—with Silas still holding the mic in the background and the cameraman still filming "It was hard. Real hard. That's why I left Knobcone Heights, even though I like this place. A lot. I always wanted to come back. I was a real estate broker way back when I was married to Flora and even before that. When she was gone, my kids and I moved to Fresno and for a while I just sort of hid there, but I got back into selling real estate, and I hope to hook up with a sales agency here soon, too."

Yet he was living at the resort for now, as his dog walker had said? Interesting. Then again, he might have in mind exactly the kind of property he wanted to either rent or buy, and was perhaps waiting until he could find the ideal thing.

Or perhaps he wanted to buy from whatever company he ultimately went to work for.

Hey, I was using my imagination the way Dinah probably did. But I didn't say anything. Just continued to listen.

"Look." Dinah was also ignoring Silas. "Today's my birthday, and my wonderful boss, Carrie here"—she gestured toward me—"is throwing me a birthday party in the restaurant. Would you like to join us? I gather you've already got someone taking care of your dogs, right, since I don't think they'd be welcome inside." She looked beyond me to where the young lady still stood with the dogs.

"That's very nice of you," Henry said.

"That is very nice," Silas said, this time thrusting the microphone in front of Dinah's face. "Are we invited, too?"

"Nope," Dinah said, aiming a false smile toward the camera. "Are we on the air? Fun! Now, wish me a happy birthday, everyone."

"And—off," Silas said to the cameraman, who moved the camera downward in response. He turned back toward Dinah. "Yes, it was a live feed for a while, including when you were talking to Mr. Schulzer and asking him what he'd been up to. We'll edit it for a later showing, too." Then he approached Henry once more. "Look, Mr. Schulzer. I'm a journalist. I can ask questions, and I'd appreciate answers next time. But I understand—"

"There'd better not be a next time," Henry exploded, then calmed again. "Look. I thought long and hard about returning here. I thought the timing would be okay, this long after … after what happened. I had no idea there would be a coincidence this crazy—and horrible—especially when I'd just moved back here for a few weeks. Holpurn let out of prison?" His voice had started to rise again, but he seemed to force himself to calm down. "Okay," he said to Dinah. "Thanks. I need to say bye to some folks and then I'll join you for your party."

"Fine," Dinah said. "We'll look forward to your joining us."

Would I look forward to it? I wasn't sure. And why had he decided to accept Dinah's invitation? I'd have assumed he would just want to get together with whatever friends he had there at the restaurant.

Maybe he was just happy that a stranger was being nice to him

After waving at his dog walker, Henry turned his back on us again, once more ignoring Silas and his assistant, and strode briskly into the restaurant.

Dinah looked toward Reed and me. Reed hadn't said anything during all this, but I knew he had my back—partly because he had put his arm around my shoulder and just stood there, watching. "I assume that's okay with you," Dinah said. "I'll pay for whatever he eats. Part of my research."

"No need," I said. "I didn't know how many were coming so there are some extra meals being cooked anyway."

As I said that, I noticed one of the people I'd invited who hadn't arrived before was now joining us: Billi.

When she reached us, I gave her a hug, introduced her to Henry's dogs—oh, and the dog walker, too, though I still didn't know her name. And then we all went back into the restaurant.

Well, all of us who were at the birthday party. Silas remained standing with his cameraman, watching us. He didn't look particularly happy. But reporters didn't always get their way when they tried to interview people. I'd even seen segments on TV that must have been embarrassing to subjects of those non-interviews who chose not to respond.

Like Henry. Oh well. He would be joining us at the party and, from what I could tell, apparently was ordering himself a drink. And if he drank even more, that should be okay, too, since he didn't have to drive anywhere.

Like Dinah, I was a bit curious about the guy and how he'd handled being widowed the way he was. I wouldn't ask him anything about it—but I'd listen while Dinah did.

When we were back at the table, Dinah asked some of those who'd remained seated to move, to provide a seat near her for Henry. Not surprising. I knew she wanted to talk to him. Interview him, perhaps gently—and at least not as intrusively as Silas had.

Did Henry understand that? He might just have thought she was being nice, inviting him to her birthday party.

I waved to Stu, to request that he bring a side salad for Henry, and I also asked him to check on the drink Henry had ordered from the bar—which wound up being a rum and Coke, heavy on the rum.

"What's going on?" That was Neal, from across the table.

I told him, "Dinah very nicely invited Henry to join us."

My brother's expression turned justifiably skeptical. "Got it," he said with a small shake of his head that indicated he didn't get it at all. But Neal kind of knew Dinah and the fact that she loved to write and research, so he probably wouldn't be surprised when I gave him a better explanation later.

"Wish I could hear what they're saying," Reed whispered into my ear.

"Me too—but excuse me turning my back for now. I want to listen, catch what I can." I reached over, squeezed his hand, and turned again toward Henry and Dinah.

I caught a significant portion of what she said, or so I thought. Dinah was again being her sympathetic self—or wearing that aspect of herself like a caring shawl draped around the newcomer to the table.

"It must have been so hard," she was saying. "I mean, there you were, a major player in the local area, its economy and politics and whatever. Or at least your wife was, so you must have been highly respected, too. And then you lost her, which was very sad. And all that extra prestige of being married to the mayor must have fled at the same time. Right?"

I wondered how Dinah's mind was wrapping around this. What was she plotting? How would she use any information Henry gave her?

"It wasn't quite like that," he said. "I ... well, what happened with Flora was horrible in so many ways. I loved my wife. But I had a career of my own. My real estate company was highly successful, so I had all the prestige or whatever I needed from that. But one of the reasons I left town was because so many people were so nice—and it hurt like an arrow zinging into me every time someone expressed

47

condolences or treated me differently, especially after her funeral and the trial of that SOB who killed her. And—"

"Well, talk about a huge coincidence. Or not." That was Silas's cameraman, who'd just appeared behind Henry. "Guess who—"

"Hey, Henry," someone called. "Good to see you." The tone of the shout sounded just the opposite, and I saw three men stride into the dining room, followed by Silas wielding his microphone.

"Oh no," Billi blurted from across the table. "That's—"

"It's that SOB I was just talking about." Henry rose, glaring toward the approaching men.

"That's Mike Holpurn?" Dinah also stood. The expression on her round face was so rapt that I felt as if she believed a cherished wish had come true. "Wow."

"Yes, that's Holpurn," the cameraman said.

Heck. I was tired of having the cameraman hanging around without knowing more about him, so I asked, "What's your name?"

He looked at me as if I'd insulted him. "I'm Wilbur," he said. "Wilbur the Wise." He grinned. "But just Wilbur will do." He was short, with alert hazel eyes and a determined curve to his mouth, and he seemed welded to the camera he held.

"Do you know who the others with Holpurn are?" Dinah asked.

"His brothers, I think," Wilbur replied. "Or at least Silas has told me Holpurn has a couple of brothers who helped get him out on parole."

They'd reached our table. I assumed the guy at the front had to be Mike Holpurn. He was tall and probably in his early forties—which meant he'd been in his early thirties or so when he murdered the mayor. His hairline had receded, and his remaining brown hair, maybe the mixed color of a raccoon, was short. He was dressed casually, in a long-sleeved black sweatshirt that seemed too warm for the August day, plus jeans and athletic shoes.

48

Nothing about his appearance suggested he was a murderer. But he began shouting as he reached our table—at Henry. "I saw you on TV a few minutes ago, on the news—and that's why I came here. I saw you acting angry about even hearing that I was being paroled. But you're the reason I was in prison, you son of a—"

"What the hell are you talking about?" Henry's hands were fisted at his sides, but he didn't take a swing at Holpurn. That was probably a good thing, since the men who accompanied Holpurn looked ready to jump in and fight, too. I could see some resemblance among them, or maybe that was just because I'd been told they were brothers. Neither looked as much like Holpurn as Neal looked like me.

"You know exactly what I'm talking about." Mike Holpurn's glare at Henry appeared lethal. "You framed me, set things up so conclusively that to save my life I had to take a plea bargain that made me admit to a murder I didn't commit. Fortunately, I still had people who gave a damn, and—well, you see that I got out early, on parole. There were questions in the supposed evidence, and—hell, I don't need to tell you anything. Except that you'd better admit to killing your own wife, once and for all."

"You know I didn't kill her or frame you or anything else," Henry shouted. It wasn't a very loud shout, but it didn't need to be for everyone in the restaurant to hear it. There were no other conversations going on anywhere around us.

"You were a liar then, and you're a liar now," Holpurn growled. "I came back to town to try to take back my old life as much as possible. I didn't imagine I'd see you here. Did you come back to gloat or what?"

"So, Mr. Holpurn," Silas called out, edging closer to the side of the table where Henry sat. "Tell me why you believe Mr. Schulzer killed Mrs. Schulzer." He held the microphone out toward Holpurn, and I could see Wilbur beside him, filming.

"Back off, jerk." Holpurn shoved Silas's hand with the microphone away.

"Were you mad that the mayor went back to her husband after her affair with you?" This time, it wasn't Silas asking but Dinah. She must have found some time to do research online, assuming the affair had been gossiped about ten years ago. So the alleged affair had caused tension, along with whatever problems there were with the remodeling of the mayor's residence.

"Lies!" Holpurn shouted. "All of that was lies. I did some work for the mayor, and she and I were alone in the residence sometimes. We talked now and then about the restoration and redecoration, and that was all."

"Is that what you believed, Mr. Schulzer?" Now Dinah turned to face Henry. "Or maybe … did you think they were up to more, as was suggested? Were you mad enough to kill your wife and frame Mr. Holpurn?"

"Why the hell are you asking things like that?" Henry now was standing up and glaring down at Dinah. I glanced quickly at Reed, who'd started in their direction as if to protect Dinah—or at least I hoped that was the reason.

Dinah was wise enough to get up and back away from the table. By now, lots of people in the dining room surrounded us, and I saw excitement and curiosity in many pairs of eyes. I considered calling one of the contacts I'd made in the Knobcone Heights Police Department, Sergeant Himura, or even Chief Loretta Jonas, but if anything was going to happen, it would go down before any cops could arrive.

"Sorry, Henry." Dinah looked down at the floor momentarily before glancing back into Henry's face. "My imagination is on overdrive, as it always is. I don't know what happened back then, though

I'd like to find out the truth—as anyone here would, I imagine. I'm a writer, mostly of articles and short stories, but I'm working on writing something with more substance, a thriller, something maybe based on a real story but fictionalized. If I base it on a real situation, like what happened to Mayor Schulzer, I want to know what's real and what's not, no matter what I put into my story. And—"

"You'd better back off this, young lady," Henry shouted. "If you base a story on my wife's death and fill it with lies, like saying that I was involved, I'll sue you. Or worse."

"What, you'll kill her, like you did Flora?" Mike Holpurn now stood right beside Henry. His grin was menacing. Horrible. And it let me see how he could have been considered the main suspect in Flora Schulzer's murder.

Or maybe that was my imagination at work.

"Of course I won't. And I didn't," Henry snapped. "*You* did. But she'd better watch it. I have resources, and I have contacts this young lady couldn't begin to know about. In fact, you'd better not write at all, about this situation or anything else," he said to Dinah. "I can ruin that kind of career, and I'll definitely ruin yours even before it begins. Count on it."

Dinah's mouth had dropped open. She looked horrified, as if she believed Henry's threats. For surely they were just that. There wasn't anything he could do to end her cherished and anticipated writing career—could he?

"But you can't do that," Dinah finally responded, her voice low and hoarse.

"Just watch me." And with a glare at Dinah, which he then turned on Holpurn, and finally on Silas, Henry Schulzer once again stomped out of the restaurant.

SIX

DINAH REMAINED STANDING THERE, staring after him. The look on her face remained shocked. At first. And then it turned into a glare.

"I have every right to research what happened back then," she said through gritted teeth, her hands fisted at her side. "And to use it in a book, as long as I keep it a fictional account without naming any real names, and make it clear that I took poetic license, and—"

"And it's your birthday," I reminded her, now standing beside her. "Sit down and forget about—well, I know you can't forget it, but at least don't focus on it."

Dinah seemed to focus instead on the dining room and the people at nearby tables who were staring at her. And then she looked at Mike Holpurn and his brothers, if that's who they were, who approached her.

"You're a writer?" Holpurn asked. "Well, if so, you should write about that SOB who just threatened you. He means it, you know. I did talk to his wife a bit before … before she died. She told me how he'd harmed her in other ways, then. Threatened her political career by claiming he'd tell the world the truth, though she knew he meant lies that would make voters hate her. Oh yeah, Henry Schulzer was the one to—"

"Say that all again," Silas said, thrusting the microphone into Holpurn's face.

Which made Holpurn scowl and back away.

I wondered if he'd said this ten years ago when he was arrested for murder. Or had he thought all of it up while languishing in prison—after confessing? Had he changed his story to get himself out on parole? But that surely wouldn't make a difference.

Well, I wasn't going to ask Holpurn about it, so most likely I'd never know.

Dinah, on the other hand, with her curiosity and drive, would undoubtedly question Holpurn if she communicated with him again. And that could endanger her, if the man's confession ten years ago had had even a semblance of truth to it.

Of course, I didn't know what he'd said in his confession and plea deal. Dinah might know from her research. And if she didn't, she would undoubtedly find a way to learn it.

"Dinner's served," said Reed.

He'd stood up when I had, remaining behind me, obviously not wanting to interrupt. But I knew I could count on him to keep all of us safe, even if that just meant calling the cops. He was a good guy. Cared about people as well as animals.

"Time for us to sit down," I said to Dinah.

That was apparently a cue for Holpurn and his gang to hurry out of the restaurant. Or maybe the fact that Silas wasn't leaving him alone contributed to or caused it.

The drama had ended, at least for now. I sat down and so did Reed. I looked up at Dinah. At first she stared after those who'd left, but then she, too, sat back down at the head of the table.

To get everyone back in party mode—hopefully—I raised my wine glass again and said, "To Dinah. Happy birthday and many more to come." Which I meant. I hoped she hadn't endangered herself. And I didn't want to say anything else on that subject, even to mention Dinah's obsession—er, fascination—with research.

Once more, calls of "hear, hear" circulated the table. Servings of chicken Kiev joined our salads and I began eating, looking at Dinah. She seemed to stare at her plate for a long moment before glancing in my direction. The smile she sent me appeared a bit wry, but then she, too, started eating.

Soon I was chatting with Dinah about other birthday parties she'd had over the years, and some of my own celebrations.

She eventually turned and talked for a while with her fellow assistants, and I, too, turned and began talking with Reed.

"Everything okay?" His gorgeous, dark brown eyes seemed to study me, as if he was trying to look into my mind and learn what I was really thinking.

"For now," I said.

"For now," he agreed with a nod. Then he glanced across the table toward Neal and Janelle. "Does your brother have any plans for the rest of the night?"

I knew how to interpret that. "I don't know if he's coming back to our place or not … but I could pick up Biscuit and join you at your house. Assuming you're willing to get up tomorrow as early as I do to get to work."

Reed rested one finger on his strong chin and raised his eyes upward. "Gee—what a novel idea."

I gently prodded him with my elbow. "Okay, wise guy. One way or the other, yes, I want to spend tonight with you."

"And I with you." His tone now was deep and throaty, and as sexy as a voice could be.

Which made me look forward to the end of this party.

But I still enjoyed the rest of my dinner, as well as the conversations I got involved in. Fortunately, Dinah didn't return to the subject that undoubtedly was weighing on all our shoulders now, thanks to the earlier ugly exchanges. Instead, she talked about the Barkery and Icing and how much she enjoyed working at my shops.

Sure, Dinah could have been trying to flatter me, since I was throwing the party for her. But we'd talked often about how glad I was that she'd stayed when I bought the shops. I'd relied a lot on her to teach me how to operate bakeries, in terms of both the baking aspect and the business aspect. I hadn't been able to learn about either while working as a vet tech, though I'd wanted to do something like this—to become my own boss—for a long time.

Dinah had helped me achieve that successfully.

Which was part of the reason I'd wanted to do something special for her birthday.

I watched with amusement as Billi chatted with Neal, Janelle, and my other assistants at the opposite side of the table. As a city councilwoman as well as a businesswoman, Billi was never at a loss for things to talk about.

Arvie showed up at the party after things had calmed down. I'd invited Dr. Paul Jensin as well, although I hadn't been certain if he would join us. But he knew Dinah, partly because she'd used him as a research resource, and he'd said he'd be glad to come.

When Arvie arrived, he hurried to where Dinah sat, bent to hug her, and then gave her a gift—never mind that I'd told everyone not to, since Dinah said she didn't want gifts. But it was sweet of him.

Then he headed toward me. "Sorry I'm late." No white medical jacket on him now. He, like Reed, wore a suit. "An emergency at the hospital."

"What was it?" Reed stood to greet our wonderful boss. People at Reed's far side moved down so Arvie could sit beside him.

"Two sibling bulldogs decided it was time to show each other who was boss, and neither won." At my gasp and Reed's shake of the head, Arvie put his hand up. "Neither lost much, either. They'll both be fine."

In a short while, Stu had brought over some wine for Arvie, as well as his salad and entree.

I felt so glad that everyone, particularly Dinah, seemed to be having a great time. She opened Arvie's present after saying to the group, "Now, I really meant it about not wanting gifts, but I can't help checking this one out, can I?"

She pulled off the wrapping paper—and pulled out a small notebook with a really pretty, mosaic-like cover.

"Oh, this is wonderful," she gushed toward Arvie. "Thanks so much."

"Well, I'm always hearing about how much you like to do research. Now you'll always have something to jot down your findings in."

Sweet, but it almost made me want to kick Arvie, since for a while all of us, including Dinah, had put aside what had happened earlier—which was, in a way, a byproduct of Dinah's research.

But Arvie didn't know that. And Dinah made an obvious gesture of holding up the notebook, pulling off the attached pen, and jotting something inside. "Just noting that this was a very sweet present on my birthday this year from amazing veterinarian Dr. Arvus Kline. Not that I'd ever forget that anyway." Then she picked up her large purse from the floor and put the notebook inside.

The rest of the meal also went great. Dinah laughed a lot, accepted another glass of wine, and almost shrieked with joy when maitre d' Ruth marched into the restaurant with the lovely, ornate birthday cake in her hands as Stu and others on the wait staff marched behind her singing "Happy Birthday." The candles were already lit, and Ruth placed the cake on the table in front of Dinah, who looked around at everyone, glanced upward as if making her wish, and then blew out the candles.

Although one took an extra try.

Well, I knew what the superstition was about that. It could mean that Dinah's wish wouldn't come true—or that she otherwise would have bad luck. I wasn't going to mention it, and the whole thing was just a fun but silly tradition anyway.

From the still-huge smile on Dinah's face, she wasn't concerned at all, which was how it should be.

The cake was covered in vanilla icing and decorated with lots of pastel swirls around Dinah's name. Inside it was chocolate, which became obvious when Ruth cut it and Stu began serving it. Another server brought coffee to those of us who wanted it.

So fun. Such a great celebration.

But when we'd finished the cake, our meal was over and so was the party. Dinah stood and came around the table to each of us, saving me for last. I stood to join her. She hugged me and thanked me and said she would see me tomorrow—and not to worry about her, although she wasn't specific about why I might worry. Then she said good night, took the rest of the cake that the servers had packed for her, and walked out with Vicky and Frida. Billi and Arvie, engrossed in conversation, followed them.

The party was definitely breaking up. Reed stood beside me, and Neal and Janelle joined us. "Great party," Reed said. The look in his eyes appeared admiring ... and sexy.

"Hey, sis," Neal said. "Thanks for the fun, and good night. Janelle and I are continuing the celebration at her place."

Which answered my question. I didn't want details about their planned celebration, but now Reed and I could continue celebrating at my house instead of his.

"Sounds good," I said. "Janelle, you're scheduled to work in the shops tomorrow, aren't you?" I knew the answer was yes, but I wanted to let her know I knew—and thereby remind her in a roundabout way that she'd need to get up early in the morning.

No matter what the nature of their celebration.

Well, so would I. I said good night to my brother and my assistant, and Reed and I headed to the parking lot, which was a lot less crowded than before.

"I assume you'll pick up Hugo, then join me at my place?" I asked Reed as he walked me to my car. I made it a question, though I hoped I knew the answer.

"Of course. We'll be there soon."

We shared a nice, long kiss after I opened my car door, a harbinger of what was to come. Which made me grin as I got into my car and drove home.

Biscuit was glad to see me, and I was happy to see her. I took her on a short walk beneath the streetlights outside, and then we went inside to wait for Reed and Hugo, his smart Belgian Malinois.

They arrived soon. I'd opened a bottle of wine so we could continue the celebration that way, too. Once more, I was in Reed's arms. He'd changed into more casual clothes, and I really liked the feel of him against me and the taste of the wine on his lips.

It was getting late, though, for someone like me who had to get up early to start baking. So we went upstairs to my bedroom and got into bed. Together. Still celebrating.

I had no trouble falling asleep after a while. Then, in the early morning, the clock radio awakened me as always and I started getting out of bed.

Reed was used to this and got up with me as he often did, although sometimes I let him sleep in for a few minutes. "Good morning," he said, and once more I was in his strong arms—but not for long. I didn't have time.

After we each showered, we took the dogs outside briefly. Dawn was just suggesting its arrival by a hint of lightness in the sky.

When we went inside again, I realized my curiosity was getting the best of me.

"You know," I told Reed, "I'm curious whether any of Silas's interviews are on TV this morning, and if so, how he'll portray Schulzer and Holpurn and anything related to them."

"So you want to watch a little TV? Do you have time?"

"I won't watch for long."

Together we went into my living room, and I used the remote to tune in to the KnobTV channel and its morning news. Although I usually wound up getting a commercial first, this time the screen contained a banner about *Breaking News*.

I hadn't expected Silas to be live at this hour, since he'd worked late last night ... but there he was.

The background picture was of the Knobcone Height Resort's main building, where we'd been less than twelve hours ago.

"What's going on?" I asked Reed, as if he would know. I must have sounded upset, because both Biscuit and Hugo came over and nudged my hand with their noses. Or maybe they were just begging for a treat.

"I guess we'll see," Reed said.

On the screen, Silas pointed to the resort building. "We don't have any information yet," he said, "other than the fact that resort management called the Knobcone Heights Police Department just a little while ago to report the death of one of its guests."

"What?" I exclaimed. "Who?"

"I wonder—" Reed responded, and then we knew.

A banner began scrolling at the bottom of the screen as Silas spoke into his microphone. "According to initial reports, Henry Schulzer, the widower of former mayor Flora Morgan Schulzer, was found dead in his hotel room. Apparently his dogs started barking and woke other hotel guests. We have no further information yet, but we're staying at this location to learn what happened. Stay tuned."

I looked at Reed, who looked solemnly back at me. "Henry?" I said, my mind racing back to the clashes at Dinah's birthday party last night. "Oh no."

SEVEN

SHIVERING, EVEN WITH REED'S arm around my shoulders, I sat there and watched the end of the report, which didn't continue much longer. Silas didn't say how Henry had died. A heart attack?

A homicide?

Sure, the latter was the direction my mind went since I'd dealt with so many murders lately, like it or not. But even if his death was due to natural causes, it still would have made the news considering who the guy was in Knobcone Heights. Either way, I felt sorry for him.

And for his dogs? Where were they now? What was going to happen to them?

"It might just be natural causes." Reed echoed my thoughts.

"It might," I agreed.

"But you don't believe it."

"Not till I hear what the coroner says. And that'll show up eventually on the news. But—" I glanced again at the TV, where a commercial for life insurance was running, and shook my head.

"Do you want to watch any more or leave for your shops?" Reed asked gently. His arm tightened, and I briefly put my head on his shoulder.

"What I want is not to have heard this. For it not to have happened, no matter how. But you know I need to go to my shops."

"I figured. Hugo and I will go back to our place. It'll be a while till I need to get to the clinic. And before you ask, yes, I'll watch the news a bit before I leave, and I'll call you if there's any more information."

"Thanks." I turned off the TV, feeling as if I wanted to punch it instead. But it would do no good to kill the electronic messenger.

I locked the house behind us after Reed, the dogs, and I entered the garage, then opened the garage door. Reed's car was right there in the driveway. Before he headed toward it, he took me into his arms again. "Just think," he said, "this could turn out to be another murder for you to solve."

"I hope not," I said quickly. "And aren't you going to tell me not to get involved if it is a murder?"

"How many ways have I tried that, and not been successful at getting you to back off?"

My laugh held no humor. "Well, at least last time my nosiness helped to prove your innocence."

"Yes, and I'm still grateful." We shared a hot but quick kiss. "I'm sure we'll be in touch today," he said.

"I'm sure," I acknowledged. "I have a shift at the clinic this afternoon, so we'll at least see each other then."

He bent to give me another kiss, then walked off with Hugo toward his car while I fastened Biscuit in the backseat of mine.

I flipped from one radio station to another as I drove the short distance to my shops but didn't hear any news, maybe because it was only around 5:50 in the morning. Biscuit and I stayed in the car a few extra minutes so I could listen on the half hour—and sure enough, one of the local stations had news on.

The lead story was about the death of the husband of the former mayor. Which was definitely news.

And it was news to me when the low-voiced female announcer said, "Police suspect that Schulzer's death was a homicide. An investigation has begun." She then went on to the next story.

Or maybe this wasn't completely unexpected information. Henry had shown no indication of poor health yesterday. But he had shown a tendency to infuriate a lot of people.

Including me.

Would I be a suspect again this time? Surely the two local police detectives, who had each become an odd sort of buddy to me, wouldn't go that direction. After all, what motive could I have?

No, the direction they were more likely to go, I hoped, was an investigation into Mike Holpurn or the men who'd been with him. The fact that Holpurn had been paroled didn't mean he was innocent, as he claimed, in the mayor's murder years ago—let alone in the apparent murder last night of the mayor's husband. And Holpurn's friends—supporters—brothers? They could be guilty instead. Or as well.

And … uh-oh. My mind was now heading in the direction I'd been avoiding. There could be plenty of people who also hated Henry.

But I'd just reached the shops, so I quickly parked my car. I got Biscuit out of the backseat and, after locking the vehicle, walked my dog on her leash to the front of the building. I used my key to unlock the Barkery's front door and we went inside. I relocked the door behind us and let Biscuit off her leash.

As I turned to go into the kitchen, my phone rang and I pulled it out of my pocket.

It was Dinah.

She was due to come in today, as she was most days, but not for another hour. I answered as cheerfully as I could. "Good morning, Dinah."

"Good morning." She stumbled over the words. "Are you at the shops?"

"Of course," I said.

"Me too." There was a sudden knocking on the glass of the Barkery's front door. Sure enough, there she was.

I unlocked the door again and let her in, then once more relocked it, this time behind her. Her round face was pasty and her blue eyes huge beneath her messy brown hair as she looked at me. Her voice continued to rasp as she said, "Carrie, did you hear ... did you hear about Henry Schulzer?"

"I did," I said. The possibility of Dinah being his killer had of course leaped into my mind, but I'd been thrusting it out—as well as I could. I didn't want to ask her.

She addressed the topic anyway, saying what I hoped she would. What I hoped was true.

"He and I argued, Carrie," she said. "You know that. So do a lot of other people who heard us. It wasn't much of an argument, but the timing, now ... And he argued with other people, too. But—" She hung her head, and I hugged her as she finished with a sob. "I didn't like him, Carrie. But I didn't kill him. Honest."

———

Dinah had cried for a while, and I'd held her, knowing only too well how it felt to be a murder suspect. But so far we didn't have any details—not just about how Henry had died, but also about who the police were looking into as possible suspects. Dinah might be completely off the hook, depending on whatever evidence the police had found.

Or not.

Even my little Biscuit had shown her sympathy to my wonderful and upset assistant, jumping on Dinah's legs while we were still in the Barkery and rubbing her head against them.

Yet I couldn't help wondering—was Dinah's extreme reaction the result of feeling guilty…

No. Dinah researched bad stuff, sure. But actually doing any of it? I'd need to see some real evidence of that, not just her usual desire to discover the truth for her plotting or writing.

When Dinah had calmed a little, she leaned on the counter near the glass display case and said, "Sorry, Carrie. I guess the way I'm acting is because… well, I made notes when I got home, mostly in the adorable notebook Arvie gave me. And as always, I let my imagination take control, so I also came up with some scenarios— all fiction, of course—that could result from our conversations with those guys yesterday, including Henry."

"Scenarios in which he was murdered?" I had to ask.

I knew the answer even before Dinah whispered, "Yes."

"And where is that notebook?" I figured that if the detectives considered her a possible suspect, they'd visit her home and look for evidence there.

"In my desk. If anyone sees it, they'll read the scenarios—including one in which Henry killed his wife, and that guy Mike Holpurn resented how he'd been in prison and therefore killed Henry now. And one in which Henry killed Holpurn instead. And one where those men with Holpurn were the ones who'd killed the mayor way back when. Or—"

"I get it," I said. And hopefully there was enough speculation and variety in Dinah's scenarios that no one would assume she was guilty of what had actually occurred.

Leaving Biscuit loose in the Barkery, we came into the kitchen and washed our hands well, and both of us started baking—me on the Barkery side and Dinah on the Icing side.

We talked mostly about general and innocent stuff—although my mind kept leaping back to the situation playing out in Knobcone Heights that might somehow involve the birthday party I'd thrown for Dinah last night. Her eyes sometimes glazed over as she kneaded dough, too, and I figured her mind was doing something similar to mine.

But the time seemed to pass quickly, as it always did when I worked hard to ensure we had enough baked goods for both shops to start the day. Soon it was nearly seven o'clock, our opening time.

The kitchen was filled with mixed aromas of sweet human treats for Icing and the more tart, meaty aromas of doggy treats for the Barkery. Sheets of both kinds of goodies had been fully baked and were out on the appropriate counters cooling. It was time to place them on plates and get them into the display cases.

I headed into the Barkery first, with a couple of plates, sending Dinah to the door that led into Icing. Biscuit was sitting near the front door of the Barkery, looking out and wagging her tail.

I guess I shouldn't have been surprised to see Detective Wayne Crunoll standing outside. He'd kind of gotten into the habit of this when I was a murder suspect, and he hadn't changed his habit while investigating subsequent murders. He didn't have his dachshunds, whom he claimed were his wife's, with him today, so he probably wasn't going to use buying treats for Blade and Magnum as an excuse for coming to my shops.

Maybe he'll just ask my opinion of what happened, I thought as I headed to the door to let him in. After all, my amateur sleuthing, intentional or not, had helped Wayne and his partner, Detective Bridget Morana, solve several murders recently, and they even asked my opinion now and then—sort of.

Well, I'd let Wayne lead this conversation. And if I had to, I'd make it clear I was innocent of anything bad that had happened... and I'd attempt to protect Dinah, too.

The detective didn't wait for an invitation to come in when I opened the door. "Hi, Carrie," he said as he slipped by me. Biscuit was still loose inside the shop and hurried over to say hi, standing on her hind legs and wriggling against him. He bent to pet her.

Leaving the door unlocked, since it was nearly opening time, I strode up to Wayne.

As usual, he wore a white shirt and dark gray pants. The dark facial shadow that matched his short, straight hair seemed a little more visible than usual this morning, shadowing his round face. His light brown eyes locked on mine. "So, Carrie—" he began.

"So you want my take on who murdered Henry Schulzer," I said in a casual tone. "It's a bit early, so I haven't figured it out for certain yet. Who do you think did it?"

Not Dinah, I hoped. Or me.

He just laughed. "You know how it works. Even if we have suspects, we can't talk to the public about it. And you're a member of the public, not the Knobcone Heights PD, no matter how many murders you've helped to solve." He grew more serious. "I did come here to find out if you'd heard about the murder. And, yes, it's a homicide."

"Right." I maneuvered around him to pick up Biscuit and deposit her gently into her high-sided pen at one side of the room. I didn't want her loose when customers began opening the door and coming in. I gathered my thoughts quickly—then decided to ask the most obvious question. "So why did you really come here this morning, Wayne?" I wanted to keep the situation as informal as I could, so I called him by his first name.

"Because I know you're already involved." His grin toward me was more than ironic. It seemed both amused and irritated.

"What do you mean?" As if I didn't know. But I wanted the detective's take on it before I admitted to being involved. Or getting more involved.

He shook his head slowly, again as if amused. "Come here, Carrie. Let's talk." He gestured me over and sat at one of the small tables in my Barkery. I crossed the blue tile floor with its brown dog bone decoration at the center.

"I don't have much time," I said, obeying him. I was glad Dinah was in Icing. I decided to tell her anything Wayne told me that she would need to know.

"Right. So here's the thing." Wayne spoke quickly as he explained that Henry had been found partly thanks to his dogs barking in the middle of the night.

I of course had to interrupt him. "Are the dogs okay? Where are they now?"

"We learned about the dog walker he'd hired when we got to the hotel, but for now we've taken them to Mountaintop Rescue. Councilwoman Matlock has been notified and she's agreed not to adopt out those dogs, at least not until we have a better sense of Mr. Schulzer's current family situation. If a relative wants to take in his dogs, that might be the best situation for them."

"Agreed," I said, hoping it would be. But I would still look into it. Plus, I'd certainly visit the spaniels at Mountaintop Rescue and talk to Billi about them. "Sorry, I interrupted. Please continue."

He did. Not surprisingly, he had heard about the altercation in the restaurant the previous night involving Schulzer, Mike Holpurn, Holpurn's comrades—brothers?—and me. And birthday girl Dinah. "As you know, we'll need to talk to everyone who was there, and I gather that includes not only you but your shop assistants."

At least he hadn't jumped on Dinah right away. But that didn't mean she wasn't being viewed as more than a birthday celebrant.

"And your brother," Wayne added. His expression had grown a bit more detached, a bit more professional—until he said that. He was teasing me, and yet not teasing me. Neal might not have been at the top of whatever suspect list they were developing, but that didn't mean he wasn't on it. Like me. "And his lady friend Janelle, yet again. Oh, and I heard your main squeeze, Dr. Reed Storme, was there, too." He knew of my relationship with Reed, of course, because of how I'd helped clear Reed during the last local murder.

"That's right," I replied. I needed to be as cooperative as possible and make sure my assistants—as well as Neal and Reed—were as well. I would protect them all, of course. Help clear them, assuming they all were innocent. And of that group, Dinah was the only one who I had any doubts about—given how Henry Schulzer had threatened to destroy her career as a writer. But it was only a mere smidgen of suspicion.

"Okay, here's the drill, and I'm sure you won't be surprised," Wayne continued. "If you cooperate, as you usually do"—this was kind, and not always true, but I wasn't going to object—"then things should go faster and easier for all of us."

He proceeded to tell me that the Knobcone Heights PD wanted to question everyone individually down at the station. He'd let me help set up a schedule that shouldn't be too bad for my schedule at the shops or otherwise, as long as each of the people involved cooperated and made themselves available at times that also worked for Wayne and his partner, Bridget, and whoever else they might pull into the interviews—otherwise known as interrogations.

But at least, if we all cooperated, it sounded as if the cops would make things as easy on us as possible, at least if or until they zeroed in on one or more of us.

Which I hoped didn't happen.

"Sounds good," I said.

"Great. I'll email you a little later with times that will work best for us, as well as the order in which we'd prefer talking to people."

"Fine." I rose, too, as Wayne stood.

"And now," he said, "I'm ready to buy a few treats for Blade and Magnum."

"Glad to hear that." I pondered quickly whether I should just give him some treats for his dogs—not as a bribe, but to keep up the currently good relationship between us. I made an internal compromise. As he picked out a couple favorites, some with carob and some with liver, I added a few extra biscuits to each bag and made sure he was aware of it.

Wayne paid and was ready to go. He was even standing at the door—and that was when Dinah walked in from Icing.

"Oh," she said, her voice cracking a little. "Hello, Detective."

"Hello, Dinah." Wayne and my assistant already knew each other a little, partly because of Dinah's never-ending research. "Carrie's going to get you set up for an interview with us." He was grinning, but there was a hint of suspicion in his gaze.

Drat. They might already have Dinah at or near the top of their suspect list.

"Really? Because of the death of Mr. Schulzer?" Her tone was stronger now. I hoped that was a good thing.

"That's right. We know about your birthday party and what happened. Just want to be clear on who said what and all."

"Got it." And then Dinah aimed a great, big, pleased smile at him. "But don't be surprised if I ask you some questions, too."

EIGHT

BEFORE WAYNE LEFT, I reminded him again of others who'd been at or around the party last night besides my friends or assistants—particularly Mike Holpurn and his buddies. Sure, the detectives could question whoever they wanted, but they should keep their minds open till they had enough evidence to arrest the real killer.

Wayne wound up smiling at me ironically as he thanked me in advance for my assistance. "Carrie, it would be fine if you allowed the KHPD to figure this one out without your help. But—oh yeah. You're already involved." He waved an unofficial salute at me and walked out the door—with his dog treats and the bonus biscuits I'd thrown in.

The kind of salute I considered waving at him wouldn't exactly have been appropriate, so I instead bent to give Biscuit a quick pat on the head.

I didn't have time to talk to Dinah right away since the stores were now open. But I did discuss a possible time for her to go to the station to be interviewed by the detectives—which had to be sometime when at least one of my other assistants was working, and when I wasn't at the clinic for a shift.

"I guess I'll need to take even more notes now for my research," Dinah said, but her expression was downcast, unlike the way she looked when digging into her research with gusto for a story idea.

A thought penetrated my mind that I immediately shot back out again. Could Dinah have murdered Schulzer for the experience, as part of her research? She wouldn't do such a thing with someone she liked, but she clearly hadn't liked—

"What's wrong, Carrie?" Dinah's tone was sad, almost as if she knew what I was imagining.

"Nothing," I said. "Nothing at all, except that I'm concerned about our schedules until everyone who was at the party yesterday is finished being questioned by the detectives."

"Oh. Right." She didn't even try to hide her skepticism.

"Okay," I said. "With all your research, and skills in reading people, you know what I'm thinking, like it or not. I believe you when you say you didn't harm Henry. But I may be the only one who believes you, at least for now, since so many people heard him threaten you, and you arguing with him."

"I know. But Carrie, like I said and as you know, others were arguing with Henry, too. And although I might write about people hurting others, you know I wouldn't—I couldn't—" Her sharp and sincere retort was cut short by the sound of the bell in Icing. I'd had bells installed on the shop doors for just this kind of situation. No, not discussions about potential murder suspects, but having nobody in one of the shops when we were all busy in the other shop or the kitchen. We needed to know whenever a customer came in.

Fortunately, Janelle and Vicky were scheduled to work later that morning. Frida had the day off. But after figuring out which of my three assistants that day could be sent to the police station, and then checking with them and emailing with Detective Crunoll to confirm the times, I felt good that I had accomplished something.

73

As long as none of them got arrested while they were there… meaning, mostly, the possibility of the cops assuming Dinah was guilty.

Because of that possibility, I found a time when all three were staffing the shops to pop into my office at the rear of the kitchen. Sitting at my desk, I called Ted Culbert, the local attorney I'd gotten to know since unfortunately becoming involved in solving murder cases in Knobcone Heights.

"Hi, Ted. Have you heard about—"

"—the murder of the husband of that mayor who was also murdered?" His voice was sharp as he interrupted me. "Yes, I've heard about it. Another murder in town, and you're involved with this one, too?"

"Not by choice, any more than with the others." As Ted laughed, I explained the situation to him, including the excitement at Dinah's birthday party. "I don't know that any of my employees or I, or my brother or Reed or Arvie, will be genuine suspects this time, but if so, you might be asked to represent one of us."

"Sounds like your assistant Dinah may be the lead suspect this time."

Ted sounded more relaxed now, but I leaned forward on my chair. "How do you know that?"

"Ever since I heard about Schulzer's death this morning, I've been following what that reporter Silas Perring says on TV and online."

"And he's been talking about Dinah? Accusing her?"

"Now look, Carrie," Ted said, his voice more appeasing than before. "He's a reporter. He's being neutral in what he says about the situation and the potential suspects, but yes, he's mentioned several of the people who were at the resort and it sounds as if yesterday's birthday girl is one he's particularly interested in. That could mean the authorities will be, too."

I shook my head, as if he could see it. "Well, I believe in Dinah. Yes, she may wind up being your client, but I really hope the cops land their sights on someone more likely—like Mike Holpurn, the confessed murderer who just got paroled. The timing just sounds ideal for him to have done it, don't you think?"

"Unless whoever did it decided to use that timing…"

I shook my head even harder. "Maybe. Well, I hope I won't need to be in touch with you again, but at least I'm glad you're aware of the situation."

"Bye, Carrie," Ted said, amusement ringing in his voice.

"Yeah, bye," I said and hung up. I half wished I hadn't called him, but just in case his services were needed by someone I cared about—or even by me—it was better to make sure he was aware of what was going on.

Time to get back to work, I thought—and get my mind off all of this.

I succeeded in half of that. I worked hard for the rest of the morning in the Barkery, then Icing. Wayne asked that Janelle be the first one interviewed, which I assumed was because they really had no reason to suspect her—this time. She'd been accused of committing one of the other murders I'd looked into, but, fortunately, the police had succeeded in finding the real culprit.

I wanted to go visit the Joes at lunchtime but Janelle wasn't back from her interrogation yet, so I hung around to make sure we were fully staffed—and also because I wanted to talk to Janelle on her return. I spent much of my time in Icing selling some of our people treats, mostly to longtime and loyal customers I recognized. Vicky took care of the Barkery, while Dinah mostly stayed in the kitchen baking additional treats for one shop, then the other. I gathered that she was hiding, somewhat, since she knew she'd been mentioned in the news.

Janelle finally returned. My brother's girlfriend looked harried and unhappy as she came through Icing's door, wearing her usual purple athletic shoes beneath her light slacks and *Barkery and Biscuits* T-shirt. "You'd have thought I was a suspect again," she said, taking me aside so we were near the wall behind Icing's display case. "Detective Morana kept asking me about every little detail I could remember about Dinah's birthday party, including when Henry Schulzer joined us, and when Mike Holpurn and his brothers showed up. They were apparently his brothers, based on what the detective said when she quizzed me about what went on."

So Bridget Morana had taken on the first official interrogation—but not of a major suspect this time. Interesting. But it didn't really mean anything, at least anything I could feel better about.

I had a vet tech shift at the clinic that afternoon. Fortunately, it was scheduled early. And Wayne had seemed fine with having Dinah come in to talk to them late in the day.

I wished I hadn't had to do that to her. Being there late might make it easier for the cops just to keep her around after they were done talking. But I had to work things out with my own schedule, let alone the cops' requests, and this had been the best I could do.

After checking with all my assistants to make sure they could handle the current not-too-large crowds in the shops and that this wasn't a bad time to leave, I wrapped up some dog biscuits that weren't as fresh as the rest to take to the clinic, as well as for a brief visit to Mountaintop Rescue that I planned for later—never mind that I'd just taken treats there yesterday.

I took Biscuit for a brief walk before fastening her into the back of my car, and we took off for the vet clinic. As always when we didn't walk, I parked behind the clinic and brought Biscuit into the doggy daycare area, where Charlie checked her in because both

Faye and Al were playing a game with several of the other pups in their care.

"Hi, Carrie," Faye and Al both called, and Faye opened her arms to welcome Biscuit into the game. Of course I smiled.

I went to the locker room, where I changed into my vet tech scrubs. I looked up and down the hall as I headed to the reception area, hoping to see Reed and Arvie, but both must have been busy with patients.

The reception room was filled with people and their pets. Fortunately, I saw none who appeared particularly ill and hoped their visits were mostly just for checkups, shots, and reassurance.

Kayle was again the tech in charge of the area, and, after handing over the leftover treats for our patients, I stood beside him for a minute as he gave me the rundown on who was where, and in what exam room I'd be needed.

It was, fortunately, the room Reed had just entered to perform an annual physical on an aging Weimaraner named Gadsy. Gadsy's owner was getting up in years, too, and didn't look particularly strong, but even though the dog was a somewhat large breed he was well behaved.

The exam didn't take long, and while I helped to maneuver Gadsy into the positions needed to check him over, I kept catching Reed's eye. He sent me more than one inquisitive look.

When the exam was over, we briefly went into his office and I let him know about the interviews my staff were undergoing at the police station.

"I figured," he said. "I got a call, too, since I was there last night. I don't have the sense I'm one of their main suspects this time"—as he'd been for the last murder in town—"but they want to ask me some questions."

Which probably meant Neal would have to go in sometime, too. I'd check with my brother later.

Then there was Arvie. I was fortunately asked to help him with a cat who needed shots, and I learned that he, too, had been strongly urged—well, commanded—to drop by the police station to provide his recap of what had gone on at Dinah's party.

And Billi? I'd find out when I spoke with her later.

My shift seemed to go fast, and soon it was time to leave. I picked up Biscuit quickly since we needed to get back to the shops soon, but I intended to stop at Mountaintop Rescue both to check on Henry Schulzer's dogs and to say hi—and possibly more—to Billi.

Biscuit and I soon reached Mountaintop Rescue in my car. Once again Mimi was the receptionist, and her shirt today, peach in color, said, *You had me at woof.*

After I handed her the bag of treats I asked, "How are your new residents Duke and Prince doing?"

"The adorable cockers who belonged to the guy who was killed yesterday?"

Before I could answer, another voice, from the hall off to the right of the reception counter, said "They're doing great." Billi strode toward me. "Would you like to come see them?"

"Absolutely." This would also give me a little time to talk to Billi. I didn't even need to ask Mimi if she'd keep an eye on Biscuit. She just held out her hand for the leash and smiled. I walked my little dog behind the reception desk, where she greeted Mimi effusively. The shelter employee took charge of her, and I hurried back out again toward Billi.

As usual when in this role, Billi was dressed appropriately for running an animal shelter: she wore a somewhat frilly white T-shirt that said *Mountaintop Rescue* over jeans. Her highlighted dark hair was loose over her shoulders, and there was a wry smile on her attractive face, with its high cheekbones and full lips.

"So how are you?" she asked as she led me through the back door into the shelter area—a large yard outside with lots of fenced enclosures and buildings to house the animals.

"Okay," I responded. "But I assume you know—"

Stopping on the pathway beside me, she laughed wryly, her voice raised above the barks and clamor from the filled shelter. "About the latest murder in town? Of course I know. And of course I'm not surprised you're asking. Are you involved in solving it already?"

My turn to laugh. "You know me well. But there's a good reason."

"There always is. And I think I know what it is this time."

We reached the area where the window-filled buildings began. The dog area came first, filled with kennels separated by metal fencing that was decorated with rows of decorative circles on top. They contained a bunch of really wonderful-looking dogs of all sizes and breed backgrounds. Cats, too, in a farther-back area. The animals' backgrounds, to the extent known, were recorded on cards that visitors could read at the front of their enclosures.

Billi stopped near the second building and looked at me. "I understand that everyone who attended Dinah's birthday party is being questioned by the police. Right?" Her voice was raised a bit to be heard over the current din.

"Right. Have they contacted you?" I spoke loudly, too. Would the police even question a city councilwoman who happened to attend part of a party where a murder victim had been the night of his demise?

Of course they would. And as smart, astute, and politically knowledgeable as Billi was, she would know how to handle the situation, as she did everything else.

But it was a shame they were bothering her, too.

"Yes, they have. I'm heading to the station in a short while to talk to Chief Loretta Jonas."

Not one of the detectives, then. That made sense—unless the chief somehow believed that Billi had more involvement than simply seeing Schulzer at Knobcone Heights Resort at the time of the party.

And Loretta was smarter than that, or so I believed.

"Anything you want to discuss with me first?" We were buddies and Billi knew my history of helping to solve murders. As smart as she was, she would undoubtedly want to know all the background information she could learn before talking to the cops.

"Do you know who did it?" she countered, cocking her head slightly as she seemed to study me.

"I know who I would like to have done it."

"Not anyone you invited last night," she guessed.

"That's right. And that includes the guest of honor."

Billi laughed. "I figured. Anyway, let's go see those pups. They're adorable."

"I know." I began following her again. "I met them first at my shops when Henry Schulzer brought them in for treats, though I didn't know who he was then." As she stopped by a door into an enclosed building, I asked, "So what's going on with them? With their owner gone, will they become available for adoption? Or have you found a family who'll take them in?"

"Still working on answers to that." Billi turned and opened the door into the building.

The cockers weren't the only dogs inside. Most of the canines in this building were small, no more than thirty pounds, and their backgrounds were varied, which was the norm in a shelter. They included Chihuahua mixes and other toy dogs, as well as several varieties of terriers and more.

"Yep, they're very cute," I said as we stopped outside the enclosure that held Henry's now-orphaned dogs. They ran to the mesh and wriggled against it, both obviously begging for attention.

"If we're given the go-ahead to find a new home for them," Billi said, "I'll try to work things out so we do it at one of the Barkery adoption events."

"Great. I was going to suggest that."

"Too bad they can't talk to us. They apparently were there when Schulzer was killed. They probably have all the answers inside them and could save all of us getting grilled by the cops."

"And I was going to mention that, too," I said, catching Billi's eye and matching her rueful grin. "Now, I've got a few questions for you."

NINE

WE GRABBED A COUPLE of leashes off hooks on the building's wall and took Duke and Prince for a walk outside on the shelter's walkways. I recognized one of the volunteers heading our way with two people, who looked like a middle-aged married couple—potential adopters? Yes, as it turned out.

After Billi welcomed them, learned what size and breed of dogs they were most interested in, and then made suggestions to the volunteer about which dogs to introduce these visitors to, we continued on. Meantime, Prince and Duke had welcomed the visitors, too, by wriggling and sidling up to both of them, which hopefully got their hearts even more in gear for figuring out who to take home—assuming they found a dog they liked and they met all the shelter's adoption criteria. Not Prince and Duke, though. Not yet, at least.

When we were no longer in their presence, I finally asked what had been on my mind all along. "Has there been any feedback about the latest murder from City Council or the mayor's office? I assume the heads of our local government are all aware of it, or have you spoken with any of them?"

"You know me well enough to be sure I've had a discussion, or two or six," Billi said. There were seven City Council members, including Les Ethman, a really sweet, older friend of mine. Like Billi, he was a member of a prominent family in town. Les loved Knobcone Heights and was obvious about it. I assumed he was one of the people Billi had talked to first.

"And what does Les say?" I asked

"I was aware of the original murder ten years ago, and I was sorry then about what had happened to the mayor, but Les and his family were actually close to them. I didn't get to talk to him for long, but I got the impression that Les was really sad to hear what has happened to Henry Schulzer."

"Then he believed justice was done when Mike Holpurn was incarcerated for the crime?"

"Yes, I think so."

I'd already figured that I needed to talk to Les, and now I was sure of it.

For now, though, Billi just told me that the other council members were all horrified and sad and eager for justice to be done—all the standard kinds of public pronouncements I expected, though so far maybe they were just relating them to one another. She hadn't spoken with Mayor Sybill Gabbon yet, but maybe someone had. I liked our current mayor and presumed Billi did, too. Mayor Gabbon had recently adopted a couple of dogs from Mountaintop Rescue at one of our events.

"Is City Council going to look into it any further? Hold any kind of memorial for Henry?"

Billi shrugged, and the movement got the attention of Duke, whose leash she held. The cocker, who'd been sniffing an area just off the walkway that dogs frequently used for their outdoor activities, moved over and sat down in front of her as if expecting her to give a command.

She laughed, and so did I. "Good dog," I said, and Prince, who must have thought I was speaking to him, stopped pulling on his leash and also sat down.

"Good dog." This time it was Billi who spoke, to Prince. Then, looking at me, she said, "One way or another, I intend to be certain that these two get good homes, preferably together. It's got to be hard to lose a person as close to them as their owner must have been, and then wind up at a shelter, even for just a while, and no longer be the center of someone's attention."

"Plus, they apparently saw what happened," I reminded her again. "Talk to me, guys." I was joking, and yet not for the first time, I wished we could communicate better with our pets. We often read their thoughts—for example, I could usually tell which of my Barkery treats were a dog's favorite. But the dog couldn't explain why.

And as far as revealing a murder they'd seen? The dogs just looked from one of us to the other, then both stood and began sniffing the ground around us once more.

"Let me know if there's anything else I can do to make sure these two remain okay, besides holding an adoption event when you're ready," I said.

"And you let me know if there's anything I can do to help find out who killed their owner." Billi looked at me with sincerity in her gaze. "Yes, I know that's more my responsibility than yours—or at least, I should make sure that City Council does what it needs to in support of our police force, as well as make it clear that the town needs answers in this situation quickly and accurately."

"Which means Knobcone Heights needs my help." I grinned to show I was joking—mostly.

Billi's return grin was one of the most ironic I'd seen on her. "Unfortunately—or perhaps fortunately—that may be so."

I left soon afterward, but not without pulling out a couple of the Barkery treats I'd shoved far down into my pockets and handing them one by one to the poor, orphaned, sweet dogs.

Would I—could I—be the one to adopt them?

Under other circumstances, I would have considered it. I love dogs, of course, and always felt sorry when things changed for the worse in a dog's life. At least I assumed it was for the worse here. I'd seen Henry with them at the Barkery and he seemed to be very kind to them, despite how he acted toward people. But had he been a good dog parent? I'd never really know.

Although that did spur me to try to speed up something I'd been intending to work on anyway.

After saying goodbye to the two sweeties and to Billi, too, I picked up Biscuit from Mimi in the lobby. And yes, I learned from her that the people we'd seen had found a dog they liked and were currently playing in an enclosed area with him to get to know him better.

Biscuit and I got back into my car. There, I used my Bluetooth to call Neal before pulling out of my parking space.

Fortunately, he mustn't have been too busy at the resort's reception desk and picked up right away.

"Are you okay, bro?" I asked him.

"You mean, have the police been hanging around here asking me, and everyone else, all kinds of intrusive and accusatory questions about last night, and how we each happened to know Henry Schulzer, and whether we killed him? Yeah, sure, I'm okay."

I was used to my brother's sarcasm—mostly. But now I said, "I get it. I'll tell you more about who they're questioning, and how, later. I want to come to the resort for dinner tonight. Maybe just to the bar, but is everything open?"

"Everything but the part of the floor where Mr. Schulzer's room is on," Neal responded. "Not that I'm surprised, but I guess you're nosing your way around another murder, right, sis?"

"If the cops didn't seem to think that someone at Dinah's party last night had something to do with it, I would stay away," I assured him.

"But they're latching onto—who? Dinah?"

I started to answer, but Neal's voice changed. "Welcome to the Knobcone Heights Resort," he said with the phone clearly away from his mouth, obviously talking to someone who'd come up to the registration desk. And then to me he said, "We'll talk later, when you get here."

"Great," I said. "And ask if Henry's dog walker could join us for dinner. Could you try to find out something about her, too?"

I hung up and started driving back to the shops. But I used my Bluetooth on the way to call Reed. Not surprisingly, considering it was still during clinic hours, he didn't answer, but I left a message inviting him to join me for dinner again at the resort tonight. I didn't explain why, but Reed had already jumped to the conclusion that I was getting involved in trying to solve this murder.

Did I want to?

Did I have a choice?

And did I want to argue with Reed again about it?

The answers weren't yes to any of these questions, but I now had a history of doing such things, especially when someone I cared about happened to be a major suspect.

"But this is all so odd, Biscuit," I said as I pulled onto Summit Avenue, where my shops were located. "I haven't lived in Knobcone Heights long, but I never heard of murders being committed here before—except, now, for that mayor's in the past. But the rest of them? Why is this happening while I'm here?"

My sweet dog, in the backseat, sat up when she heard my voice, as I could see in the rear-view mirror. But she didn't attempt to answer my question even by body language, other than to wriggle a bit because she'd heard me speak.

We were soon parked behind the shops and I walked Biscuit to the front to take her into the Barkery. I realized it was getting late. Too late for me to see Dinah before she had to take off for the police station?

Fortunately, Dinah was still in the Barkery, waiting on a customer who held a Papillon mix in her arms and was feeding the little dog a biscuit—one of my liver treats with cheese. A bag sat on the counter and Dinah was ringing up the woman's order.

"Hi," I said to the customer. "Welcome to Barkery and Biscuits, and I'm glad your pup has been given a sample."

"Two samples," the woman contradicted with a smile. "This is so nice. I haven't been here before but I'm buying little Pappy some treats, and you can be sure we'll be back."

"That's great," I said, smiling at Dinah as the customer thanked her again and left.

She'd been the only customer in the shop, so I asked Dinah, "How are things?"

"Okay, but I'm glad you're back. I was going to ask Janelle to come in. It's time for me to go."

"I figured." I went around the counter and hugged my dear helper. "I hope it all goes fine. Just another avenue of research for you. Be sure to give me a call when you're done and let me know how it went."

"Do you want to be the recipient of my only call when I'm arrested?" Dinah retorted, and unfortunately didn't sound as if she was kidding.

"They're not going to arrest you." At least not tonight, I thought, but I didn't say that. Nor did I add that I hoped what I said was true. "In fact, just so you know, I'm meeting Reed at the resort tonight for dinner so we can talk, and hopefully I can meet with the dog walker Henry was using. I'd like to talk with her."

"Me too. Okay, if that's an invitation to join you, I'll give it a try."

"Great," I said, meaning it. This way I would learn how the cops treated her right after the fact.

It was around three o'clock now, and we closed the shops at six. All went fine for the rest of the day, with Janelle in the Barkery and Vicky in Icing and me popping back and forth between them.

My mind jumped often to anticipating what would go on that evening, which was silly in a way. Maybe I'd learn more about Henry and what had happened to him, who his dog walker was, and how some of the people I cared about were reacting to this latest murder, but I didn't expect too much would happen on this next visit to Knobcone Heights Resort.

Reed and Dinah had agreed to meet me at the resort bar around six thirty. I decided to also call Les Ethman and told him briefly why I cared about the Henry Schulzer murder situation. I got his agreement to meet us at the resort.

I went home to drop off Biscuit, after serving her a nice, wholesome doggy dinner. I changed clothes, too. I didn't get very dressed up but wore something fancier than my working day attire. Then I drove across town, without calling Neal in advance to let him know my arrival time. It didn't matter. He would be there anyway, since his working hours on Thursday ended around seven.

Neal had already told me this would be another of those evenings when he couldn't validate my parking ticket. But it would be worth the price if somehow my discussions led to even a few answers, or at least helped to start me on the right track.

After finding a parking spot, I strode into the lobby, where a lot of people were hanging out. I wondered if the police had shut down the restaurant at all during their investigation, since Henry had been there, but if so, at least it wasn't currently cordoned off with crime scene tape. And Neal had said only Henry's room was still being examined.

Yet Henry had been with us in the restaurant for a while. Even though that didn't necessarily turn the restaurant into a crime scene, the cops might want to ask questions of even more of the people who'd seen Henry there.

If they'd closed off the area, I bet it hadn't been for long. The Ethmans—Les's extended family—owned the resort, and they held a lot of sway in Knobcone Heights. They wouldn't be happy about any decrease in revenue while some of the facilities were being examined. That might even be true of the hotel room where Henry had been killed.

Even so, I'd decided to eat in the bar, avoiding the restaurant. No need for anything tonight to resemble last night's party. Besides, the people I was meeting with would be happy in the bar, I felt certain.

First, though, I hurried over to the end of the lobby where Neal worked. My nicely dressed, good-looking brother fortunately had no one with him so I joined him briefly, let him know where I was going, and asked softly, "Did you find out anything about Henry's dog walker?"

He nodded. "I've seen her around here before, you know, but I never had occasion to talk to her or ask her name. She was here earlier today, obviously without Henry's dogs, and she looked a little lost. That gave me good reason to go greet her."

"And ...?" I prompted.

"She's named Mysha Jorgens. I assured her I'd introduce her to a couple of new hotel guests who just got here with their dogs, as long as she joined us this evening."

"And will she?" I asked, somewhat excitedly. But I knew the answer. Why else would Neal have mentioned it?

"She will," he confirmed.

"Excellent! I'd better go reserve seats in the bar."

"Yes," he said, "you'd better grab some—though I already told the staff to put a few tables together on the patio. It's not that cold outside, and they can turn on some heaters if necessary."

"If you weren't working I'd kiss you," I told my brother. Even so, I blew him a brief kiss. Then I headed across the lobby, ducking between groups of people, toward the bar.

Les Ethman was already standing inside the door, not near the crowded counter where quite a few patrons were watching a soccer game on a TV hung on the wall. He held a tall glass of beer. "Hi, Carrie," he said immediately.

"Hi, Les." I responded to his outstretched arms and drew closer so we could share a brief, friendly hug. I was careful not to bump into his hand holding the glass.

As a town elder, Les had been on the City Council for as long as I'd lived in Knobcone Heights, and for I didn't know how many years before that. Tonight he wore a dressy, pale yellow shirt and brown slacks. His hairline seemed to have receded since the last time I'd seen him, and as always I basked in his friendly smile.

But I had to tease him. "So are your relatives comping you here tonight?" I nodded toward his hand holding the drink. With his family owning the resort, it probably was true, but it wasn't as if Les, as wealthy as the resort owners or maybe even more so, couldn't have afforded his drink. Or parking in the resort lot, for that matter.

"Shhh," he whispered. "I don't want word to get around."

I laughed along with him. "Okay, let's go grab the tables outside on the patio that Neal reserved for us."

"I'll let the bartenders know where we are, so they can tell the others who'll be joining us," Les said. "Let's see. Does that include Dr. Storme?"

Les was a close enough buddy of mine to know that Reed and I had been seeing each other socially for a while. But I threw my hand up to my mouth and gasped. "Oh dear, did I forget to invite someone?"

"I don't think so." Les was suddenly looking over my shoulder, and I turned to see why. Not surprisingly, Reed was there.

"Hi, Carrie," he said. "Les. Good to see you."

"I'm especially glad to see you, now that I don't have to worry that my reputation will be besmirched by hanging out with a murder suspect," Les said. "Although that goes for both of you."

I laughed. "Okay, don't rub it in."

We followed him through the bar, and he gave a heads-up to the bartenders about where we would sit. When we went outside, into the August air, it was unsurprisingly still warm. Sunset was on its way, but there was still some daylight.

We took our seats at a couple of empty tables that had been moved together. Reed and I ordered drinks—his an imported dark beer, different from the lighter ale Les was drinking, and I asked for a merlot.

I stared at the lake, whose shores were at the bottom of the stairway that led down from the patio. There were a few boats out but not many. I wasn't sure how long we'd be outside, but I always enjoyed the view from the resort at night, with the lights reflecting on the water.

"So why are we here tonight?" Reed asked.

"To enjoy each other's company," I answered. "Oh, and to ask Les if the City Council happens to have any insight on who killed Henry Schulzer." I planned to bring up the topic of the dog walker later, especially if she joined us, but I had no reason to believe she knew who'd killed Henry.

On the other hand, it wouldn't hurt to ask her. The dog walker had seen more of the man than I figured most people had during the last days of his life.

"I already talked to Billi," Les said. "She told me she spoke with you this afternoon about—surprise—the same subject. I doubt I know any more than she does. But I did know Henry's wife, Flora. I wasn't a councilman back then, but I had political aspirations, so I got to know people in local government whenever possible." He paused. "She was a nice enough lady if she wanted something from you—and as mayor, she wanted a lot of things from a lot of people."

"What if she didn't want anything from you?" I prompted, then took a sip of wine.

"It depended on who you were. Since I was an Ethman, she was never nasty to me, but I saw she could get nasty to others, especially those who got in her way."

"Like Mike Holpurn?" I had to ask.

"As far as I could tell at the time, that was an interesting situation. She used Holpurn—in a number of ways, including, I gathered, as a bedmate. Did her husband know? I'm not sure. Did the mayor break it off and thereby give Holpurn a motive to kill her? Again, I don't know. But that seemed to be part of his confession. And—"

"I am so sorry," interrupted a female voice that almost sounded hysterical. "I wish I could tell you, Ms. Kennersly, who killed Mr. Schulzer. He was a nice man. His dogs are wonderful."

I looked up and saw that the person who'd interrupted was the dog walker… what had Neal said her name was? Oh yes. Mysha Jorgens. I hadn't paid much attention to how she looked when I'd first met her, only to the dogs in her care, but she was an attractive young woman with a pale complexion and large brown eyes. Now she wore a fluffy top and long skirt over boots. She didn't appear to be ready to walk dogs at the moment—and she didn't have any with her.

She was followed by Neal, who stood behind her and shrugged his shoulders, an apologetic expression on his face.

"Henry's dogs certainly are wonderful," I assured her.

Before I could say anything else, Mysha started speaking again. "You've got to do it, Ms. Kennersly. I've heard that you've solved murders around here before. Find out who killed Mr. Schulzer. Fast. He deserves justice. Please, Ms. Kennersly. Please."

TEN

"Um…" I BEGAN, ready to tell Mysha that I appreciated her desire to have a quick answer but that I could make no promises—and that I hadn't really wanted to get involved in solving all those murders in the first place. But instead, seeing the plea on her face—plus, she'd knelt down on the patio to look straight at me as I sat there—I couldn't just brush her request off.

And I was certainly curious about what her relationship with Henry had really been. Was she only his dog walker? Based on her emotionalism, I doubted that. Unless she was just generally an emotional human being.

Neal bent down to help Mysha back to her feet. "We'd like to have what happened resolved as fast as possible, too, but let's leave those details to the cops, okay?"

"But—"

I interrupted, since Mysha was resisting Neal's efforts to help her up. "Here, please have a seat." Although I was happy she'd agreed to join us, I also hoped she would calm down and become less emotional. Most of all, I hoped she would give us some helpful information.

"Would you like a drink?" I asked. Mysha appeared young but not too young to drink—maybe early twenties.

"Oh. Yes. Yes, I'd love some wine. Like yours. And oh, Ms. Kennersly, I've been wanting to talk to you. When you told me that you own Barkery and Biscuits, I knew you must love dogs, especially since you're also a vet tech, as your brother told me. I'm a dog walker, you know—and Mr. Schulzer was my main client lately. I need to find more now."

In other words, she was kind of out of work.

Could I help her? Maybe. Did I want to?

Again, maybe. She was so sad, so emotional, that I didn't think she could be the murderer.

Then again, all of this could be a ploy to send my suspicions in a different direction. Not that my opinion mattered much. The cops would have to agree either way.

But word had somewhat gotten out about my prior successes in solving murders, so much so that someone like Mysha could assume that convincing me of her innocence would go a long way toward convincing the authorities as well.

Within a minute, Neal had brought three more chairs to our table. I assumed Janelle would join us soon, too. One of the bartenders came over and jotted down our orders, and then there we all sat, looking at each other again.

I had my questions for Mysha ready. "So, how did you get the job walking Prince and Duke?"

Her expression lit up. "Oh, you know them! I'm not surprised. They must have stopped by your Barkery, right? Anyway, Henry moved to the resort a few weeks ago and had his dogs with him. I was already doing some work for another guest, so I went over to Henry and gave him my card—and he called me. From that point on, I spent a lot of time with his dogs."

And with Henry? My suspicion about whether there'd been more to their relationship than dog walker and owner continued to grow. Otherwise, why had Mysha been so emotional?

But that didn't matter, unless she'd killed him.

"Yes," I told her. "I met Henry at my shop, and I saw his dogs this afternoon, too."

Mysha half stood. "Really? Where are they? I've been wondering since . . . since yesterday."

I explained to her that the authorities had turned the dogs over to Mountaintop Rescue, with the understanding that relatives of Henry would be sought first to see if they would adopt the dogs, and if not, this wonderful local shelter would take care of them till the right new dog parents could be found. "Mountaintop Rescue is the greatest," I assured her.

I half wondered if Mysha would make an offer to adopt the dogs but doubted it. Owning dogs was more expensive than walking them for profit.

Her drink and Neal's arrived then, and behind the server came Janelle, who also sat down. She shot a curious glance toward Mysha and I introduced them.

Then the dog walker said, "Well, I'm really glad that Duke and Prince are being taken care of, but—"

"But I'm sure you're concerned," I acknowledged. "You know, I agree with you that it would be a good idea if Henry's death was solved quickly. That might make it easier also to rehome the pups." I saw that Janelle, Neal, and Les had entered into a conversation, among themselves—one I couldn't hear. That was probably a good thing, since I could take advantage of the situation. "You'd been working for Henry and the dogs for a while," I said to Mysha. "Do you know of any people he met here, or who he otherwise had contact with? Of course, there was the situation with the man who was convicted of killing Henry's wife many years ago, but did Henry argue with anyone else that you're aware of? You might not think one of them could be his killer, but it would be helpful for the police to know of anyone like that."

"They've already asked me," Mysha replied. "But because you … well, since you've helped them before, here's what I told them, though it's not much. I saw that Mr. Schulzer was friends with some guests here at the hotel."

"Really? Do you know their names?" I knew that Neal would be a good source for finding out more about these guests, whoever they were.

"No, but they were apparently staying at the resort for a while, as … as … as poor Henry was." Mysha's voice choked up and tears ran down her cheeks. "I think their room was next to his, or at least close by."

That might not be enough for Neal to go on, but he was listening now and I glanced at him.

"I did see Mr. Schulzer in the lobby several times with some guests I believe were his neighbors here," Neal said. "I'll talk to them and ask them to get in touch with you, Carrie." In other words, he was protecting the hotel guests' privacy, which I understood. That was part of his job.

But Neal clearly knew priorities around here—at least mine. The sooner I could talk to as many people as possible who potentially had knowledge of the murder victim and what might have happened, the better. With another glance at me, Neal excused himself as if to head for the restroom, but I suspected he was going to make a phone call related to this latest info.

Meanwhile, since I knew I'd be able to speak with everyone else at the table later, I encouraged Mysha to keep talking about the various dogs she walked and their owners, especially Henry and anyone who might have known him.

Sipping my wine and toasting Henry, Duke, and Prince now and then, I learned a lot about Mysha's favorite paths around the resort area and even around downtown Knobcone Heights. She seemed to relax, and even to enjoy the conversation. She asked me more about my Barkery and how I created the treats I sold there, and I told her a little bit of my background.

But having a fun discussion wasn't exactly on my agenda. Eventually, I motioned to our server and requested that he bring us more wine, and some of the others at the table requested more, too.

Then, before our new drinks arrived, I said to Mysha, "You know, I only met poor Henry recently. He went through a lot here in Knobcone Heights all those years ago when he lost his wife. I take it you're aware of this now, but did you know it when you first started working for him?"

"Well, sort of. My other customers who knew him a little have lived in town for a while, and they let me know that horrible story. But I never learned the details." There was no sorrow on her youthful face now. Instead, her wide-eyed expression appeared—well, fascinated. "He was such a nice man—most of the time. He sometimes chewed me out for being late to pick up the dogs or whatever, but—well, I understood, in a way. People hadn't always been kind to him. I still can't believe that someone killed the poor man's wife when she was mayor of this town."

"Right," I said, shaking my head sadly. "At least it appeared the guilty man was punished for it." I was still looking straight at Mysha, but she didn't react, so maybe she didn't care that the confessed killer of Henry's wife had recently been paroled. Not that it mattered.

What did matter right now was who'd killed Henry.

"And now … someone … someone just murdered him." Mysha swallowed a sob. She seemed genuine, and yet …

"Do you think it's because he got angry with someone, the way he did with you?" In other words, I wanted her reaction to Henry getting angry with her, in order to sense whether his anger had sparked anger—or revenge—in Mysha herself. She might just be a darned good actress … and murderer.

"You never know, do you?" Her voice was still choked. "I always apologized to him if he got mad at me. It was usually justified, you know? I never meant to be late, but it happened, especially when I'd walked other dogs first. They sometimes took their time, and—well, you know. And the stuff I saw Henry get upset at other people for—well, they deserved it, too."

But did they react to it as she claimed to, and accept it? Or did they use it as an excuse to kill him?

There had certainly been anger between Henry and Mike Holpurn—and maybe between Henry and Holpurn's brothers, too.

And, justified or not, he had also become angry with Dinah about her research and had spewed his venom at her.

Dinah wouldn't have killed him for that, or anything else.

I hoped.

Okay, maybe it was out of line, or too soon, or—well, inappropriate, but I decided to ask her directly. "You said Henry sometimes got mad at you, even justifiably." I took a sip of wine as I looked Mysha in her big brown eyes. "Did you ever get mad at him?"

Those eyes widened even more. "Did I—how did you know that? I always try to keep it to myself if I get upset with people or I'm liable to lose their business. I love their dogs most of the time, but—" She scowled suddenly, apparently recognizing what I was doing. "I've heard a lot about you, Carrie, like I said. You figure out who killed people. Is this how you do it, put them on the defensive until the bad guys actually confess?"

I just raised my eyebrows and smiled without answering.

Still holding her wine glass, Mysha continued to glare at me. "I'm not confessing, Carrie Kennersly. I really liked Mr. Schulzer, even if I sometimes got mad at him like he got mad at me. And if you think I'm going to confess to killing him—well, you're wrong."

"I understand," I said. But if Mysha didn't confess, that wouldn't mean she hadn't done it.

And in her rant against me and the way I was acting toward her, she had become defensive.

Which might mean nothing other than that she remained emotional over Henry's death, the loss of payment to walk his dogs, and whatever else was on her mind.

But she hadn't exactly denied that she was the killer.

Good thing I'd pretty much completed what I'd wanted to ask Mysha about, since she suddenly stood up. "You know, I think it's time for me to leave. I know you're just trying to be helpful and all that, but I've told you everything I'm aware of about Henry and his dogs. If you happen to hear of anyone else needing a dog walker, please let me know." She reached into her pocket and pulled out a business card.

Interesting. She was a professional of sorts.

The card had Mysha's phone number on it, as well as a website address, but it didn't say where she lived. It could nevertheless be helpful if I needed to find her again … or send the cops after her.

But I had no reason to do that, at least not now.

"Thanks," I told her. "And you know where to find me, at my shops, if you think of anything else that might help us figure out who killed Henry."

That was hopefully bland enough to indicate that I wasn't pointing to her as the murderer. Not yet, at least.

But if the detectives were zeroing in on Dinah, or even if they weren't, it wouldn't hurt to at least let them know there might be more to Henry's relationship with Mysha than her being solely his dog walker. I still suspected this despite Mysha's story.

"So." Neal slid to sit across from me once Mysha was gone. "Did the dog walker know anything helpful?"

"If she did, she didn't tell me," I told my brother. "She may just be an innocent dog walker, as she said."

"I gather from the way you phrased it that she might not be." Neal could always read my attitude even if I didn't express all that was in my mind.

"Exactly," I said.

Janelle had scooted over closer to Neal. "And you hope she at least knows more for Dinah's sake," she said.

"You got it."

I glanced around and noticed that Reed and Les were standing inside near the bar, talking. I wondered if they'd rejoin us anytime soon.

Neal, Janelle, and I talked a little more about Janelle's interview with Detective Morana. The cops hadn't revealed anything to her while she was at the station, but she recognized that she hadn't been very helpful to them, either.

"Are you going to talk to them some more?" she asked me.

"Probably, although I'd rather they talked to me," I said with a wry grin.

We continued sitting there, drinking a little as Janelle described their questions in more detail than I'd heard before. Then both she and Neal looked over my shoulder, and I thought I knew why.

I turned. I was right. Dinah had just hurried in. She sat down with us in the chair Mysha had vacated, her skin pale and her expression haunted.

"I need a drink," she said. "Now."

ELEVEN

No matter what had happened at the police station, no matter how they'd treated Dinah, I was thrilled that she was there. She was still free—at least physically.

Not under arrest.

But I didn't say anything to her about that. Instead, I made sure she got the glass of wine she wanted.

Until it arrived, Dinah remained fairly quiet. She merely said she was glad it was over with.

"Me too," I told her sincerely. But was it really over with?

"For now," she added, answering that question I hadn't asked.

When the server brought her wine, Dinah picked up the glass and glared at it. What, it wasn't enough? I decided to buy her another glass later if it made sense.

She took a couple large gulps and stared into the distance. I started a conversation with Neal and Janelle about their plans for the upcoming weekend.

"I intend to have a great weekend, too," Dinah eventually broke in. "And not just while I'm at the shops." She looked at me. As usual, she was scheduled to work over the weekend and get next Monday and Tuesday off.

"Great." Then, though I was a bit worried about what she might have in mind, I asked, "Any exciting plans?"

"Yes, and you'll identify with them."

My heart plummeted a little. I had a feeling I knew what Dinah meant. "You won't be doing any writing, I gather." I added a humorous tone to my voice.

"Well, yes, but I'll be plotting based on reality." She stared at me, apparently waiting for my reaction.

"That sounds interesting." And scary, but I wanted to keep my reaction bland.

"You could say that." Dinah looked from me to Neal, then to Janelle. "I'm going to figure out who killed Henry Schulzer in order to get those miserable cops off my back."

Which was what I figured she meant.

Should I discuss the process of solving a murder with her? Just because I'd had some luck with it didn't mean I really knew what I was doing.

"That would be a great plot for a book," Janelle said. "But using your imagination is best." I figured Janelle knew what I was thinking—and maybe she felt the same way, too.

Of course, Janelle had also been a murder suspect. She had also tried to figure her case out, just as I did when I'd been a suspect and not merely a nosy, detectivish civilian.

There could be frustration involved.

And danger.

I figured Janelle was trying in her own way to keep Dinah safe—as safe as she could be while the cops tried to find evidence to arrest her.

"I will use my imagination, at least to some extent." Dinah took another big sip of wine, then leaned over the table toward Janelle. "Still, maybe it'll be a nonfiction book, after the fact. Maybe I can write a step-by-step story of how I figured it out before the police did. You could do that too, Carrie, one of these days, with any of the murders you solved. Once I get this story done, I'll be able to help you even more." She'd turned toward me, and her smile was broad—and seemed challenging.

I just hoped Dinah would stay safe—and free—while she conducted her research.

"Maybe so," I said noncommittally.

Just then, Neal stood up and looked across the patio toward the door inside. I turned to see what had caught his attention

Two people stood there, maybe in their forties. The woman held a Chihuahua close against her.

"Hang on a minute." Neal hurried toward them.

"Who are they?" Dinah demanded, as if I knew the answer.

"I think they're hotel guests," Janelle said. "I've seen him talking to them before."

He conversed with them briefly, and then all three came to our table and stood near us.

"I'd like you to meet the Banners," Neal said. "They're—er, they were—neighbors of Henry Schulzer."

"We've only been here about a week," the man said. "Henry was so nice, telling us lots about the town and things to do and see."

"We didn't know of his background here," said the woman, "or that he had good reason to know a lot more about Knobcone Heights than we did."

"Would you like to join us?" I asked. I didn't know how much the Banners could or would tell us about Henry, but it wouldn't hurt to find out.

"There's a very good reason to join us," Dinah said. "Your little guy, there." She pointed to the Chihuahua. "This is Carrie Kennersly." Her finger moved from the dog to me. "She owns Barkery and Biscuits, this town's excellent bakery of healthy dog treats. Oh, and she also owns Icing on the Cake, the people bakery next door."

"We've been to those shops," Mrs. Banner said with a grin. She she sat down, dog on her lap, once her husband brought chairs over.

It turned out that Kris and Paul Banner were visiting from Portland, Oregon, after some friends who'd stayed at the Knobcone Heights Resort hadn't stopped talking about how wonderful it was.

I couldn't help piping in. "In case you want to see more of the area and enjoy hiking, Neal here loves to lead hikes."

"Really?" Kris, whose black hair was short and nose was long, sounded impressed, and my brother shot me a grateful smile as he started describing the thing he liked to do best.

Dinah rolled her eyes. She also waved over the nearest server and asked for another glass of wine. She'd finished her first before the rest of us had.

Dinah also changed the topic when Neal stopped to take a breath. "It must have been difficult to lose a new friend and tour guide that way," she said. "When Henry Schulzer was killed, I mean."

"Yes, in many ways," Kris said. "Our dogs loved each other and we went on some walks together. And we kept picking Henry's brain for more to do in the area."

That didn't make for a very pretty image of their friendship, I thought. And I still didn't really know how Henry had died. Had his brain been picked?

"And we shouldn't complain," Paul said, "but we had to change rooms when he was killed." He looked older than his wife, with salt-

and-pepper hair—what was left of it. "The police have been spending a lot of time on our floor, and we were right next door to Henry."

"At least we had some vacancies on the floor above you," Neal said. I wondered if he had been kind enough to suggest their relocation or if the police had insisted on it.

I also wondered how friendly Henry had really been with them. I'd seen no indication of any differences between them, but who knew? Maybe he'd insulted their little dog and they'd retaliated.

I'd at least try to find out more about the Banners before eliminating them as possible murder suspects.

"Did the police talk to you?" I asked. "I mean, did you ever see poor Henry arguing with anyone, or—"

"Oh yes," Kris responded right away. "Once, on a walk we took with him, someone must have recognized who he was and started bawling him out for something I guess his wife, the mayor, did years ago—something about signing a bill that increased some local property tax or whatever, which they claimed nearly made them lose their home."

Interesting. That sounded, though, as if whoever it was would be more inclined to get rid of Flora than Henry.

Maybe.

I asked, "Did you happen to mention that to the police?"

"We did," Paul said. "They seemed really grateful."

Which sounded strange. Maybe that was just Paul's impression, or maybe the detectives were glad to have any additional information on possible though unlikely suspects. How would I know?

I did get an idea, though. I thought about asking this couple, who'd been displaced from their room next to Henry's, about it.

But it would make more sense for me to ask my sweet, usually accommodating bro about it. And hopefully soon.

I wanted to know exactly where the Banners' room had been.

I wanted to visit that floor, although I probably wouldn't be able to get into what had been Henry's room. Not yet, at least. But maybe something in the vicinity would give me some more ideas about what had happened to Henry.

About *who* had happened to Henry.

For now, though, I just reached into my pocket. As usual, I happened to have a dog treat there. I pulled it out and showed it to them before offering it to their pup.

"May I?" I asked.

"Of course!" Kris said. "Marshmallow will love it."

Marshmallow? The little Chihuahua was golden brown and didn't resemble a marshmallow. But it was still a cute name.

I noticed Dinah stir beside me and I turned to share a smile with her before handing the yam treat to Marshmallow.

Of course, Dinah's smile was sad. But I suspected she and I were sharing similar thoughts about the Banners. And looking for more people who'd met Henry. People who'd seen him argue with someone else, who might wind up being useful witnesses even if they weren't obvious suspects.

I figured their names and relationship with Henry would soon be jotted in Dinah's new notebook.

The Banners stayed for just a little while longer … and I tamped down my urge to follow them when they stood and began maneuvering their way around the tables on the patio, then through the door into the bar that seemed filled with even more patrons now.

I stayed put, though. I didn't know if the Banners were returning to their room, and even if they were, their current room wasn't on the floor where Henry had been murdered. I wasn't likely to learn anything more just by hanging out with them.

But I really, really had an urge to see that floor. Better yet, the room where Henry had been killed, though I had no doubt that it was still blocked off as a crime scene.

I wanted to get at least an idea of the layout, though. Maybe visiting the floor just above or below would give me a sense of what the area and rooms were like.

The person who'd be able to show me at least some of these locations sat across from me. I caught Neal's eye as he sat beside Janelle, sipping his beer. His eyebrows raised, as if in amusement or understanding or both.

My bro knew me very well.

But this wasn't a good time to even hint at what I wanted him to do. Instead, still sipping my merlot, I eavesdropped on Janelle's conversation with Dinah. I figured Neal was, too, as well as Reed, who'd returned to our table without Les; Les had asked him to pass along his goodbyes to us. Reed also drank as he sat beside me, sometimes rubbing my hand or shoulder gently, but otherwise staying still.

At Janelle's encouragement, Dinah was describing her discussion with—interrogation by—Bridget Morana. Of course I wanted to hear all about it, but I hadn't wanted to embarrass Dinah at the resort or upset her any more than she was already upset. At least not for the moment.

Janelle apparently had no such qualms. They were, after all, friends as well as coworkers now, and Dinah could tell Janelle to back off if she didn't want to talk.

But Dinah was talking. And making notes on a pad of paper extracted from her purse, though it wasn't the notebook Arvie had given her. Maybe she felt more inclined to jot drafts on this less formal pad now.

"I saw no sense in lying to the police," she was saying. "I admitted that my little exchange with Mr. Schulzer—Henry—hadn't been particularly friendly. You saw that, Carrie. But he was irritated with other people as well as me. That guy Holpurn, who'd been in prison for killing Henry's wife—well, he had the nerve to accuse Henry, right there in public, of committing that murder instead of him and framing him for it. So it wasn't a surprise that Henry would be peeved."

"That's what I figured, too," Janelle agreed. "But—well, Henry left your party. I assume that was okay, and the end of your contact with him, but—"

"Not exactly," Dinah said in a low voice. "When I left, and Vicky and Frida had gone on their way, I looked around the lobby and outside in case he was still around. And he was. Walking his dogs in the parking lot. And I approached him."

Uh-oh. "What happened then?" I had to ask.

"They went inside the resort building next door and I followed them. That's when I noticed that we weren't exactly alone. Mike Holpurn and his buddies must have been in the lobby, and now they were following me. And that reporter, Silas, followed them. Plus, there were other people around the lobby."

"So whatever you said to Henry, there was a potential audience," I said. An audience could be a good thing—or just the opposite, depending on how Dinah's interaction with Henry went. And judging by her apparent uneasiness, I assumed it hadn't gone well.

She wound up confirming that. "Since Henry didn't seem angry anymore," she continued, "and didn't run away like he had in the restaurant, I started asking questions about his wife's death. Did she, as mayor, have any enemies? Had he—her husband—felt like an enemy when word got out that she was apparently having an affair? Did he remember what the evidence was against Mr. Holpurn? I didn't look at him when I asked all this, but I sensed him moving a little farther away from me. I reminded him that I was doing research and might write a book about what had happened, despite what he'd said inside about ruining my career. And—well, he blew up at me again. I guess I shouldn't be surprised. He ... well, he made me feel terrible. But this time I got angry, too."

Dinah hung her head, and Janelle bent toward her and gave her a brief hug. When Dinah looked up again, there were tears in her large blue eyes but a stubborn lift to her chin.

"The thing was," she continued, "he told me that someone like me, just nosy and stupid and pushy, couldn't possibly write a good book or do anything else worthwhile. He questioned what else I did, how much money I earned, how intelligent I was—and I knew he was just doing it so I'd go away and leave him alone, but I couldn't."

I kind of wished now that I'd followed Dinah out when she left the restaurant. But Vicky and Frida had been with her at the time. And I'd had other things, and other people, on my mind—like Reed.

Dinah didn't stop talking. "Our argument didn't go on much longer, but I purposefully accused him of possibly killing his wife back then, and he said again something like of course he didn't do that, but at least he was smart enough to do so if he'd chosen to. Although—well he did look over at Mike Holpurn, who was watching, and say it was a good thing Holpurn confessed since he wasn't the smartest guy around."

I shook my head, wanting to hear more ... yet wishing that second confrontation simply hadn't occurred.

Dinah looked at me through increasingly teary eyes. "I knew he wasn't completely making sense but was just goading everyone. He threatened me again, too. Said he'd come after me if I dared to accuse him."

I gasped and nearly stood up.

But Dinah didn't stop. "I promised I would do it, just for fun— then realized this was dumb, since the guy actually could be a killer. I decided it was time to stop and just walked away, and then finally I left the resort. But people heard him insult and threaten me—and not just my writing this time. They saw my reaction, and ..." She looked at Janelle, then at me. "I hated Henry at that moment, sure. And yes, we'd argued twice that night. But I never would have killed him—at least not for real. If I wrote about him in a novel, well, that would be different." She seemed to try to smile but didn't exactly succeed.

I wasn't smiling either. I really cared about Dinah, but I could really understand now why she was on the cops' radar as a possible murder suspect. "So what did you tell Detective Bridget when she questioned you? All of it?"

Dinah nodded and took another sip of wine. "Yes, all of it," she said defiantly. "And that includes that I was peeved, sure. But the only way I'd have harmed the guy is on paper—or, really, on the computer. Honest, Carrie. You know me. I could have baked Henry some red velvet cupcakes, for example, but I'd never have poisoned him for real. Although ..."

"Although?" I prompted. I still didn't know how Henry had actually died. Poison?

Neither, apparently, did Dinah. "I wish I knew how he did die. I guess that'll eventually come out in the news. If I knew it now, I'd be able to start working on showing that however it was done, it couldn't have been me who did it."

That didn't sound good. Sure, Dinah had an imagination, but saying that it might take a while to come up with a good defense against whatever the cause of death was certainly didn't convince me that she didn't do it.

No, I liked Dinah. Trusted her ... mostly.

And I'd certainly jump into this case as I had others, to try to figure out what had happened.

Figure out who'd killed Henry, and how and why.

I only wished that, at this moment, I felt more certain it wasn't my wonderful, full-time, research-loving, dedicated—and apparently now angry—employee.

TWELVE

JANELLE STARTED ASKING DINAH questions about her research methods and what she would write if she started a new story at this moment, trying to draw her focus away from how nasty the encounters with Henry had been. Or at least I hoped that was Janelle's goal, and also the result.

Meanwhile, I remained jazzed—and curious. And worried.

I caught Neal's glance. He kind of rolled his eyes but also shrugged his shoulders in a direction that suggested I should follow him. He probably knew what I would be asking.

I turned to Reed, then, and did the same, so that he would come along too. "Excuse us for a minute," I said to Dinah and Janelle. I thought about offering an excuse like a potty break but decided that saying nothing wasn't such a bad thing.

I followed Neal through the crowded bar and out the door, and Reed followed me, holding my hand. In the lobby, which was filled with people, too, I said to Neal, "Can you show me the floor above or below where … well, you know. Whatever most closely resembles the floor with the crime scene. It won't tell us much, but still …"

"Still, you'll get a better sense for who could have been roaming around, how easy it would have been to see them, how they could have gotten into the room and all that," Neal finished for me.

"At least it should be safer with the cops around than it was before," Reed said, now standing beside me, "even if they're not on whatever floor we visit."

"Exactly," Neal agreed.

I wondered if Dinah knew which room Henry had been staying in ... and figured that unfortunately, Dinah being Dinah, she probably found out.

We walked outside and stood in front of the main building for a moment. I saw that the parking lot appeared full as usual, and some drivers appeared to be looking for spaces. It was late enough for dusk to have arrived, so most of the illumination came from pole lights around the parking lot.

"This way." Neal motioned for us to go to the left, toward one of the two resort hotel buildings. It was the one I'd assumed Henry had been staying in, thanks to where I'd seen him and also his dogs, while they were in Mysha Jorgens' control. I'd apparently guessed correctly.

I wasn't sure why I felt so nervous—except that it made sense not to feel completely relaxed when we were about to enter the building where a murder had recently occurred. In any event, I was glad to hold Reed's hand as he reached for mine, and all three of us walked together.

I wasn't surprised to see police cars and other official vehicles parked by the entrance. Their lights weren't flashing, but I didn't think anyone would doubt that the people who'd come here in those vehicles were in charge.

"Henry's room was on the second floor," Neal said in a low voice. "I helped to get the Banners moved to the third floor, and it's pretty much the same layout. Some of the rooms on the first floor are smaller, so I think you'll be happier checking the top floor instead."

"Sounds fine with me," I told him.

"We'll take the nearest stairway as long as it's not blocked off. That way we'll be less obvious to the cops."

"Also fine," I said. Inside, though, I felt a bit queasy. The cops. Even my detective "buddies" wouldn't be thrilled to see me there. They undoubtedly wouldn't be surprised, since they'd already indicated that they expected me to try to solve this murder, too—partly because some of the suspects were my friends. And I knew Chief Loretta Jonas wouldn't be surprised to see me either, nor would Sergeant Himura. But most of the Knobcone Heights PD probably only knew me by reputation, and wouldn't be thrilled to have me nosing around the area of the murder scene or otherwise.

I swallowed my unease. Uncomfortable or not, I was going in. I would look around, see what the layout was, scan for anything that would give me an idea of how to look around more thoroughly later, when I could.

And at least I had my relationships with the chief, sergeant, and detectives to refer any other cops to, in the event we were stopped and questioned.

Hopefully that would help.

"You ready?" Neal said.

"Ready," I said firmly and looked at Reed. He nodded, sending me an amused smile.

"Let's go," he said, and we followed Neal to the outside door on the nearest side of the long building.

After we got inside, still following Neal, Reed and I entered the stairway. A flight went downward to the building's basement, and another one headed up. We started slowly up the latter one, Neal still in the lead.

"I know you're not going to try to butt into the cops' crime scene investigation," Reed said. "Not exactly, at least. But I hope you're at least going to be careful." His voice was low, but it still echoed a bit in the stairwell, as did the sounds of our feet on the steps.

I turned to glare at him. "Please keep your voice down," I whispered. "I'm not butting in anywhere. We're just going to look at the layout of the rooms on that floor by checking out the one above it."

"Oh," he said and continued after me.

We climbed up the two flights. I kept my ears open particularly when we reached the second floor and heard muffled voices from somewhere around there. Cops and crime scene investigators, I figured. When we reached the top floor, Neal opened the door. It wasn't locked, and I assumed that was for safety, in case people who were staying in the building needed a way to get to the ground floor in an emergency. Plus, some people just preferred stairs to elevators.

I followed Neal, with Reed still following me.

I'd visited quite a few locations in the Knobcone Heights Resort—including the beach below the main building, probably all the public establishments in the main building, plus some of the offices there, too—but I didn't recall ever visiting the hotel room of anyone staying in the resort. The hallway was wide and well lit, its white walls matching the outside of the buildings, with a wooden floor and recessed doors made of a decorative wood leading into each of the rooms. The room numbers were on plaques on the walls just outside those doors. There was a nice-sized window near the door to the stairway that we'd exited from, and I assumed there was another window at the far end of the hall.

No one was out and about in the hallway. It could be that, considering what was going on one floor below them, everyone was taking their time returning to the hotel this evening. Or maybe some had shut themselves into their room for the night already.

Or maybe this simply wasn't a popular time for traversing this hallway—except for us.

We walked along silently for a few minutes, passing the elevator lobby and a couple more recessed areas containing ice machines and soda and snack vending machines. I figured that a few unmarked doors led to closets or rooms containing the staff's cleaning equipment.

I moved ahead a bit to catch up with Neal and asked quietly, "Which room are the Banners staying in now?"

He pointed ahead and to our right. "Number 308."

I wondered if they were inside currently but had no intention of knocking. Instead I had another question. "And the room downstairs where Henry…was?"

"It's number 212."

There was a catch in my brother's voice. I doubted he'd been a particular fan of Henry's—I doubted anyone was—but still, it was a shame the man had been murdered here, at the resort where Neal so enjoyed working. Heck, it was a shame Henry had died at all, let alone by murder, regardless of his well-earned lack of popularity.

But what Neal had told me caused me to halt right outside room 312. I stood there for a minute listening—and thought I again heard some sounds from the room right below us.

"Are there any vacant rooms on this floor?" I asked. I wanted to see inside one, just to use my imagination about how things might be going during the investigation on the second floor. The likelihood of Neal having a key to get into a vacant room was slim, of course, but I had to ask.

"A couple," my brother said. "And yes, before you ask, I happen to have one of the generic key cards that housekeeping uses to get inside to clean rooms. I assume that's why you're asking—you want to get inside one."

"You assume exactly right," I said. "But do you know offhand which ones are vacant?"

"I will in a minute." Neal drew his cell phone from his pocket, swiped at its face and pressed it a few times, then said, "Either coincidentally or by design, this one doesn't have any guests in it." He gestured toward room 312.

I couldn't help smiling. Apparently there was a special app for resort employees. "Then can we go in?"

"Why not?" He pulled the card key from his pocket and pressed it against the raised metal gadget attached to the door handle. The light on it turned green and I heard a click. Neal took hold of the handle and pressed it down, and the next moment, we were in the room.

And a very nice room it was. It appeared to be a mini-apartment, with a kitchen area as well as a living room with a sofa, which was probably a pull-out bed, facing a wall-mounted television. There was a door that most likely led to a closet, and an open one for the bathroom. Pictures on the wall appeared to be mostly of the lake just below the resort.

"Not bad," Reed said, putting his arm around my shoulders. "I'm sure it's not cheap." He looked at Neal.

"Good guess," my brother said.

"And the room below us is about the same?" I asked.

"Nearly identical."

I wandered for just a few minutes, allowing my imagination to go to work. Henry Schulzer had chosen a room just like this, and he had apparently stayed here for a while with his two dogs—on the second floor, not the first, so he had to take them down in the elevator or stairway when they needed to go outside.

I gave my imagination free rein as I examined the place. How Henry Schulzer had died, exactly, still hadn't been made public. Had he been in his bed, asleep? How had the killer gotten in? Henry's dogs had barked, alerting neighbors, but had they started barking when company arrived or not till their master was hurt?

I looked into the kitchen. It contained a small refrigerator, a stove, a toaster oven. Had Henry invited a guest in and served drinks or food—only to have the person slip poison into whatever he was ingesting?

Or—I opened a top drawer near the sink... and found, as I'd wondered, some flatware—including a couple of sharp carving knives.

Could one of those have been used?

Or maybe the bad guy—or girl—had brought a weapon along, premeditating what they were about to do here.

Or—

The unit's door slammed open and I screamed, though just a little. Were we about to be attacked? But surely, with the police just downstairs...

The police. That's who had opened the door. One of my friendly nemeses now stood there: Detective Wayne Crunoll.

"Why am I not surprised to see you, Carrie?" he asked. As usual when I saw him, he was dressed professionally in a white shirt with dark slacks. No beard shadow today on his pudgy cheeks, but there was a nasty scowl on his face.

Reed apparently noticed that scowl, since, nice guy that he was, he maneuvered around to place his shoulder between the detective and me. But I took a step so Reed and I were side-by-side as I made myself smile at the detective.

"I'm certainly not surprised to see you here, Detective," I said. "But I figured you'd be hanging out on the next floor down, which I understand is the crime scene."

"I was, but people heard footsteps in the stairwell, then up here. There are still hotel patrons staying here, but we decided it was prudent for one of us to come take a look at what was going on, just in case we might have a … situation brewing."

"Like a serial killer?" I asked.

"That or something else," Wayne replied. "I gather we have a something else—a nosy citizen perhaps butting in again."

"But this time, the nosy citizen has kind of been asked to get involved, at least in scheduling police interviews for people who were with the victim last night before he was … harmed."

Wayne sighed. "Yes, you're right about that. And—well, when I was told to come up here and take a look around, my first thought was that it could be you up here snooping. Someone mentioned seeing you in the resort bar tonight, so it was a logical conclusion on my part."

Neal had planted himself near the detective. Playing his real role as a hotel employee, he asked, "Is there anything the Knobcone Heights Resort can do to help out in your investigation? I'm sure you've talked to people with a lot higher authority around here than I have, but I know we're all supposed to cooperate with you."

"Right, so the resort won't get blamed for what happened. That remains to be seen, of course. Anyway … well, unless you're renting a room on this floor, Carrie, I'd suggest you all leave."

I thought of a million reasons to protest—well, maybe not that many, but a few. I'd seen what I hoped to, though, so I said, "Sure, Wayne." I paused. "But do you have any idea when the room where … where it happened is likely to be released?"

"You want to see it." It wasn't a question but a frustrated sigh. "Why am I not surprised? Don't answer that. I'm aware that you'll want to stay involved since some of the people we're questioning are friends or employees of yours. I get it. And I also know that telling you to stay out of this one won't work. But I do want your promise to keep us informed if you find something that could lead to an arrest in this case."

"I'd be glad to, if that promise is reciprocal." I grinned. Wayne didn't. I nevertheless added, "The whole world—or at least the part of it here—is filled with curiosity. Can you reveal Mr. Schulzer's cause of death yet?"

"I gather that we will soon, but I'm not in a position to discuss that with you."

I didn't mention that since we were in private, except for Reed and Neal, we were definitely in a position where he could disclose what would be made public soon anyway. I might not agree to remaining uninvolved in trying to figure out the case, but I would agree to keep my mouth closed about it, at least for now.

"All right, Wayne," I finally said. "I understand. You have a protocol to follow and all that. But I'm sure you can recognize how concerned I am. Yet another murder here in Knobcone Heights—and like the others, it seems to involve people I know and care about as potential suspects. I'd of course like to know who you're looking at most closely, and I hope that includes Mike Holpurn." It was probably unnecessary to say so, but it didn't hurt to mention him. "And if it turns out that none of the people I care about is truly considered a suspect, then I'll be able to back off. I like to spend my time in my shops, after all, and as a vet tech." I turned briefly to grin at Reed. "So—"

"So you know that if our protocol doesn't allow me to even mention the cause of death, I can't discuss possible suspects with you, Carrie."

"I figured. But—well, you've seemed to appreciate my help before, if not my nosiness. Just know that I'll try to be a good citizen and stay in touch with you when it matters."

Which really wasn't saying anything. I was making no more promises than he was.

"Gee, thanks, Carrie." Wayne realized what I wasn't saying. "And now, I really think it would be good if all of you left the building."

I glanced toward Neal first, then Reed. Both nodded, Reed more vehemently than my brother.

"Okay, we're leaving," I said. "I'm sure we'll be in touch again, Wayne. Most likely soon, depending on how things go. Meanwhile, please say hi to Bridget and Chief Loretta for me, okay?"

"Okay," he grumbled through gritted teeth, and I led Neal and Reed into the hallway to head for the elevator.

We didn't need to hide that we were leaving.

THIRTEEN

WE WENT BACK TO the bar and joined Janelle and Dinah again. They were just finishing a snack of sliders, and since we hadn't eaten dinner yet, Reed, Neal, and I ordered some too—along with a quick good night drink. Then, while waiting, we described the little we'd seen in the resort hotel.

"Guess I should have come along," Dinah said, sounding dejected. "It would have been research, after all. But I didn't realize that was where you were going."

"I think right now it's a good thing for you to just take care of yourself and not worry about research," I responded. Unless, of course, she could find the nugget of information that cleared her from being a murder suspect.

Then again, despite how the cops had apparently acted toward her at her interrogation, I didn't know for certain that Dinah was a major suspect. It wasn't as if Detective Crunoll was forthcoming with such information.

We soon were done and everyone expressed an interest in leaving, so we did.

"I'll be at the stores early tomorrow," Dinah promised as we walked outside into the parking lot.

"Great! Me too." And I felt fairly certain I'd see her, since Wayne hadn't alluded to having found anything that would cause the police to arrest anyone yet for the murder, let alone Dinah.

But I'd also learned, since I'd begun my unintentional sleuthing, that you couldn't count on anything to happen ... or not happen.

Once Dinah headed toward her car, the rest of us had to decide, as was often the situation, who was spending the night where. Once again, Neal was heading for Janelle's, which meant that Reed would go pick up Hugo and meet Biscuit and me at my place.

Sure, we sometimes all spent the night in one house. But we all felt more comfortable when each couple had an abode of their own to sleep in—and perhaps do more. Later that night, after Reed and Hugo arrived and the four of us took a short walk, we all went to bed—dogs on the floor and Reed and I engaging in some fun to help us sleep better. Which it did.

We woke up bright and early, as always, the next morning, since I had to dress and dash off to my shops. But once the alarm clock had gone off, Reed was the one to reach for the remote and turn on the TV. The morning news was on, but it wasn't Silas who was reporting. This wasn't surprising, since he usually came on later in the day, although as I'd seen now and then, particularly recently, Silas would show up any time if there was a major news event to report.

Honey Raykoff, an attractive lady in her late thirties who did appear on camera at that early hour, mentioned that the apparent homicide of the husband of the town's former mayor was still being investigated. Then she went on to other stories, so apparently nothing exciting had been determined overnight. "Nothing new yet," I said to Reed.

"Not yet," he agreed. "Do you trust those detectives to figure out what happened?"

"I certainly hope they do this time."

He laughed as we both finished dressing and took the dogs outside.

Soon Reed and Hugo were on their way home, while once more I fastened Biscuit into the backseat of my car and drove to the shops.

Sure enough, Dinah came in early. By silent agreement, we didn't mention the elephant sitting on our shoulders and squeezing our minds with its trunk, or at least that's how it felt to me to be thinking about the murder and its investigation and wondering what would happen next.

Vicky came in soon, then Frida. It was Janelle's day off. I wasn't sure what time Neal started to work on Fridays, but figured they might have a nice leisurely morning to spend together.

And me? Well, I was delighted, as the morning progressed, to have a good number of customers in both shops after we finished baking and opened the doors. But I still felt uneasy, as if another very large shoe was about to drop. And, perhaps, land on the head of one of my assistants, most likely Dinah, during the investigation of Henry's death.

Standing behind the counter, placing dog treats into a paper bag for a woman who'd come in carrying an adorable Westie who loved our yam treats, I found my mind wandering ... and certainly not for the first time that day.

"Here you go," I finally told her, giving her dog another sample and ringing up the sale with a smile. I then aimed my smile toward my Biscuit, who, as always, sat in her enclosure looking happy and inquisitive and adorable.

I knew what I needed to do: find Mike Holpurn and talk to him and his brothers. They were the most logical murderers, weren't they? Holpurn had already admitted to committing one murder in his lifetime, no matter that he now denied it and his incarceration had been cut short.

I wasn't sure where Holpurn was staying, or if he even remained in town—although under the circumstances, and given that he was on parole, I figured the cops must have given him orders to stay around. But considering his background, would he obey them or would he simply choose to defy them?

How would I know?

I decided to leave word with my friends and brother to tell me if they happened to see him.

That gave me a wonderful excuse to grab some coffee at Cuppa-Joe's later that morning. I had a shift at the vet clinic scheduled for after that, so I'd let people at the clinic know as well, although I didn't think Holpurn owned a pet, since he'd just gotten out of prison. I'd also visit Mountaintop Rescue, since although Holpurn might not be likely to stop in there, Billi spent time in a lot of other venues where she might see the guy, such as at her spa or even in City Center, when she went there to fulfill her role as City Councilwoman.

Besides, it would be fun to see her, to work on setting up our next adoption event at the Barkery next week, and to find out if Prince and Duke were likely to be among the pets seeking a new home at that time.

Around eleven o'clock, there was a bit of a lull in both stores, a good time, I figured, to go to Cuppa's. Dinah was still working in the Barkery, and before even telling her I was leaving, I popped into Icing to check in with Vicky and Frida—and to ask them to be sure that one of them always hung out with Dinah while I was gone. My full-time, number one employee, while doing her job just fine, was a bit slower than usual and seldom smiled. She clearly felt some stress and needed company. I didn't have to explain this to my other assistants that day. Both knew what was going on.

Soon I popped back into the Barkery and got Biscuit's leash. I waved goodbye to Dinah, who was waiting on a customer. Then Biscuit and I started our walk to Cuppa-Joe's.

The August morning was warm, and the stroll from the shops across the town square to Cuppa's was pleasant, especially because Biscuit got to trade a few nose sniffs with other dogs romping on their leashes in the square.

Soon we reached the coffee shop and walked inside. I didn't see the Joes at first, but Sweetie lay under a table in a corner of the main room, leashed there so she couldn't dash out the door. She was a good girl and I doubted she'd try to leave on her own, but in a place as busy as this, it was undoubtedly difficult for the Joes or their staff to keep a close enough watch on her to make sure she didn't attempt an escape—or that a customer didn't attempt to walk out with such a cute, friendly dog.

Since Sweetie was there, I assumed the Joes, or at least one of them, would join their dog soon, so I headed that way with Biscuit. I pulled an empty chair from a nearby table, since there were only two at the table that was my destination, and put it down at a good spot. Biscuit hurried under that table to greet her buddy.

"Hi, Carrie." That was Kit, the server, who approached right away. She appeared a bit harried, which was unlike her, but she still looked cute and efficient, and the knit shirt she wore that day, with its traditional coffee cup logo on the pocket, was blue.

"Hi, Kit," I said. "Are the Joes here?"

"They're in the kitchen but will be right back out. They wanted to refill their coffees and sit here while the news is on."

Only then did I notice that the TV that hung on a nearby wall, catty-corner to this table, was on, with its sound muted. News anchor Silas Perring was on the screen, talking into a microphone. Below him was a red and white banner that silently shouted *Breaking News*.

What was going on?

I asked Kit, "Is it possible to turn on the sound for just a minute?"

"The Joes intend to do it when they—oh, here they come."

Both Joe and Irma Nash hurried in through the door to the kitchen, Irma in front. They each held a mug presumably filled with coffee. Joe maneuvered his way around the table just below the TV screen, pulled the remote from a small shelf just below it, pressed a button, and the sound came on.

Soon both were sitting at the table with me. "Hi, Carrie," Irma said softly, nodding her head and sending me a smile, then shifting her attention to the TV screen.

"There's supposed to be a big announcement now," Joe said as he clunked his mug down on the table. He turned his back toward me so he could face the screen.

Kit hurried over and placed a cup of coffee with cream in front of me. I thanked her as I listened to Silas.

"The police are about to hold a brief news conference," he was saying, just as Chief Jonas, in full uniform including her dark jacket with its many medals, came to the lectern. "Hello, Chief," Silas called. "What can you tell us about your investigation into the death of Henry Schulzer, husband of our former mayor, the honorable Flora Morgan Schulzer?"

"This is an ongoing investigation," Loretta said into the microphone held by Silas. "What we can say is that it appears to be a first degree homicide." Just as we knew, a murder. "The cause of death was several stab wounds, apparently with a knife." Aha! The cause of death was finally being made public. Loretta went on to pat the police, investigators, and coroner verbally on the back, but she didn't relate any further details about the killing or the crime scene.

When she was done, Silas asked, "Chief Jonas, do you have any suspects who might have committed this murder?"

"Yes," she said, "we do. But since it's an ongoing investigation, I can't reveal who we're zeroing in on. Not yet. But we hope to have our answers soon."

I hoped they had their answers soon, too—and that they found the real killer, who wasn't Dinah or anyone else I cared about.

Was that wishing too much?

In any case, I wasn't about to back off and quit my own snooping. Not now. And if I solved this case first, too? Well, the local cops had never seemed thrilled about my apparently unwanted yet somehow pleasing ability to do better than they did in this area, but they'd sort of accepted it. Even acted somewhat friendly at times.

I stopped my thoughts for now, though. The news conference seemed to be winding down. Hearing the official cause of death was helpful. Now that I knew what the murder weapon was, I had assumptions about where it came from, though I couldn't be certain. Not yet, at least. Let alone of who had been the one to use it so viciously.

"Is there anything you would like to say to the citizens of Knobcone Heights?" Silas asked Chief Jonas.

"Yes," she said. "Be careful. Don't attempt to solve this situation on your own. It's too dangerous."

The thought crossed my mind that she was talking to me, which was absurd. How could she even know I was watching this?

Although there was always the possibility I'd see the news conference rebroadcast.

"If you have any thoughts or evidence to share," she continued, "please call the KHPD as soon as possible." She paused, then glared into the camera. "In any case, you can be certain we'll figure this out." I felt that she was talking to the murderer now. Maybe that was the impression she intended—to make him or her feel scared, perhaps do something dumb that would make it clear whodunit.

A good idea, of course, but unlikely.

"Thank you, Chief." Silas started to move away.

But she leaned forward, over the microphones. "One more thing. There will be a memorial service for Mr. Schulzer a week from Sunday at the Knobcone House of Celebration. We've contacted his family, and that was their request. It's scheduled for eleven in the morning."

I'd have to go to it, of course. Maybe I wouldn't bring my weekend staff members, though. I'd have to discuss it with them, but we had more than a week to figure it out.

The news conference was over. Joe rose and approached the wall that held the TV, using the remote to turn it off.

"Hope you didn't mind watching that, folks," he called out to the coffee house's patrons. "But I figured we should all know any information the authorities can provide. And first and foremost, listen to the chief and be careful—and keep out of attempting to figure anything out yourself."

As he made his way back to the table, maneuvering around filled tables, his eyes were on me.

When he sat back down, I leaned forward and looked into his wrinkle-framed eyes. "Was your comment intended for me?" Like Chief Loretta's statement? I didn't mention that, though.

"You know it was," Joe grumbled. "We're all very impressed that you've figured out so many murders lately, but you can be sure we're always worried that whoever did it will protect himself by doing the same thing to you as he did to the victim."

I was glad to hear Joe refer to the killer as a "he." That was the generic thing to do, but if the Joes, who knew a lot about what went on in town, believed the killer was Dinah, he'd have referred to the killer as a "she."

"I appreciate that," I said. "And I'll be careful." What Joe said made me hesitate to bring up the next thing I wanted to ask, so instead I started a friendly conversation about how I was hoping to hold another pet adoption in the Barkery soon. Joe and Irma had adopted Sweetie not long ago from Mountaintop Rescue, and they'd always been supportive of me as a vet tech and then a Barkery owner as well as a bakery owner, so talking to them about dogs always worked well.

But after a while, I knew I needed to return to my shops. "Thanks so much for hanging out with me here," I told the Joes as I stood up, giving a soft pull on Biscuit's leash. Sweetie and she had been snuggling up together under the table and I hated to stop that, but I knew they'd get the opportunity to chill out together again soon.

"Thanks for coming," Irma said, approaching me. We hugged, and I also hugged Joe.

Before saying goodbye, I had to finally address what was on my mind. "You know," I began, "everyone in town comes to Cuppa's sometime. Right now, I'd love to get the opportunity to chat with Mike Holpurn, the guy who was imprisoned for killing Mayor Flora Schulzer—maybe I can get a sense of whether he was the one who killed Henry Schulzer."

Joe glared at me, shaking his head. "I knew you'd ignore what I said and continue to be nosy about this murder."

"I'm not ignoring you," I chided softly. "I'll be careful, like Chief Loretta advised, too. But ... well, you may already know that Dinah argued with Henry Schulzer the evening before he died. Twice. Holpurn did too, at Dinah's birthday party. I know Dinah didn't kill Henry, but I haven't had a chance to form an impression about whether Holpurn is guilty or not, and I'd like to talk to him just in case."

"And you don't think the police will check Holpurn out for the same reasons?" Joe asked wryly.

Irma, though, seemed a lot more understanding. "We know Dinah's your friend as well as your employee, Carrie. We understand why you want to make sure she's not arrested for something she didn't do." Then Irma hesitated. "She couldn't have done it, could she?"

"Of course not." I wished I felt as sure as I sounded.

"Well ... look, dear. We don't always know who our patrons are anyway, but if we happen to see that Holpurn man, we'll call you— but only if you promise to stay here to question him, then let one of us or one of our employees accompany you to your stores or the clinic, wherever you're going. And also if you promise then to be very careful and watch out for him, in case he's really insidious and tries to hurt you afterward."

"That's so sweet, Irma," I told her. "And I'll be very happy to do as you say. I don't want to be hurt or anything else, so I'll definitely try to be smart. And I won't just stay on the lookout for Holpurn, either. He's had two men with him every time I've seen him, who are apparently his brothers. I'll have to watch out for them, too. And you be careful as well. If Holpurn was horrible enough to kill the mayor, no one really knows what he, or his cohorts, are capable of now."

"Maybe we'd better not serve them," Joe stated, crossing his arms.

"Or maybe he got paroled early because he really was innocent," I said. "We just don't know. But we're smart enough, all of us, to be careful—right? If nothing else, please take this conversation as a warning, since we've had another murder in this town with no answers so far. Who knows what the motive, or state of mind, of the killer might be? Everyone could be in danger."

I hoped not. But the Joes meant a lot to me, and if anything happened to them as even a remote result of anything I said or did, I would never forgive myself.

Biscuit and I left a short time later, after I insisted on paying for my drink and tipping Kit. I hugged Irma and Joe yet again and promised to come back soon.

And to be careful. And smart.

FOURTEEN

DINAH WAS LATE COMING to the shops the next morning.

Fortunately, I'd scheduled Janelle to come in first to help with the baking, and she popped in early, all jazzed and ready to work. I gathered that she had spent an enjoyable night with my brother. While standing across from me in the kitchen, kneading dough for some Icing cookies, she told me they had gone to see a new movie that had just come out, all about a photographer—which is what she was in her spare time.

"Great film," she said, "all about how people nabbed some wild-life poachers by taking their pictures in a sanctuary." Janelle took photos mostly of people, from what I knew, but I was aware she was an animal lover, especially of dogs, as demonstrated by her love for her own pup, Go. Goliath, as he was officially called, was her beautiful, black, purebred Labrador retriever. She sometimes brought Go into the shops to keep Biscuit company but hadn't this week. She did have a nice and reliable dog walker take Go out a couple of times a day when he stayed at home, though.

"Sounds like a good movie," I said, making a mental note to try to see it, preferably with Reed.

We finished our baking in time to fill the display cases in both shops before opening time at seven. Dinah was due to come in then—but she didn't. I had some work to do in my office but it had to wait, since at the moment Janelle and I were the only ones around to tend to the shops, and we had some customers in both immediately, which was a good thing.

I didn't mind taking care of those customers in the Barkery. Not at all. Plus, I got to see that Biscuit had settled down in her enclosure and mostly lay there watching people come in, sometimes with their dogs, to buy treats.

But I was concerned about Dinah. Surely she hadn't been arrested overnight—had she? I considered calling her between packing treats into bags or boxes and taking care of payments at the front counter, but I decided to wait, at least for now.

If she didn't come in before, say, nine o'clock, then I'd definitely call her.

She arrived at eight thirty, entering the Barkery from the kitchen door, dressed in a yellow *Barkery and Biscuits* T-shirt over black jeans and wearing a large smile like she used to wear nearly all the time—but not over the past few days.

"Hi, Carrie," she called out, walking directly to the glass counter where a new customer had just appeared with a miniature pinscher mix. Dinah immediately opened the counter's rear door and removed a couple of treat samples for the delighted min-pin. Since she'd entered from the kitchen, I assumed she'd done the usual: left her purse on the bottom shelf of a supply cabinet and shut the door, then washed her hands carefully before coming into the shops. She had been following that routine longer than I had owned the shops.

Dinah continued to smile and act happy as she waited on her customer. I wondered about the origin of her happiness. Was it just because she hadn't been arrested? Because she was aware someone else had been, and since I'd been here in the shops I hadn't heard? Because she was engaged in conducting some research she enjoyed, whether or not it was related to Henry's murder?

The good thing was that our shops were busy that morning. I'd been going back and forth between the Barkery and Icing and just didn't have time, with people coming in and out, to take Dinah aside and chat. I was glad she appeared happy, but under the current circumstances, I was very eager to find out why.

I was about to hurry over to Icing and once more see how Janelle was getting along there and help out if necessary. But as a matter of habit, I looked toward the Barkery door as it swung open, making its small bell ring.

I didn't move when I saw who entered, since I felt shock zing through me. Not that I should have been surprised, no matter who walked through the door. We'd had some unusual customers at times, some of whom were downright nasty and others who simply seemed a bit nuts.

But something didn't feel right at all when Mike Holpurn and his brothers suddenly stood inside the Barkery, all of them scowling, with their arms crossed.

And staring at Dinah.

Biscuit started barking, which was unusual for her. She loved people and generally stayed quiet no matter how many customers we had or how stressed any of them seemed to get about long lines or whatever.

"It's okay, Biscuit," I told her, heading over to pat her head. She quieted but still seemed tense, the way she sat there and stared.

Her bark had been loud enough to attract Janelle's attention. She poked her head into the shop from Icing, then backed out again with a worried look on her face.

Fortunately, we weren't crowded at that moment. Our most recent Barkery customers had just left. I didn't like what was happening, whatever it was, but at least no patrons were here to see it—or possibly to be in danger, no matter that I'd told Biscuit it would be okay. I certainly didn't trust Holpurn the confessed killer, nor his buddies, and their apparent attitude didn't help.

"You're Dinah Greeley," Holpurn said, glaring in Dinah's direction. "We've met before."

"Yes, I am, Mr. Holpurn," she said, with a small, happy grin on her face. "And please remind me who the gentlemen with you are?"

Very nice way to ask, although I doubted that either of them would rise to the level of a gentleman.

"My brothers, if it's any of your business," grumped Holpurn. "Bill and Johnny."

Aha! I finally knew their names. All three guys were tall and had receding hairlines, although Mike seemed to have the least hair. One brother had much darker hair than Mike, and the other's was slightly lighter. I'd already figured Mike was in his forties. One of the brothers appeared to be older and the other younger.

I still had loads of questions, such as had Holpurn actually murdered Mayor Flora? Had one or both of his brothers been involved? Had they helped to get him out of prison? In any case, how and why had he been paroled?

But at the moment, what I really wanted to know was why they were at the Barkery—and what they wanted with Dinah.

I was about to ask, but Dinah beat me to it. "Welcome, Mike, Bill, and Johnny," she said, aiming her smile at them. "I'm so glad you came by today. I wasn't sure I had the right phone number when I texted Mike with the invitation." This was probably why she was smiling, then. Her research bug was buzzing. "Now that you're here, what can we do for you? Do you have any dogs? Would you like to buy them some treats from the Barkery? Or would you like to buy yourself some treats from Icing on the Cake? We might even give you a free sample or two if you're nice to us."

"We have no intention of being nice to you, Dinah Greeley," Mike growled. "You've certainly not been nice to me. That's why we came here today, on your invitation."

Uh-oh. What did that mean?

"Oh, do you mean that Detective Crunoll told you what I said about you? The thing was, he was questioning me in great depth, as if I'd had something to do with Henry Schulzer's murder. I just suggested he ought to look further and mentioned some of the things about you I'd found out during my research. I'm a writer, you know, and I'm always conducting research. Right, Carrie?"

All eyes moved to stare at me, and I gave a faint smile back. "Definitely," I said. "But research doesn't always provide answers right away." I was hoping to say something to get these men to back off—and I also wanted to find a way to call my buddy Wayne Crunoll and let him know what was going on.

"No, of course not," Dinah said. "And what I do with it is create fiction, anyway, although I still haven't published much. I haven't had a lot of time to do anything yet, but I was trying to figure out how you got paroled only ten years after confessing to the mayor's murder, and—well, I got the idea that there was more to your confession back then, that you might have been attempting to protect someone by pleading guilty. But you eventually came to believe that Henry Schulzer had killed his own wife. Which meant you no longer needed to take the blame to protect someone. Who were you protecting back then?"

Ah. More research.

Mike Holpurn made a startled motion from where he stood near the doorway. "What do you mean?"

"Okay, you still don't want to talk about it. But I gather the authorities finally bought into the possibility that you were innocent, despite your confession, and gave you parole. And once you were out, you decided to pursue your theory that the mayor's husband was the killer, right?"

"Now, look." This was either Bill or Johnny. "We're just here to make sure you know we're aware that you've been pointing fingers at Mike about the Schulzer murder, as if Mike did it and not you. Well, we know otherwise, and we've already told the cops, but in any case we want you to shut up about Mike. Got it?"

Dinah's expression froze. "I don't like to be threatened," she said softly.

"Then shut up and we won't threaten you," said one of the brothers.

This needed to stop. But before I jumped in to tell them to leave, Dinah said, "I'm sorry—kind of—that I mentioned you when I was being questioned. But ... well, it was partly to try to get them to stop grilling me that way, as if they were certain I'd killed Mr. Schulzer—which I didn't, by the way." She waved her hand as Mike took a step closer to her on the tile floor. "I didn't tell them you did it, either—although I also didn't tell them you didn't do it. I was just trying to figure out if they had other people they considered major suspects. And I shouldn't be a suspect, by the way, just because I kind of argued with the man. We were in public, and he was giving me a hard time, and—well, never mind."

It was a good decision to stop talking, I thought. Mike had taken yet another step toward her, and she wisely slipped in behind the counter.

140

"Okay," I finally broke in. "Let's just take the position that no one in this shop right now was the person who killed Henry Schulzer, all right? At least as far as the cops are concerned. We can suspect anyone we want to, but we'll keep it to ourselves when we're discussing the situation with the authorities."

"That's not gonna work," said one of the brothers. He'd moved toward the front of the store, which concerned me. Was he attempting to block us if we tried to run outside? Or maybe he was making sure no customers came in, since I thought I saw a couple of people with dogs come up to the front window.

But they weren't the ones to open the door. No, it was detectives Wayne Crunoll and Bridget Morana who walked in.

"Hello, all of you," Wayne said. "Now, what are all of you doing here together? Confessing? Were you in collusion when you murdered Henry Schulzer?" He was grinning broadly, so I figured he was kidding. At least I hoped so.

"Oh, we were just discussing other possible suspects to sic you onto," Mike lied, looking first at the detectives with a similar grin, then turning back toward us with what appeared to be a warning scowl. "Right?"

"Close enough," Dinah said. "Mike and I know we've each been pointing fingers at the other when we've talked to you, and we've agreed not to do that anymore."

That seemed to appease Mike, at least somewhat, since he nodded and his posture appeared to relax a little. "I think it's time for us to go," he told his brothers.

Which made me relax. Especially since the detectives were here.

I considered sending the Holpurns out with some sample people treats from Icing, just to ease any remaining tension—although it wouldn't stop any of us from suspecting the others. But I mostly wanted them to go, so I didn't even suggest it.

In moments, they'd walked out the door, and I inhaled deeply, only realizing then that I'd been holding my breath.

"Thanks for coming," I told the detectives. I decided to give them some samples, both from the Barkery for the Wayne's dogs and from Icing for themselves.

"Any time," Detective Bridget said. "Oh, and you can thank your assistant Janelle for calling us rather than 911. Since we've already spoken with her about this case, she knew of our involvement—and interest."

As if she'd overheard, which she probably had, Janelle pushed open the door between the two shops and walked in.

"Are you two okay?" She headed toward me with her arms outstretched for a big hug.

I reciprocated. "We are, thanks to you," I said. I pulled back and looked at the detectives. "And to be fair, the Holpurns didn't exactly threaten us, but they were clearly unhappy that Mike's name had come up in your questioning of Dinah, and maybe elsewhere."

"And maybe that's because we haven't removed any of them from our list of suspects," Wayne said. "Nor have we removed anyone." He looked straight at Dinah. "No matter how well our interviews seem to go. So if any of you want to confess right now, we're ready." That smile of his reappeared.

"Thanks," I said, "but not right now. Or ever. But if we happen to figure out who actually committed the murder and come up with some proof—"

"We'll let you know right away," Dinah finished.

FIFTEEN

DINAH CAME IN TO work on Sunday, as scheduled, and then took her regular days off on Monday and Tuesday. She and I kept in touch by phone calls and text messages now and then—something I encouraged so that I could remain certain she still hadn't been arrested. Plus, I was doing some nosing around on my own to try to ensure that neither she nor anyone else who'd been at her birthday party was taken into custody by the cops.

Not that I had any real idea about who killed Henry. Not yet, at least.

Things remained fairly normal at the shops over those next few days, as well as at the vet clinic, where I had a couple more shifts while my helpers did their usual things at the Barkery and Icing.

No visits from Wayne or Bridget during that time, either—not even when Dinah was working. Nor did either of them stop in to get my current take on who'd killed the former mayor's husband, despite my successes in figuring out past murders.

Soon it was Wednesday, and I was in the kitchen baking, and Biscuit was inside the Barkery as usual. Of course my mind kept slipping to the current murder situation, but fortunately not much appeared to be going on. In fact, I felt rather complacent with nothing in particular happening, at least that I could see. Dinah remained free, and so did everyone else.

Which meant, of course, that the cops hadn't gotten enough evidence to arrest anyone … yet. But I had no doubt that they would. Eventually.

Now, placing the dough for some of our very special red velvet cupcakes into the white pleated paper cups we used, I couldn't quite keep my mind off it—maybe because Dinah would arrive at the shops soon.

We'd talk, I felt sure. In the meantime, I'd been encouraging her to do her favorite thing and keep me informed about her research into who might have had something against Henry.

Like she did? Henry's threats against Dinah had been fairly serious—potentially ruining her writing ambitions, or her life. But heck, her altercation with Henry had been too spontaneous and too brief for me to consider Dinah much of a suspect. Both arguments had happened on the same night, and they seemed related to the stress of the party. Most importantly, I knew Dinah. I just couldn't accept the possibility that she might be guilty.

Still, I'd feel a lot better when the real culprit was caught.

Someone else who'd been at the resort restaurant that night?

One interesting thing was that Dinah had found out, after our little meeting with them, that Mike Holpurn and his brothers Bill and Johnny had rented an apartment from an Airbnb host. She wasn't sure how long their commitment was, but at least we now knew where we could find them—maybe. Their renting the place didn't mean they were staying there, and even if they were, that didn't mean they were doing anything other than sleeping there at night.

I didn't have anything new to ask the Holpurns...yet. But of all the possibilities, I still believed Mike was the most likely suspect, notwithstanding his still-unexplained early parole from prison for the prior murder.

Dinah had also conducted other research about the Holpurns in her hours not working at my shops, and she kept me informed. For one thing, brothers Bill and Johnny had apparently lived nearby, in the town of Lake Arrowhead, way back when Mike did his remodeling work for Mayor Flora, and they'd moved down the mountains to San Bernardino when Mike went to prison.

But they were back in town, at least for now. All three of them. And if Henry Schulzer had killed his wife, did that give one or more of them a motive to have—

"Hi, Carrie," called a voice from behind me. Well, speak of the devil. Or angel. It was the very person I'd been thinking about. The one who'd bring me up to date on her research, maybe right now while we finished baking.

I turned to face Dinah. She looked good, which made me happy. No news, then. She apparently hadn't been confronted by the detectives, and neither had I.

"Hi, Dinah. Good to see you. Ready to get to work?"

She came farther inside, washed her hands, and put on one of our special aprons over her *Icing on the Cake* T-shirt and jeans. "I'm always working," she reminded me.

"Of course. Now help me finish the biscuits for the Barkery—and tell me what you've most recently found in your research."

She had nothing new to tell me, though. Nor did I learn anything helpful later when I took a coffee break at Cuppa-Joe's, or at my shift at the vet clinic or a visit to Mountaintop Rescue.

It was a normal day, just like one when no murder had been recently committed.

So were the next few. I did spend several evenings with Reed, of course, and a couple of nights as well.

Then Sunday arrived—the day of Henry Schulzer's memorial service at the Knobcone House of Celebration. Apparently Henry and Flora's now-adult children had worked things out with the coroner and a nearby cemetery, and would be in attendance.

Fortunately, Frida and Vicky agreed to watch the stores while I went to the memorial for Henry. Reed was accompanying me, and Neal and Janelle were going, too.

So was Dinah. A good idea? Yes, for her research—maybe. But would it look suspicious if she was at a memorial held to celebrate the life of Henry Schulzer?

The life that the police might believe she ended?

The day before, I'd told her she could have Sunday off but probably shouldn't come to the memorial. Her response was a good one: Would the memorial be an opportunity to research? Yes, maybe a little.

"But I also want to pay my respects," she'd said. "Partly to show I didn't kill Henry and partly because it's the right thing to do."

I had to agree with that. Not that I could have prevented Dinah from coming anyway, but her motives were good.

And her motive for possibly killing Henry? I couldn't think of a good one and was glad about that. The public arguments they'd had certainly didn't rise to that level, thank goodness.

So now the five of us from my shops joined the crowd waiting to enter the Knobcone House of Celebration. Crowd? Yes. I was kind of surprised at how many people there were, considering that Henry hadn't been living in town for very long—this time round. But he had, after all, been married to one of the town's former mayors.

The Knobcone House of Celebration was along Knobcone Lake, about a half mile from the resort. I wasn't sure of its architectural style but it was attractive, a streamlined structure on the outside that appeared to be a couple of stories high. Not counting the office in the back, there was only one large room, which could be divided into several spaces depending on what was going on inside.

As the crowd milled around, I saw people I knew, such as quite a few of my customers. I waved to those who caught my eye.

Standing nearest to the door was what I believed to be the entire City Council. At least Billi was there, and so was Les Ethman. They were all dressed up and talking to others whom I didn't know well but nevertheless recognized from the media as being part of city government.

Then there was the current mayor, Sybill Gabbon. And some other Ethmans, including Neal's bosses, owners of the Knobcone Heights Resort.

Wandering among them all was Silas Perring. He was holding his microphone and interviewing one after the other, perhaps recording them for an upcoming broadcast, since I suspected the interviews weren't appearing immediately on live TV. His cameraman Wilbur the Wise was filming it all.

Silas wasn't the only journalist there, either. Francine Metz was also walking around talking to people. She was the editor of the *Knobcone News*, and I knew her because she was pet-friendly and sometimes came to the adoption events at my Barkery.

Quite a few people I knew or recognized there had pets that they brought to the Barkery or to the vet clinic, and some of those pets had been adopted from Mountaintop Rescue. But it wasn't a surprise that none of the people brought their pets to this sad event.

Then there were also people I'd met over the past week or two because they knew Henry: Mysha Jorgens, the dog walker, and Kris and Paul Banner, his neighbors at the resort hotel, who all stood together talking. Mysha was crying. She must really have cared a lot for Henry. Or his dogs, who were no longer in her care.

There was something about Mysha, though ... or was I just hoping to zero in on someone at the service as Henry's killer? The young woman wasn't very large, but she certainly could have grabbed a knife in the resort suite's kitchen and used it ...

Okay. Enough.

We stood around for quite a while, and I talked to the members of my small group about the upcoming pet adoption event Billi and I were planning for the Barkery, and other things totally unrelated to our reason for being here.

I eventually saw Chief Loretta Jonas and my two detective contacts arrive. Did they think someone would confess to killing Henry during his memorial? Or had they just come to pay their respects? Perhaps it was a combination, but I wasn't about to ask. They saw me too, though. We traded glances, and Wayne nodded toward me before turning away.

Finally the doors opened and we all walked through the tall, wide front entrance. I hadn't been at the House of Celebration often, but I clearly remembered the silvery, matte metal walls with the many windows. The gleaming wood floors were as I recalled as well, as were the rows of chairs, all facing the large, raised stage area.

The people filing in filled the seats closest to the stage first. We ended up sitting about halfway back and near the end of our row, which worked well as far as I was concerned. Not that I had any intention of sneaking away, but I still preferred having the flexibility to edge my way out of the service if I chose to.

Dinah wound up sitting in the aisle seat, which concerned me a bit. Would she be the one to sneak out—or get up and start questioning people for her research?

Or, if anyone suggested that she was a murder suspect, would she dash out of here?

But this was a memorial to celebrate Henry Schulzer's life, not to solve his murder.

I heard noise from behind us as the crowd seemed to talk louder. When I turned, I saw why.

Mike Holpurn and his brothers had just walked in. They immediately grabbed seats at the back, but I wondered why they'd come. To rub it in that Henry was dead now, too, and not just Flora?

I also saw where both Silas Perring and Francine Metz were sitting—next to each other, as it turned out, and also near the back of the room, probably so they could see everything and everyone better than if they disappeared into the rows of mourners. Both stood and looked at the Holpurns, but neither was unprofessional enough to go interview them now.

I figured they would later, though, when the service was over.

We didn't have to sit there long before two people climbed onto the stage, a man and woman who appeared to be in their mid-twenties. Henry's kids?

My guess proved to be right. "Hi, everyone," the man said into the microphone at the right side of the stage. It was too loud at first, and I cringed as a casually dressed guy, presumably someone who worked there, came onto the stage and adjusted microphone.

"Hi, everyone," the speaker said again, and this time the tone sounded normal. "I'm Henry Schulzer, Jr. Just call me HS. This is my sister, Mabel." He gestured toward the woman at his left. "Just call her Mabe."

I didn't see a resemblance in either of them to their tall, scruffy, gray-haired father, which was the way I remembered him. HS was tall but appeared to have some bulk beneath his black suit, and his hair was light brown. His sister, Mabe, was shorter than him despite her stiletto heels, and her long, straight hair, decorating her short-sleeved black dress, was a similar shade of brown.

HS went on to talk about his parents, and their family living in Knobcone Heights years ago. How his mother had been the mayor —and how she'd died here. How they'd left the area and his father had moved on with his life. "And I suppose," HS said, "that the biggest mistake of his life was coming back here."

A murmur of agreement moved through the room, and I saw Mabe raise a tissue to her eyes.

My eyes were drawn, then, to the area of the room just below the stage, on the right side, where I believed all of the City Council now sat. There was no way of picking Billi out now, but I wondered if she'd spoken with the Schulzer children yet about Henry's two dogs, now sheltered at Mountaintop Rescue. My first impression of HS and Mabe was positive enough for me to think one or both of them might make a good guardian for the now-orphaned Duke and Prince.

I thought so even more after HS finished his sad speech and turned the microphone over to his sister. Mabe said she missed both her parents fiercely and then went on to talk a bit personally about herself, saying that she hadn't been able to bring herself to marry or have kids because she'd seen what the loss of someone so beloved had done to her father.

I thought that was a bit off, since why not marry and enjoy the time you had together? And this somehow caused me to glance sideways toward Reed.

He glanced at me the same way, which caused a little shiver to run through me. We were always saying we needed to discuss our relationship, and we sometimes did, but we didn't really delve into its possible future much.

I made myself concentrate on Mabe once more. She was describing her memories of growing up in Knobcone Heights while her mother was mayor. Her father often acted as if he was both parents since their mom was so busy. Henry, being in real estate, had also been busy, but his hours were a bit more flexible.

Mabe kept talking for a while, and I felt so sorry for her and her brother, and her mother and father, and the dogs, too.

She wound up introducing her aunt, Tula Schulzer, who'd just joined them on the stage—their father's sister. I wondered if they had any other close family members at the service or if they were otherwise alone, but that wasn't really my business.

When Tula was done talking about her brother, HS took the microphone back. "I know our father didn't live here very long this time, and most of you probably don't remember him from before, but would anyone else like to come up here and say something about him?"

A few hands went up, but not many. Mysha waved vehemently, and HS told her to come up to the stage.

Mysha sweetly described the dogs and how much she had enjoyed helping to take care of them, but she also described what a good doggy-dad Henry had been. She was sobbing by the time she ceded the microphone back to HS.

"Yes, we all love dogs," HS said sadly. "Our mom raised the spaniels who were the forerunners of the two dogs our dad had when he died. Thanks for helping him, Mysha."

Les Ethman then got up to speak, since he had known the Schulzers when Flora had been mayor. He eulogized both of them, though admitting he hadn't known Henry well recently.

A few other people also got up to talk, but things seemed to be winding down.

Yet before saying goodbye, HS, holding the microphone, seemed to look over the large room for an entire minute before his gaze stopped somewhere in the back.

He then said, "Mr. Holpurn, would you like to come up here and say something? Preferably something nice about our late mother, whom you admitted to murdering? And I wouldn't be surprised, since you're out of prison and back in town, if you're the one who killed our dad, too. Care to admit it now?"

A loud murmur exploded through the mourners now, and I stood and turned quickly to try to catch Mike's reaction. He was already standing, but he didn't make any attempt to head toward the stage.

Instead he yelled, loudly enough to be heard over the noisy crowd, "Don't make accusations without substance, Mr. Schulzer! There was a good reason for me to be paroled, and I didn't kill your father. But I've also good reason to believe that the real murderer is here today. Your father wasn't a very nice man, and he liked to fight. He exchanged some pretty bad words with someone the night he died. Twice. My opinion? That person was the one who stabbed him. Who is it? I think the police know."

With that, Mike Holpurn and his brothers stomped out of the House of Celebration, which now felt like a house not just of mourning but of malevolence.

Had Holpurn spoken that way to deflect accusations from himself, despite being convicted of the crime? Or did he really believe he knew who the killer was, and that the person was here at the service?

He said he had seen some of the people at Dinah's party have "bad words" with Henry—which included Dinah. Had Mike just accused Dinah?

And, as I'd feared, did the police believe my dear assistant had been the one to stab Henry?

SIXTEEN

IF SO, THE POLICE didn't do anything about it during the memorial, such as get up and speak to the crowd or make any accusations against Dinah or anyone else. But all three—Chief Loretta and detectives Bridget and Wayne—waited outside the House of Celebration afterward, greeting the mourners just like Henry's relatives were, as if they were somehow hosts.

Most likely, the police were doing that for a reason—perhaps seeing who'd been interested enough to attend, or even in hopes that HS's request at the end of his speech—that the guilty person step up now and admit it—would still cause someone to confess.

I didn't see or hear any sort of confession.

But the silence on this topic didn't seem to make a difference to the police, who remained on the walkway outside the House of Celebration, across from the grieving family members and a little farther toward the parking lot.

"Let's go say hi to the cops," I said to Reed.

"Why?" he asked, looking at me as if I'd gone crazy. "Do you think they're going to tell you whatever's on their minds?"

"No, but I want to at least let them know I'm here—although they probably noticed me. And if Dinah will join us—well, I'd really like to see how they act around her now. Let's go offer our condolences to Henry's family first, though."

I turned to let Neal, Janelle, and Dinah know the plan. "Good idea," Neal said, nodding. Janelle seemed to agree, too.

And Dinah? Her smile was sad but her eyes were wide, as if she was prepared to watch while she listened and, hopefully, learned something for her research. Something that would also wind up clearing her from suspicion.

And talk to the cops? She was apparently willing to do it.

We got into the line along the paved walkway to meet with the family, with about ten people in front of us. The line moved quickly, since we were all supposed to just introduce ourselves and convey our sympathy. Henry hadn't been my favorite person, but as I'd thought often, I also hadn't wished for him to die—let alone be murdered.

We were eventually next. But before we could take those final steps, Silas Perring and his buddy Wilbur the Wise butted in front of us, microphone and camera clearly ready to roll.

"Hello, Schulzer family." Silas then introduced himself and Wilbur. "We were at the service and heard your very touching presentations. And now we would like you to tell our viewers what you think, how you feel." Without waiting for their consent, Silas announced, "Let's begin." He held the microphone to his own face and told his audience who these people were. Then he faced them and held out the mic. "I saw you, HS, ask for whoever killed your father to come forward now and confess. Has anyone done that?"

"No," HS snapped, then calmed a bit. "But we're ready to hear it. Maybe it wasn't someone at the service, but they may be watching your show. It's not too late. Come forward and tell the police now," he said to the camera.

Silas then did the same with the other two family members, then returned to HS. "Do you happen to know of a motive anyone might have had to harm your father that way?"

"None at all," Mabe said sadly, stepping in front of her brother and looking straight into the camera. "It was so hard to lose our mother all those years ago, right in this town. And now our father, too … it's terrible. We'd never visit again, but we're going to have our father buried next to our mother, and she's here."

"I understand," Silas said. "Are you working with the police to try to get some answers?"

"We're cooperating," HS said. "But we don't have any answers. You were there when we were talking before. Like you said, I asked for the guilty person to come forward, and now—" He turned back toward the camera. "Let me repeat that I'm still asking this, and for anyone who knows anything to go talk to the cops. There are a couple of really good detectives working on this case. They've spoken with us, and I think maybe a clue or two would really help them."

I liked the way HS was handling himself now—and the message going out to the world via Silas and the TV station. Would it help to solve Henry's murder? Who knew?

As the interview wound down, Silas asked Tula what she thought, and I gathered that Henry's sister thought very little, or at least nothing she intended to discuss on camera.

And when it was over, and Silas wasn't asking the Schulzers anything else, I figured he was through. But he wasn't. He held out his microphone to me, and Wilbur aimed the camera at me.

I thought of waving my hands in front of my face, running away, anything to prevent what was clearly about to occur.

But I'd been interviewed by Silas before, and it hadn't been so bad. Plus, this time I had an ulterior motive—protecting Dinah and the others who'd been at her party and argued with Henry, including myself.

"And you, Ms. Carrie Kennersly. You've been helpful in figuring out who committed some other crimes in this area recently. Have you zeroed in on who was involved in this one?"

"No, I haven't." I hoped to leave it at that.

But Silas continued. "I'll bet you have some ideas. Are you sharing your suspicions with the local police? I assume you're at least looking into this murder."

"I'm strictly an amateur," I said to the camera. "I hope this situation gets resolved quickly. But in the meantime, I'd like to invite your viewers to visit Barkery and Biscuits, and Icing on the Cake, the shops I own that sell treats for both dogs and people. And—" As I'd hoped, Silas pulled the microphone away from me, and the camera, too, was focused on other people by Wilbur.

Which made me smile. With a small gesture near my hip to the people with me, I moved forward.

My group and I stopped in front of the Schulzers, and I looked first toward HS and introduced all of us. "I don't think any of us knew your father well, though we met him. We're all very sorry for your loss, and—"

"You're Dinah." Mabe was looking at my assistant as if a banshee had come to greet her.

"Yes, I am," Dinah said, stepping forward. "I take it you've heard about what happened at my birthday party." She sounded sad.

"Yes, we did," HS said. "And out of everyone that people have mentioned around here, we think you—"

"You think I was the one to kill Henry," Dinah finished.

I could see Neal and Janelle exchange looks, and Reed shot me a glare as if I'd caused this confrontation. Maybe I had, in a way, just by suggesting that we convey our condolences right here and right now, personally.

"Didn't you?" HS demanded. I noticed his phrasing. Rather than "did you," he seemed to be taking the position that of course Dinah had, although she might deny it.

I was the one to step forward this time—just as I noticed that Silas and Wilbur were recording and filming us now, too. "No," I said firmly, "she didn't. We can understand, if you heard about the little disagreement they had that evening, why you might wonder whether anyone involved could have harmed your father—but, as I said, it was just a small disagreement. And I have to say that your father's attitude at that time seemed to be encouraging a lot of little disagreements."

"Well, one of those turned deadly." That was Tula, who'd otherwise been quiet. "And it could have been any of you, right?"

"No," I contradicted her. "That's not right."

Fortunately, the people right behind us in line chose just then to interrupt. Had they been listening and decided enough was enough? I thought the woman looked familiar—perhaps one of my customers, though if so, she must not be a regular. "Sorry," she said, "but we have to convey our sympathy now since we need to leave."

"Sure." I nodded toward the others with me. Then, with a glance back toward the Schulzers and resuming the sympathetic expression I'd had on my face before, I led my group forward.

Toward the cops.

I noticed that Silas didn't pull away as soon as the people behind us got the Schulzers' attention. Was he going to move forward, too, and also butt in on my conversation with the cops?

Apparently not, since, fortunately, Silas seemed to have come up with another question for the Schulzers—or at least he stayed there as the other mourners spoke with them.

"Let's go talk to the cops now," I said to Reed, who had remained by my side.

His expression turned wry, and I couldn't help but stare at the gorgeousness of his deep brown eyes. For a moment, at least, till he responded to what I'd said. "They're not my favorite people these days, and I'm not theirs, either," he said.

"No, but you're no longer a suspect in any murder. Just because you happened to be present at Dinah's party—as were the rest of us—it doesn't mean they'll pay much attention to you. Not this time." Unlike last time, when Reed was highly involved in the situation and probably the prime suspect until that case got solved—largely thanks to me.

"But what about you? They do seem to like you, at least more than before."

"Sure, they're much nicer these days to me," I said. Sort of, at least. "But not too friendly, at least not all the time. Maybe they think I'll dump my other careers and try to take over their jobs if they give me too hard a time."

I aimed a wink at him that made him laugh. He took my hand and we walked the few feet to where the police now talked to Les, Billi, and a couple of other City Council folks who'd come up to them.

Detective Bridget Morana seemed to notice me immediately. "Ah," she said, "here's our favorite amateur snoop. Er, sleuth. Did the memorial point your suspicions in any directions we should know about, Ms. Kennersly?"

"Not really," I said. "How about you?"

"Do you really think we'd tell you if it did?" That was Wayne, who simply stared at me, no particular expression on his face.

"Of course not," I responded. Maybe it was useless to even think about talking to the cops now. But I did wish I had a better sense of who they were zeroing in on.

I of course feared it was Dinah.

Wayne seemed to read my thoughts. Or maybe, since I'd been a thorn in the cops' sides in the other recent murder cases, he knew what I was thinking—since things were similar, in some ways, to what had gone on before.

"Well, all those nice employees you sent over to talk to us at the station, in accordance with our request, remain in our sights," he said. "In case you were wondering. And you've learned, I'm sure, over the past months that we tend to go after the most obvious suspects, at least at first. The most obvious aren't always the most guilty," he said more hurriedly as I opened my mouth to comment. "But sometimes they are. And if you have any evidence, or even ideas, to lead us away from your buddies"—he looked over my shoulder, and I turned briefly to see Dinah in his line of sight, unfortunately not unexpectedly—"we'll be glad to listen any time."

Really? Fine for him to say so, but I figured that if I planted myself at the police station and demanded a discussion, they wouldn't be too pleased.

Not unless I could lead them to the proverbial smoking gun, which wouldn't work in this case anyway, and not only because Henry hadn't been shot. They already had the murder weapon, or at least that was what they had indicated.

"Then who are those buddies of Ms. Kennersly's that you think could be guilty?" asked another voice. Damn. Silas had left his position near Henry's family and made his way over without my noticing, since he had stayed behind me.

And approaching from the other direction was Francine Metz. I wasn't sure where the *Knobcone News* editor had been since the service but assumed she'd been interviewing people, too. She didn't have a photographer with her, but she was snapping pictures with a small tablet computer.

"We aren't ready to provide that information yet," Chief Loretta said smoothly. "Our investigation is still in its preliminary stages, and the fact that Ms. Kennersly, or anyone else, has friends who might have had a motive to commit this crime is not relevant."

Good. Any motive my friends might have had were flimsy at best. Or so I'd been attempting to assure myself.

Silas now held his microphone out to the police chief, with Wilbur filming away behind him. "What *is* relevant then, Chief Jonas? What is your procedure now to solve this murder?"

Francine was on his other side, typing on her electronic device.

"Once again, that's something we can't discuss," Chief Loretta said. "All we can say right now is that determining who committed this homicide is a very high priority of ours, and you and your viewers can be certain we'll keep on it until it's resolved."

"And how long do you think that will take?" Silas persisted.

"I think you've seen in the recent past that such investigations can take some time. We clearly want to do it as quickly, yet as accurately, as possible." Chief Loretta turned to look directly into the camera Wilbur had aimed at her. "And if any of your viewers have insight or information that might be of use to us, we would very much appreciate hearing from them."

All very good and politically correct, I thought.

"We'd appreciate it, too," said a now-familiar male voice from behind me, and I realized that what HS Schulzer was saying was true. His family wanted answers, which wasn't surprising—it was what he'd emphasized during his father's memorial service.

As I turned, Silas maneuvered around to once more stick his microphone into HS's face, asking, "What does your family intend to do now, once your father is finally laid to rest, Mr. Schulzer?"

What did Silas want to know—whether HS and his sister and his aunt were going to jump into the investigation, too?

In a way, they had more reason to than I did. But even though I hadn't seen anyone official pounce on Dinah yet, at least not too hard, there was enough I'd heard to concern me. And I would never allow someone I cared about be jumped on too hard as a murder suspect…unless I felt certain they'd done it.

I didn't believe that of Dinah—even if I couldn't exactly exonerate her completely in my mind.

I watched Francine Metz observing all this. Apparently she was willing to let Silas take the lead, at least for now.

"We intend to return to our lives." This time it was Mabe answering. She looked so exhausted and so sad that I really wished that I had hard evidence against someone that I could turn over to the police and get this over with.

But on who? No one at Dinah's party that night, despite Henry's attitude toward us and vice versa. And despite my suspicions of Mike Holpurn and his brothers, I had no more evidence against them than I had against my wonderful, research-driven assistant. Mysha the dog walker? The neighboring Banners?

Me? No, I'd been at the party, and though I hadn't liked Henry's attitude, I hadn't hated it badly enough to harm him.

The cops might have some additional evidence besides the knife they'd indicated was the murder weapon. But it must have had no useful fingerprints on it, or they'd surely have arrested someone already.

What else? Who else?

The whole situation was irritating as well as befuddling me, and I wasn't sure where I could go with it now.

"Yes," HS was saying, backing up his sister. "We both have jobs and things that we need to return to. Tula, too." He looked at the cops. "We haven't asked yet about this, but I assume we're okay to go home after our dad is buried, right? We might stay a little longer, but we'd like to make that decision later."

"That's fine," Chief Loretta said. "As long as we have all the information we need to contact you before you leave."

But the discussion suggested that HS and Mabe and Tula were suspects of sorts, too. And why not? No one had seen them around town—at least, not that I knew about—but if one or more of them had been arguing with Henry, for any reason, who knew? Maybe one of them could have killed him and returned to their home, only to come back to Knobcone Heights for his memorial and burial.

I certainly preferred it to be one of them rather than someone I really knew. Although I still hoped it was Mike Holpurn or one of his brothers. They were the most logical killers, weren't they?

"Of course," Mabe said, glancing at HS, then Tula. They both nodded.

And why not? If officials from Knobcone Heights started arrest procedures against them when they were back home, they'd probably have time to disappear. Assuming, of course, they were guilty enough to pay attention to where the investigation was heading.

"So where do you live?" Silas piped in now.

Would any of them be foolish enough to tell that to the world?

"Quite a distance from here," Mabe said, wisely. It was a response that Silas could use in his broadcast if he wanted but basically it said nothing.

"Near where your father lived after he moved away from here?" Silas persisted.

"Not exactly," Mabe responded, and the others still said nothing. Good answer. That could mean they lived in a different house from Henry but in the same neighborhood, or that they lived in the same state, presumably California, or—well, it was vague enough not to pin any of them down.

I saw Loretta cast a glance toward her two detectives. "We need to leave," she said.

"But you'll keep the media advised as to anything you find?" Silas demanded.

"Any breaks in the case will be reported the way we usually do," Loretta said. She aimed a smile at Francine, as if in appreciation of that reporter's more polite approach to the situation. Did that mean the cops were more likely to give the *Knobcone News* first crack at any update?

I had no doubt that Francine hoped so.

That pretty much ended the post-memorial reception, since nearly everyone seemed to disperse. My group, too, began walking toward the parking lot.

On the way, I saw Billi with her City Council crowd. She separated from them as our eyes met, and I slowed down when she started to walk toward me.

"Do you have a few minutes?" she asked. "I want to talk to you about Prince and Duke."

SEVENTEEN

OF COURSE I HAD time to talk. I was always happy to chat with Billi, and when the conversation was about dogs—which it often was with her—I enjoyed it even more.

Billi motioned me aside with a brisk tilt of her head. I glanced toward Reed, who'd remained near me throughout this sometimes difficult event, acting as my backup and friend and more, which I truly appreciated, as always. He must have seen Billi's motion since he sent me a nod, and, good guy that he was, he walked over to where Neal, Janelle, and Dinah were talking and joined them.

I wondered about the gist of their conversation but figured I'd hear about it later from Reed, if not from the others, if anything important was brought up.

And now I could chat with just Billi.

Since many of the attendees at the memorial service appeared to be leaving, Billi and I simply walked off the sidewalk and onto the grass beside it and let people pass us.

Because this was a somber occasion, Billi, like the rest of the City Council members in attendance, wore a dark suit that probably would have been appropriate for a council meeting. I'd always considered her to be a pretty woman, with her smooth and attractive face framed by her nicely highlighted dark hair. At the moment, though, her attractiveness was hampered by a frown.

I opened my mouth to ask what was going on with the dogs but she beat me to it. "Would you believe that no one in this supposedly caring family wants to take in Henry Schulzer's dogs?" Her scowl looked furious now, and her tone was more than irritated. "I made a point of asking them when I offered my condolences and they all looked at me as if I were totally insane for even mentioning poor orphaned Prince and Duke."

"Oh no," I said. "That's too bad. I assumed they'd want them since they said the dogs were descendants of some others raised by their mother years ago. You'd think they'd at least want that reminder of their mom. Or Tula might want them as a reminder of her brother."

"I agree. But the dogs are what matter now. I'm going to find them a wonderful new home, preferably together—and then I'll rub it in those dratted Schulzers' faces. Maybe shame them a bit for not caring more about the dogs that Henry—or even probably Flora—really gave a damn about."

"Great idea." I appreciated what she'd said. But I also figured that these people wouldn't care if the dogs were taken in by someone impressive, like a local politico or celebrity, or anyone else for that matter.

"You and I have been talking generally about holding another adoption event soon. Why not very soon, while those folks are still in town? I'll have to get them to sign all the necessary paperwork to permit the adoption, but that shouldn't be a problem, assuming they're Henry's appropriate heirs."

"And assuming they're willing to do what's right for those dogs, even if they have no interest in them," I said. Surely HS and Mabe would rather the pups find a new, loving home than stay in a shelter forever. Mountaintop Rescue was of course a no-kill shelter, but everyone's preference there was to find the inhabitants a loving family.

"I certainly hope so," Billi said. "Any chance of your stopping by tomorrow? Since it'll be Monday, I assume you'll have a shift at the vet clinic first?"

"Yes, I do," I said. "And I'll definitely come to see you afterward. We can start making plans then."

"Great. See you." With a wave, Billi turned and headed back toward a few of the City Council members who were still talking near the entry to the building.

I turned, intending to join Reed and the others—and stopped. Dinah was off to my right, near the parking lot, and she seemed to be animatedly talking to Silas—with Wilbur filming them.

Heck, didn't she know better? She was a murder suspect, even if she hadn't been arrested—at least not yet. She should keep to herself, and certainly not talk on camera. It was too easy to say something unintended that gave the wrong impression, and reporters like Silas were unlikely to erase anything that could earn them a few more viewers because of the harmful implications.

Ready to pounce figuratively on both of them, I stalked in their direction. I had a feeling that Silas was waiting for me, since he pivoted when I got close to them and held the microphone out. "Ah, welcome, Carrie. This is Carrie Kennersly, who owns Icing on the Cake and the Barkery and Biscuits bakeries, where she is Dinah's boss. We were just discussing the fact that many people like Dinah, who is relatively new to Knobcone Heights, hadn't known of Henry Schulzer's affiliation with this town. Were you aware that he was the widower of our previous mayor, Flora Morgan Schulzer?"

"No," I said, glaring into Dinah's eyes. "I wasn't aware of that previously."

"But he's been a customer in your shops recently, right?"

Dinah must have mentioned that, although I figured Silas could have learned it from other sources. Silas wasn't a customer at either shop, so he wouldn't have seen Henry walk in with his dogs.

"Not very long, but his dogs seemed to like the healthy treats we sell in my Barkery and Biscuits shop." Okay, that was a bit of a plug, but why not take advantage of this uncomfortable situation? "And now, Dinah and I need to get back to those very shops." I looked at my assistant with a gaze that I hoped allowed no dispute. She had probably driven herself to the memorial service, but I wished we were riding together so I could quiz—and chastise—her. Both could wait till we got to the shops, though.

The way Dinah kept glancing at me as we walked to the parking lot told me she expected that chastisement. She didn't try to explain herself—not now, at least.

Back at the shops, things were going fine—or at least that was what both Frida, in Icing, and Vicky, in the Barkery, told me when I asked. There were still plenty of baked goods in both shops, though, which also told me something: we hadn't had a lot of customers.

Sundays were often busy—but quite a few people had gone to Henry's memorial, so that had possibly cut back on the numbers of visitors to both stores.

I spoke with Dinah for a short while in the kitchen before either of us got back to work. "I know it wasn't the smartest thing," she said, "but most of what we talked about was how I enjoyed research, and how nearly everything I researched was fun and hypothetical. We talked only a little about Henry Schulzer and his behavior at my birthday party, sort of. And that was far from being a motive for me to kill him, though I wish I knew who did it."

"Me too." Was I relieved? Not really. I just hoped she hadn't said anything potentially harmful to herself.

Still, I got back to work in the Barkery, leaving Dinah in Icing to help out. I'd left Biscuit at home that day. Not that I didn't trust my staffers here, but I knew I'd worry less about her if there was no possibility she could sneak out. That also meant I'd try to leave the shops right on time. Soon.

As closing time finally approached—after, fortunately, quite a few customers popped in to buy treats for themselves and their pets—I was surprised to see Detective Wayne Crunoll come in. Oh, sure, he had his cute Doxies with him, Blade and Magnum, but this obviously was a work day for him. I had a feeling his dogs were just there to try to put me off my guard, as he'd attempted previously. He still wore the white shirt and black pants he'd had on at the service.

"Hi, Carrie." Wayne edged his way around a couple of customers still studying the contents of the glass-fronted display case. He held his dogs' leashes so they had to stay by his side. "How about some of your great carob treats for these guys?"

"Of course," I said warily, but when I went behind the counter I pulled out a few sample treats for now. As I gave a second one to each pup I looked at Wayne. "So why are you really here?"

"Is Dinah still around?" he asked, and I shuddered inside. Was she the real reason he'd come here this late afternoon?

If so, why?

"She's over in Icing," I said, glad he had his dogs with him. They weren't police K-9s, so he was unlikely to be here to arrest Dinah with them along.

Even so … well, I wanted, needed, to know more of what was on his mind.

"Good," he said. "Can we sit down for a minute?"

Uh-oh. It appeared I might be about to get the answers I wanted, or at least some of them. And that made me wonder if I really wanted to know.

But I still said "Sure" and led him to the table closest to Biscuit's enclosure, since it was farthest from where the customers still pondered their selection. I told them to let Frida know when they made up their minds.

Then I sat down across from Wayne.

I tried to appear nonchalant as I looked into his light brown eyes. He had more than a hint of a dark shadow on his pudgy face, probably because it was so late in the day. And the expression on that face?

It appeared … well, almost triumphant.

What was he thinking?

I found out in less than a minute. "I just got done talking with Silas Perring," he began. Which made me worry again about what Dinah might have said on camera. Justifiably so, as it turned out. "He showed me part of his interview with Dinah on his tablet. They were talking about research."

"She usually talks about that," I said, hoping that was all she'd talked about. That's what she'd said, at least.

"The thing is, she admitted that she would do nearly anything to research whatever book she thinks she's writing. Even maybe killing someone, or at least going through the motions."

What? Surely Dinah hadn't said something that absurd. "Pretend motions," I asserted. "I don't know what she said, but I'm sure she didn't mean anything more than that."

"Maybe. But she also admitted how upset she'd been after Henry Schulzer gave her a hard time at her birthday party."

"I'm not surprised about that, but it doesn't mean—"

"Oh, she didn't admit she killed Henry as part of her research, if that's where you think I'm going with this. But—well, her denial wasn't as forceful as I figured it would be under the circumstances. I intend to talk to her again. Now, in fact. But I'm not ready to bring her in again even for a further interview … yet. I know that this time you're her protector, and I shouldn't be talking to you about this. Still—it won't hurt for you to know that Dinah's now gone up a few notches on our list, so you'd better get ready to figure out who really did it." He chuckled. "You're so good at that, aren't you?" His tone sounded sarcastic. "And by the way, I warned our chief and my partner, Detective Morana, that I'd be talking to you. Neither of them objected—and we all seem to be heading in the same direction after seeing parts of Silas's interview."

Drat. Well, it would be better to get this confrontation out of the way now, when I could be there.

I told Frida, who was waiting on those customers—who fortunately seemed to have made up their minds—that I was going next door, and that she could leave after that order was done, as long as she locked the shop first.

I helped Wayne put his dogs into Biscuit's currently empty enclosure, and we went next door into Icing.

Both Vicky and Dinah were there, a good thing since a few customers remained in that shop, too. I went behind the counter where my assistants stood and asked Vicky to finish up with the people, who seemed ready to place their order.

Then I motioned to Dinah to join Wayne and me at one of the tables.

Dinah didn't look happy, but she complied. As we all sat down, she faced Wayne. "Is this about the interview I gave to Silas Perring?" she asked. Before he responded, she went on, "If so, you need to know that, sure, I'm curious. I'll do many, many kinds of research

170

if it teaches me things that I may eventually be able to use when I write a book. But if what he said, even what he showed you, made you think I'd actually hurt someone, let alone harm them, to learn how it feels to do that, you can be sure that's not what I intended. Sure, I'm curious, but I'm also a nice human being. I'd only hurt someone by writing about them, not killing them. I thought I made that clear when I talked to you at the police station."

Did she protest too much? I hoped not. She made sense to me—but I hadn't been there for her police interrogation.

"Telling the world you consider yourself a nice person doesn't necessarily make you one," Wayne said bluntly, staring at her. "Although I will say that you didn't admit to killing Mr. Schulzer. Does that mean you actually didn't? I don't think so."

"It doesn't mean she did do it, either," I interjected.

"No ... but let me tell you this, Ms. Greeley. There are quite a few possible suspects in this situation, and that includes the people who argued with Mr. Schulzer at your birthday party. From what we gathered, you were one of the most vocal of them. And now—well, if I were you, I wouldn't let myself be interviewed on camera."

I silently agreed, but it was a done deal. I still wanted to protect Dinah. "That's undoubtedly true, Detective," I said. "But she was interviewed—and I gather that, no matter what else she said, she didn't admit to killing Henry Schulzer, right?"

"Right, but—"

"But did what she say make you want to take her into custody right now?"

"No, but that doesn't mean she's innocent. It means—"

"It means that whatever she said might not look good, but it can't have been that bad, either. And now I'd appreciate it if you'd leave. We're about to close both shops."

"Fine," Wayne said. "But that doesn't mean I won't be back—or that you won't remain on our radar, Ms. Greeley."

We both looked at Dinah. Her large eyes were filled with tears and her lips were trembling. "I understand," she said. "But let me say right now—"

I held up my hand. "Don't talk to him," I insisted.

She ignored me—again. "I just wanted to make it clear that no matter what it might have sounded like, I wouldn't kill anyone, and I absolutely didn't kill Mr. Schulzer."

"Right," said Wayne, standing up. "I get it. Goodbye, ladies. Oh, and Ms. Greeley, please don't leave town." He stalked out of Icing as we both stared after him.

EIGHTEEN

DINAH AND I BOTH just stood there for a minute. She stared out the door after Wayne. I stared at her.

She finally turned back toward me, her face pale, her expression wretched. "I guess I messed up."

I wanted to say *Yes, you did*, but she was hurting enough. So instead, I said, "Well, I guess you'll know better next time." I hoped so, for her sake. And that assumed there would be a next time—as long as she wasn't incarcerated for Henry's murder.

She lifted her chin almost defiantly. "I didn't say anything that was really bad, no matter what the detective seems to think. Maybe they're just desperate to find someone to accuse, and I made the mistake of making it easy for them."

"Maybe so," I said, walking over to her. "But—okay, I don't want to make you feel any worse, but it's definitely not a good idea to go public even to describe your love of research, if what you say can be interpreted ... well, against you. And I assume this time that was the case." Trying to make the sort-of accusation less critical, I gave her a hug.

She hugged me back, but after a moment stepped away. "I know I should listen to you. You've been in the position I'm in before, plus you've helped to exonerate all those other people who were accused. But—well, it's done. And I'm still free, at least for now." She looked me straight in the eye. "Do you really think I could have killed Henry Schulzer?"

After a split second I said, "Of course not."

But Dinah was smart and intuitive, and she read the truth in my brief hesitation. "Then you're not sure. I understand. But Carrie, please believe me when I say that I'm like you were when you were accused, and like the friends you helped when they were suspects. I can understand—sort of—why I'm in the cops' crosshairs, but honestly, I really, really did not kill Henry Schulzer. And even if you're not going to continue helping me like you did the others, I intend to prove my innocence." Now her expression was angry.

At me? Maybe. Or perhaps just with the world.

"I'll help you all I can, Dinah," I promised. "But please be careful. Don't do anything that will make it look like you could have committed this crime. Things like asking too many questions, accosting anyone who may also be a suspect, being pushy with the police—"

"Fine thing for you to tell me all that when I know you do every one of those things, probably each time you work on trying to solve a murder." Dinah's tone was icy. But in a moment she stepped forward and hugged me again. "I know you're just trying to help me, Carrie. And I also know, you being you, that you're going to keep trying to figure this one out, too. So let me tell *you*: please be careful. I don't want you to be hurt on my behalf, either." She squeezed me even harder, then let go and backed off. "Time for me to go home. Tomorrow's Monday, so I won't be coming in."

I wondered if it would be a good idea for her to pop in on her days off so I could keep an eye on her, but then realized that was silly. Maybe. Still, I opened my mouth to say I'd miss her and to be careful, but she preempted me.

"And yes," she said, "I promise to stay out of trouble. I'll probably just stay home and write all my research and feelings down on the computer. Maybe someday I'll be able to read it again and just laugh at it—or use all the emotional stuff in a future book."

"Good idea," I said. "And … Dinah, you know I care about you as more than just an employee. Please call me anytime if you need to talk. But—"

"You're the greatest, Carrie." She gave me yet another hug. Stepping back, she looked at me as if she wanted to say something else, but then she shook her head, turned, and fled into the kitchen, where I knew she'd grab her purse and leave.

Which was okay with me. I just hoped she really was innocent—and that, if the cops didn't zero in on the real killer, they didn't arrest Dinah either.

I closed up both shops then and also headed home. While I was in my car, my mind swirled around what to do next.

How could I clear Dinah, or at least protect her so the police would stop hounding her?

But what if she really was guilty?

She couldn't be. That stupid argument with Henry and his threats toward her weren't a motive for murder.

But Henry had insulted her, her career, and her research. And what if she really did want to know, for her research, what it felt like to kill someone?

No! I was glad to reach home and pull into my driveway. It was time to go inside and walk Biscuit and put this situation behind me, at least for the rest of the day.

I was delighted, though, that after I went inside and my adorable pup jumped up and greeted me, my phone rang—and it was Reed. We hadn't discussed plans for tonight, but he let me know that Hugo and he were eager to come over to my place and bring dinner, if I was interested.

Was I? Heck, yes—even though I'd received a text message from Neal, who said that he and Janelle would be around our house for the night, too.

Enough had gone on that day to make me delighted to have all the company possible. That included Janelle's dog Go, as well as the other two dogs.

Knowing my brother's plans, I asked Reed to pick up some pizza and told him we'd have company. He didn't mind.

After I hung up, I put Biscuit's leash on and let her lead me outside. The evening had turned a bit cool, which was a good thing. It made me feel more comfortable taking my dog on a longer walk than we usually did at this time of night.

Of course, I generally had her with me at the shops and walked her there more often. But she was a good girl, as always. And as soon as I saw Neal's car coming down the street I ushered Biscuit back toward home.

Neal had Janelle and Go with him. After he greeted me, he got down on his knees and said good evening to his "Bug," which was the name he called Biscuit.

We soon were all in the house, hanging out in the kitchen. "Anything new in the murder investigation?" Neal asked, pulling a chair out from beneath the kitchen table and sitting on it backwards, his legs around the back of it.

"A little," was how I responded as I got four wine glasses out of a wooden cabinet near the metal kitchen sink, then set them gently on the mottled beige granite kitchen counter. I told Janelle and him about the media interviews of Dinah, and how one of those had resulted in Detective Wayne showing up at my shops.

"Glad I wasn't there for that," Janelle said.

"I'd rather he didn't come at all," I responded. "I tried to make it clear to Wayne that Silas must have misinterpreted what Dinah said to him during the interview."

"Probably he was there because he wanted to find more of a reason to keep her as a prime suspect," Neal said. "I gather they haven't grabbed onto someone else, right?"

"Apparently not," I agreed. "At least no one they feel comfortable about arresting."

We chatted for another minute about what evidence there might be, beyond the murder weapon. Very little had made it into the news, as far as I knew, which could mean police secrecy—but it could also mean there just wasn't much.

My phone played its song, and when I pulled it from my pocket, I was glad to see it was Reed calling. He said he was parked in the driveway and about to bring in the pizza.

We all headed for the front door to meet him, dogs included.

He carried two large boxes, so I figured none of us would remain hungry that night. The end of Hugo's leash was looped over his right wrist, and the sweet Malinois kept his nose in the air, obviously scenting what was in the boxes. Biscuit's and Go's noses soon mimicked his.

I checked the time. Local news would soon be aired on KnobTV, and everyone seemed as eager to watch it as I was that night. As a result, we decided to eat in the living room, where there was a television mounted on the wall.

Reed, Janelle, and I sat on the fluffy old beige couch, while Neal settled in on a matching chair beside it. We put our wine glasses and the bottle of merlot I'd opened on the coffee table in front of us, but we kept the pizza boxes in the kitchen—and out of the dogs' reach, up on the counter. We ate off of paper plates in our laps.

"Good?" Reed asked as I took a bite of pizza. He'd chosen several toppings, and the slice I currently ate had lots of cheese, pepperoni, and green peppers on it.

"Great," I told him with a grin.

A talk show about entertainment was just ending, and I used the remote to keep the sound muted for now. We all chatted about our respective days—about things other than Henry Schulzer's memorial and related subjects, for now. The dogs lay on the floor around us, sometimes begging for a piece of pizza crust, but they seldom got any, *seldom* being the key word.

Janelle talked about a new photo assignment she had just obtained, thanks to referrals from a couple who'd recently gotten married. She'd been the photographer at their ceremony and apparently they loved what she had done, since they'd recommended her to another couple who'd been attendees at their wedding. Janelle would be taking their wedding pictures in a couple of weeks. "Can't wait," she said. "I've got some wildlife photos to shoot for an article I'm writing for an online e-magazine and I love that, too, but weddings are special." She aimed a look toward me, then Reed.

Okay, I knew my brother and his main squeeze assumed that was the direction Reed and I were heading. I assumed it, too, or at least I hoped—but we hadn't made the final commitment. Not yet.

Even so, I aimed a sideways glance at the guy I believed I wanted to spend the rest of my life with—and found him grinning at me.

Interesting. Were we finally going to have that talk anytime soon?

Neal then talked about a couple of hikes he had scheduled for some of his local hiking enthusiasts as well as visitors staying at the resort. "I'll be doing a hike each day next weekend," he said.

"You didn't do any this weekend," I said. "Right?"

"Yeah, and you know how I miss it when I don't. That's why I've worked to ensure I'll have two coming up."

Reed then mentioned a couple of neighbor cats who'd had a clawing fight, and both owners had brought them into the clinic late in the day when he'd returned to work after the service. "Both will be fine, and they even seem to have taught each other a lesson, since their owners let them get together again in the office and neither attacked the other. I warned the owners, though, not to leave them alone together, in case this was just a temporary truce."

"Good idea," I said.

Most of what I'd be able to relate about the rest of my day I simply didn't want to talk about, since it was all pretty much related to the memorial and those who'd been there. I did mention that we had a good group of customers at the shops, and that was that.

And in fact it was a good thing I was ready to shut up. The news was just coming on.

I turned up the volume and sat back, my wine glass in my hand. I'd finished my pizza. Now I wanted to watch this as dessert—although I doubted it would be sweet at all.

And boy, was I right.

The Knobcone House of Celebration was in the background as Silas moved his microphone from his narrow, pursed mouth to Dinah's full-lipped one.

First, he asked why she was there. "I just attended poor Henry Schulzer's memorial service," she replied solemnly.

"Then you knew Mr. Schulzer?"

"Not well," Dinah answered.

"Okay. Now tell me about the birthday party you had a couple of days ago at the Knobcone Heights Resort."

"That's right. You were there, too. It was wonderful!" Dinah described it briefly, including her friends who'd attended, and said that her boss at the bakeries where she worked had thrown the party for her—which made me grin. She held up her hand then. "If you're asking about that because Mr. Schulzer was there, yes, I invited him to join us. But he wasn't very pleasant after a while. He argued with me and some other people. But nothing was said that would have made any of us angry enough to hurt him."

"I see," Silas said.

The camera panned away from Dinah toward the House of Celebration, and no one said anything. When it returned to Dinah, Silas said, "I understand that you work at Barkery and Biscuits and Icing on the Cake, but in addition to staffing those bakeries you're a writer, too."

"Yes," Dinah said. "I've had some magazine articles and short stories published, and I'm always working on new ideas for novels though I haven't published any yet. I'm getting close with a couple, though."

"And I gather you conduct a lot of research for that?"

She nodded at the camera. "Yes, I do."

"Does that research involve more than just reading, things like getting yourself involved in situations you hope to write about?"

"Sometimes."

"Does that mean you sometimes put yourself in the same position as your characters—say, you learn about a particular career such as baking or dog walking or driving a boat, then go do it yourself?"

"Sure. That can be part of the research. A really fun part, and I do it whenever I can."

"Are any of the novels you're working on murder mysteries?"

"Well, yes."

The interview ended then. The next part was Silas, alone on camera with the microphone up to his own mouth, a solemn expression on his face. He reminded the viewer that Henry Schulzer, widower of the murdered former mayor of Knobcone Heights, had been murdered himself.

"So far, there have been no arrests in this murder," Silas said. "The police are declining to be interviewed right now, but our understanding is that they appear to be gathering evidence that will lead to an apprehension very soon. This is Silas Perring, for KnobTV news. Now, back to the studio."

Another story came on as another member of the news team, Bobbi Hanger, began talking about a car accident somewhere nearby in the San Bernardino Mountains.

I put it on mute. Then I looked at my companions, one at a time, who had also heard Dinah's interview. They all appeared stunned, though maybe not as much as I was.

"Did I hear Dinah admit, after mentioning the altercation with Henry—which wasn't that bad an argument—that she sometimes puts herself in situations related to her research, and that she enjoys it, and that she's writing murder mysteries?" I asked, but I of course knew the answer.

"Yes," Janelle replied almost sadly. "She did."

"She didn't admit to killing Henry," Reed pointed out.

"But the implication of the possibility was there," I said.

"That reporter guy overdramatized it," Neal said.

"Yes, but … Well, I can see better now why Detective Crunoll came to my shops to question Dinah again. He told me about this interview, which was a public admission of sorts. Silas apparently told him about it, showed him parts of it."

"And now it's been aired on TV for anyone to see," said Janelle. "Poor Dinah."

Reed looked at me. "It really wasn't an admission," he said. "Although someone—like maybe the police—could read that into it."

He paused. "Still—Carrie, are you certain Dinah had nothing to do with Schulzer's death?"

"I'm sure you're not the only one who'll be asking that now," I snapped. "I just wish Dinah had listened to me and stayed far away from the news or anyone else nosy other than the police, who have the right to ask her questions."

"Too bad she didn't," Reed agreed. There was a thoughtful expression on his face, as if he was analyzing what I'd just said—and what I hadn't said.

For I hadn't really answered his question: *was* I sure Dinah had nothing to do with Schulzer's death?

Because the answer, if I were honest, would have to be that no, despite my hopes that my employee was fully innocent—despite my belief that she had no genuine motive—I couldn't say that I was certain she was. I hadn't been sure before. And now, after seeing that interview personally, I felt even less convinced of her innocence.

NINETEEN

I THOUGHT ABOUT CALLING Dinah after watching the news report—but I didn't. What could I say to her about it that I hadn't already said? Tell her yet again that she shouldn't have let Silas interview her? She was certainly aware of that.

But now it was on TV for the world to see.

Was it really so bad? I tried to tell myself it wasn't as I went back into the kitchen to open another bottle of wine.

Everyone seemed done eating, so I first put the remaining pizza slices into a box and stuck it into the refrigerator. Then I reached into my pantry, where I kept a few unopened bottles of red wine. I chose another merlot.

As I put it on the counter and prepared to get the corkscrew from its drawer, my phone rang. I had an idea who it was, and I was correct, I saw, as I pulled my phone from my pocket. Dinah.

"Hi," I said as brightly as I could. She didn't need to know my roiling thoughts and deep concern about her.

"Carrie?" Her voice sounded choked, and I could tell, even with that one word, that she was crying. "It's horrible. You were so right. But you're always right, and ... and I—"

"I'm not always right," I said firmly. And that was true, even though I was right this time. "I take it you saw your interview on TV."

"Yes. And, Carrie, it sounded so bad. I said everything that they showed, of course, but I'm pretty sure Silas edited it. Parts of it seemed out of order, at least. I knew I kind of left the door open for anyone listening to learn about my research and that I'd do nearly anything for research, but not kill people or even hurt them. But playing the interview the way he did makes it sound like I'd injure someone or worse just for the fun of it, for research, even if I had no other reason to harm them, so I could make notes about it and use it in a book. That's not me, Carrie."

"I know it's not." A thought crossed my mind. "You said the interview was edited out of order? I don't know if that's okay to do." That was assuming Dinah remembered all aspects of what Silas had asked her and when, of course. The adrenaline rush of having a news person with a camera asking questions could certainly confuse someone, mess with how they remembered what had happened. Even so ... "I think this might be a really good time for you to hire attorney Ted Culbert. He can check to see if it's okay for the media to change the sequence of what people say in order to imply something different from what they meant. Maybe he already knows. And he might also be able to help you—"

"—if this leads to my arrest for Henry Schulzer's murder." Dinah's voice broke up then and I heard her crying.

I grabbed the bottle of wine along with another glass from my shelves. I needed a strong sip now as I attempted to figure out what to say next. But I had to wait till I had two hands to open the bottle.

"Would you like me to come to your house and keep you company?" I asked.

"No, thank you," she managed to gasp. "I think I'll be better off alone right now."

"Okay. But feel free to call again anytime, late, early or whatever, okay? And you don't have to be working a shift to drop in at the shops tomorrow or Tuesday, just for the company and to talk about what's going on."

"Thank you, Carrie. I just might take you up on that. Good night." Dinah ended the connection.

Reed had entered the kitchen as I was talking with Dinah and I'd given him a brief wave. Now he stood beside me as I opened the bottle of wine. "Can I guess who that was?"

"Sure," I said, "but I'll bet you already know." I poured out just a little wine and took a sip. "Dinah saw that news report, too. She doesn't deny the interview, of course, but she indicated it might not have been presented in the order Silas actually asked his questions."

"Does it matter?" Reed asked.

"I'm not sure." And I wasn't.

But I became a little more certain that it did matter, later on after we'd gone to bed, Reed and me together, Neal and Janelle in his room. The dogs were divided up according to who their owners were, which meant Biscuit and Hugo were with Reed and me, and Go was with Janelle and Neal.

I heard Reed's heavy sleep-breathing, and Hugo's slight snore, as I lay there, but Biscuit was silent. Maybe she, too, was awake, thinking. Or more likely, listening for her closest human, me, to fall asleep.

And what was I thinking about? Well, what if Silas had first asked Dinah about her research and how she conducted it, and how important it was to her, and whether she would attempt to do something she was researching? If so, and then he later brought up questions

185

about Henry and Dinah's birthday party, and the friction that had occurred there, she would have answered truthfully, as she had.

But put those two subjects in their opposite order—the way they'd been presented on the TV news—well, her dislike of Henry's behavior at her party and her comment that it wasn't enough for anyone to want to harm him, followed by her statement that she'd do anything to aid in her research ... this perhaps implied she might have killed Henry, who she was angry with, in the name of her research.

Too odd? Too ridiculous?

Too incriminating?

I eventually fell asleep, thank heavens, since I had to get up early as always the next morning. I followed the usual routine and didn't have to wake Reed since he woke up on his own. We attempted to stay quiet so as not to awaken Neal and Janelle, or even Go, but I suspected that at least Go, with his keen hearing, knew what we were up to. Even so, none of them greeted us at that early hour.

"You okay?" Reed asked when we were both in the kitchen, preparing to take our dogs out before leaving.

"Sure. Why?"

"I heard you moving around a lot last night and figured you were worried about Dinah. Either that or you were weighing who would be the best suspect in the Schulzer murder. Maybe both, combined."

I laughed, then went over to where he stood near the door, Hugo's leash in his hand. I leaned upward and kissed him, then stepped back. "I guess my way of thinking is pretty obvious to you these days."

"I guess so, you murder-solver, you." Reed was still smiling, which was a good thing. He'd had a tendency to try to get me to stop sleuthing ... until that sleuthing helped to save him. I'd wondered about what his attitude would be the next time I encountered a murder case, even though I'd hoped there wouldn't be a next time.

Well, there was one now, and fortunately Reed's attitude remained more amused than irritated.

We soon parted ways for the morning, though I had a shift scheduled at the vet clinic that afternoon. Today, I was able to bring Biscuit to work as usual, since on the outings I'd planned, like my visit to the veterinary clinic, she could come along.

I did my regular routine of starting the baking, and today Vicky was the first assistant to arrive. Janelle came in a little later with Go, and I figured my brother had to be awake now, too.

And what did my assistants and I talk about besides our food preparation and anticipation of customers that day? Dinah, of course, and her interview with Silas Perring.

"It wasn't so bad," Vicky said when we were both in Icing, filling the glass display case with cookies and cupcakes. "Sure, they mentioned the nastiness at the birthday party, and that Dinah does a lot of things to further her research, but I didn't get the impression the newscaster was stating that she was the killer."

"Maybe not, but the implication was there," I said. "He asked about what she'd do to accomplish her research goals."

"That would be a dumb reason to kill someone," Vicky said as she arranged a tray of our popular red velvet cupcakes right in the middle of the display.

"Yes," I said, "it would be. But that won't necessarily stop viewers who've seen the interview from wondering how far someone like Dinah would go."

"If that's all your detective buddies have on Dinah, it's no wonder they haven't arrested her," countered Vicky.

Janelle had walked in during the conversation but stood in the open doorway between the two shops. "No one in the Barkery yet," she said, "but I heard you two talking. I just hope that public opinion doesn't make the cops decide they have to try harder to arrest

Dinah. Yes, it didn't sound like she was confessing to anything—but it's still not helpful in making it clear that she's innocent, either."

And so it went for the rest of the morning—at least when I spoke with my assistants in private now and then, for customers soon started coming into both shops. Fortunately, none mentioned Dinah, let alone her interview, so all seemed to go fine … until nearly lunchtime, when Mysha Jorgens walked into the Barkery with a schnauzer mix on a leash. I wasn't sure whether the dog walker had been here before, but she was welcome, especially if she bought treats now and then for some of her charges.

"Hi, Carrie," she said. "This is Herr Schnauzer, better known as Herr." She pointed to her charge. "His owner is visiting the resort, and your brother or someone there referred them to me. Tell me about the treats you have available now."

They were pretty much the same as always, since I hadn't recently been developing any new ones. I let Mysha know about my favorites, such as the treats with yams and those with carob. I gave Herr a sample of each.

She chose to buy some of those, plus other varieties we had. "I won't give them all to Herr, though. I do have a couple of other clients. But … well, I miss Mr. Schulzer and his dogs. They kept me busy and I liked them, and … well, that whole thing is a shame." Mysha's head drooped as she spoke, but then she looked up at me. She looked even paler than when I'd first met her, and her clothes were a lot more casual now, too. I wondered if she'd dressed up to try to impress Henry. Had she liked him as more than a client?

Had she any reason to dislike him—enough to kill him?

I'd considered her as a possible suspect before, partly because I didn't know her well enough to be upset if the cops suspected her. But she still seemed genuinely upset that Henry was gone.

Which didn't mean, of course, that she couldn't have been the one to create that situation.

"It is a shame," I agreed, considering whether to attempt to get her to talk more about the subject.

"Do you know what's going on now with Prince and Duke?" she asked. "I've been so worried about them."

"They're still at Mountaintop Rescue," I told her. "We're going to hold an adoption event here in the Barkery very soon to try to find them a new family, since Mr. Schulzer's family wasn't interested in keeping them."

"Really?" Mysha seemed to perk up. "When?"

"I need to finalize that with Mountaintop Rescue," I told her. "But I suspect it'll be later this week. You can check back here, or at the rescue, to find out, if you want to come to see those dogs again."

"I do. Absolutely. Thanks." Mysha stopped near the enclosure to pat Biscuit and Go, and then she and Herr left.

And I continued to wonder what her real relationship had been with Henry ... and how I might learn more. Well, it sounded as if Mysha would most likely come to the adoption event, whenever we held it.

Which gave me even more reason to get it scheduled when I talked with Billi that afternoon.

We got busier at the shops around lunchtime, and I didn't have an opportunity to go to Cuppa's that day. I wished I had, since I would have loved to get the Joes' take on Dinah's interview and find out if they'd eavesdropped on other conversations about it, too.

Or, since it hadn't been conclusively a confession or anything else, were just those of us who knew Dinah worried because we cared about her? Maybe the rest of the world didn't find the interview particularly interesting.

Although what Silas had shared with the detectives had gotten Wayne to come by to talk to Dinah yesterday...

Enough. My mind had been focusing not on the customers who wanted more treats but on something I could do nothing about, at least for the moment.

I hopped into Icing and helped Vicky there for a while, since there was a lunchtime crowd who clearly wanted sweets for themselves that day. When it slowed a little, I went into the Barkery, and then I continued checking both shops until I had to leave for the vet clinic.

As always at the clinic, I left Biscuit with Faye and company in doggy daycare. My shift was fairly uneventful and enjoyable. I saw Reed, of course. And Arvie, who knew me well enough to ask what was wrong. The head vet and I were close, so I wasn't really surprised, but I didn't go into detail with him.

Yet he clearly wasn't surprised that what was on my mind involved concern about solving another murder...

My shift was over soon, and Biscuit and I headed for Mountaintop Rescue. As usual, I had a bag of slightly aging treats to make sure the dogs there got tastes of something good and healthy.

Receptionist Mimi greeted me cheerfully from behind her counter. "I bet I know why you're here."

I showed her the bag of treats. "Here's one reason."

"But not the only one. Billi has been talking about when to schedule the next adoption at the Barkery to see if we can find a new home for poor Prince and Duke. They're both great dogs and don't belong here—not that any of our charges really do."

"I get it, but if any animal doesn't have a loving family, there's no place better than Mountaintop Rescue for them to be."

"Thanks," came a voice from behind me—not unexpected, since I'd heard some footsteps as I stood there. Billi must have come in from the enclosure area.

I turned. Recently I'd seen her more in her City Councilwoman garb than her shelter manager clothing, but now she was dressed casually. That didn't mean her attractive face wasn't adorned perfectly with makeup, though. I smiled at her. "You ready to set up an adoption?"

"I sure am. Let's go to my office. I've got some other things to discuss with you as well."

Given the decisive expression on her pretty face, I had a good idea what she meant.

A City Councilwoman watched the news, after all, particularly the local news.

I believed I was about to have another discussion about Dinah.

TWENTY

WE HEADED UPSTAIRS TO Billi's office, Biscuit beside me. As always, I smiled at the sign on her door: *Councilwoman Wilhelmina Matlock, Boss of the City, Canines, and Cats.*

"Come in, you two," Billi said, referring to Biscuit and me. She was definitely an animal lover. The way she talked to pets at the shelter and otherwise was just one indication of that.

She waved toward the wooden chairs facing her desk and I chose one, sitting down as Biscuit circled, then lay down by my feet on the antique rug.

Billi didn't wait for me to start. "So what was that interview of Dinah on TV this morning? I didn't see it initially, but someone got a buzz started among the council members so I found it online. I imagine we've all viewed it by now. Was Dinah just playing games? It didn't sound like she was confessing to having killed Henry Schulzer, but the possibility was there."

I shook my head, knowing my expression must appear wry. "Honestly, I don't know what she was thinking, even though she and I discussed it. She's really upset, said something about how portions of the interview were shown out of order and that was what made her appear to be saying something she didn't mean. This may be true, but even so … well, it doesn't really matter, but I'd told her before that happened not to talk to anyone, particularly the media."

"I don't know Dinah as well as you do," Billi said, "but I gather she enjoys talking to almost everyone as part of her research." She paused. "Do you think she'll ever get a novel published? It might help if something was out there that she—or you—could point to that would show the authorities why she's asking all those questions, pushing other people to talk, maybe doing things herself…"

"Like murdering someone to see what it feels like, in the name of research?" I snorted. "She's said she's finished a couple of manuscripts, but I don't know if she thinks they're ready to get published—or whether she's trying to find a publisher or thinking of publishing them herself or what."

Billi leaned back on her desk chair. "You don't think she really had anything to do with Henry's death, do you?"

"Honestly? I don't think so. I don't want to think so. And despite any motive the police could say she had—whether for research or because Henry threatened her and her career—I just can't really buy into it as a logical reason to hurt anyone that way. Because of that, and because I know and like Dinah, I don't think she murdered Henry." My turn to pause. "But if the cops actually find some evidence against her and bring her in, I can't say I'd be totally blindsided. If so, though, they'd better have a much more convincing motive than I can conceive of."

"I understand. And you have a reputation these days for getting these things right. I hope that's so now." Billi smiled at me, then grew serious. "But unless you want to talk about it more now, let's figure out when to hold the adoption event. And then I'll take you to see how Prince and Duke are doing."

"I'm sure they're doing great," I said, "but I'd be delighted to see them."

After figuring out the details of the event, which we scheduled for that coming Friday, we went downstairs. I left Biscuit with Mimi at the front desk and followed Billi into the yard area, where the kennels were. I observed all the sweet, hopeful faces of dogs in their enclosures as we passed and wished I had the treats I'd brought with me, but I'd left them at the desk with Mimi. "Be sure to give out my samples here generously," I told Billi. "I'll bring some more soon."

"I will, and I'm sure they'll all look forward to it."

Soon we got to the enclosure housing Henry's two dogs. Billi accompanied me inside, and I knelt on the cement and hugged both lovable golden cockers. "We'll get you a new home soon," I promised them. "Hopefully this Friday."

The dogs might not be able to understand my words, but I figured they read my tone of voice as caring. They snuggled with me for a short while, but I soon stood since I had to leave.

"Let's start publicizing that adoption event right away," I said to Billi. "And of course a few other dogs are welcome, too."

"I want to make sure these two are taken into the same loving home," Billi reminded me, but that was nothing new.

"If the right person doesn't come along on Friday," I said, "we can schedule another event and start publicizing it, and the availability of these two pups, right away."

"Fine with me," Billi agreed. "And I'll start getting the word out, through my usual resources, about Friday's event."

"Me too."

It was time for Biscuit and me to leave. On our way out, Billi pointed out some of the other dogs she was considering bringing to the adoption event. The number always varied, but she did a great job of choosing ones that people tended to like right away and, often, adopt.

Mimi was playing with Biscuit when we got to the reception area, and I hated to interrupt their fun. On the other hand, I needed to get back to the shops. I thanked Mimi, said bye to Billi with a promise we'd talk again soon about Friday, and then Biscuit and I left.

I had a thought on the drive back to the shops. I knew where the KnobTV station was located, at the far side of town. Knobcone Heights wasn't a large city so it wasn't a great distance, but as I pondered, I figured going there wouldn't get me any more answers than if I called.

Which I did after checking in at the shops and putting Biscuit in her enclosure in the Barkery. I said hi to Janelle and Vicky and made sure everything was under control, then went through the kitchen to my office. I looked online for the info about KnobTV and considered just sending an email, but who knew how long it might take for someone to get back to me?

Instead, I called the main number and asked for Silas Perring.

But he apparently wasn't around. Maybe he was out and about interviewing someone else—making their lives more miserable for having spoken with him on camera.

Although some people enjoyed such things and didn't talk about matters that could hurt them.

Instead of hanging up, though, I thought for a moment and asked for the station manager, but whoever that was also was not available. I quickly came up with the names of two other on-air reporters I was aware of, Honey Raykoff and Bobbi Hanger. Fortunately, Bobbi was there, and my call was transferred to her.

I had never met Bobbi and didn't know much about her other than having seen her occasionally on the air. I doubted she had much seniority, so she might not know the answer to my questions, but it wouldn't hurt to ask.

"Hello, Carrie," she said after I introduced myself, including that I owned Barkery and Biscuits as well as Icing on the Cake. "I don't have a dog, but I love your Icing red velvet cupcakes. What can I do for you today? Although"—she added before I could respond—"I assume, since Silas Perring recently interviewed one of your employees, it has something to do with that."

"Exactly," I said. I didn't want to sound like I was accusing Silas of anything, so I just got into what some of the basics of TV interviewing entailed, such as how the editing was done.

"Depends on the air time allotted to a particular story," Bobbi said. "Those related to Mr. Schulzer's death are generally given some priority right now since that's still an ongoing investigation by the police."

"And are portions of a story ever shortened or shown out of order, or—"

"I'm sorry, but since I'm just a reporter here I can't get into discussions of the station's policies on things like that. And, frankly, my understanding is that our management is not inclined to talk about how we get our stories or what we do with things we've recorded, such as interviews. But—well, if you'd ever like for me to come over and do a story on your bakeries, that would be fun."

"Good idea," I said, trying to hide my irritation. "Let me think about that."

I said goodbye and hung up. I had another thought then. I had no reason to invite Bobbi to our adoption event, but Silas had attended a few before.

I'd be sure to tell Billi to let him know about it. Better that she invite him than me.

And after his grilling of Dinah, Silas probably would be delighted to come and interrogate my assistant again at her place of work—although I wouldn't allow him to do that. He'd already done enough damage to Dinah's peace of mind, and maybe her reputation, too. But I wanted him to come so I could grill him—rather than him grilling Dinah or me—on his station's policies about the editing and sequencing of the clips in their news stories.

I soon hurried back out to work in my shops. All went fine for the rest of the day and I closed both on time, thanking Vicky and Janelle for all their hard work that day.

Reed called me and said that he was staying overnight at the clinic since a badly injured dog had been brought in, possibly attacked by a coyote. At least it sounded as if the poor thing could be saved, and Reed was a darned good vet. If anyone could save him, Reed could. And he didn't need my assistance since Yolanda had already said she could stay there to help out.

Biscuit and I were alone that night, as it turned out, since Neal was staying with Janelle. I knew I wouldn't have slept well even if they had been around, or even if Reed had been there—although I did call him during the evening to check on how things were going with the injured dog. I fortunately caught him at a time he could talk, since the surgery to stitch up some lesions had already been finished. The dog seemed to be doing all right, so Reed was happy.

That made me happy, too. Hopefully the pup would heal fast.

So I slept the best I could, and Biscuit and I headed to the shops on time on Tuesday morning.

As soon as I arrived, Dinah called. She told me she was on her way in. It was one of her days off, but she said she just wanted some company, and working was always a good way to keep her mind off other things. This was fine with me, since having extra help at the shops never hurt.

As always, I started baking, first for Icing this time, and when I had started preparing my dog treats for the Barkery, the back door of the kitchen opened and in walked Dinah. She looked like herself, wearing an *Icing on the Cake* T-shirt and jeans.

"Hi, Dinah," I said immediately. I would have rushed over to hug her but my hands were full of carob dough. "How are you doing?"

Her gaze seemed ironic as she looked at me with somewhat sad blue eyes. "I'm fine. I hope you're not surprised I decided to come in today."

"Of course not," I said. "I'm concerned. You know that. Having you here makes me feel better, though."

"Me too," she said. "Okay, tell me where to start."

I let her do a quick cleaning job in the shops, then return to take the Icing goodies out of the oven to cool.

We chatted a little about how she'd spent her day yesterday, which turned out to be mostly on the computer. Researching. But she said it had to do with another idea she had for a story, one that wouldn't involve anything like what had happened to Henry.

With her mood as light as it was, I had to believe her.

We opened the shops on time. I asked her to hang out in Icing until Frida arrived. I remained in the Barkery, talking to Biscuit now and then as I made sure the treats I'd baked were displayed well in our glass-front cabinet.

About half an hour after I'd opened, I was shocked to see who walked in. No, not one of the detectives this time. It was attorney Ted Culbert.

As far as I knew, he didn't have a dog, so I wasn't sure why he was here—although I suspected the reason.

"Hi, Ted," I said. "Did you come to see Dinah?"

"Yes. Is she here?" He was wearing a suit, as usual. His light brown hair appeared a little longer than I'd seen it before, which added to his good looks. His gaze was intense, as always, and I noted again how blue his eyes were.

"In Icing on the Cake next door," I told him. "Are you representing her now?"

"Yes," he said. "She came to my office yesterday and we spoke. She asked me to come here today so hopefully all three of us can talk, although I'm sure you know I can mostly just listen and not say anything. I won't violate attorney-client privilege."

So I wouldn't learn what Dinah had already told him. That was fine—I hoped. It was interesting that Dinah had already decided, yesterday, to come in today.

"Sure," I said cheerfully. "The only thing is, it's just her and me here right now, so we can't go off to talk. But fortunately my other assistants should be here soon."

"That's what she said. I'm a little early, I know. She wanted us all to go out for coffee to talk."

"Fine with me," I said, although I wished Dinah had told me. I hoped Frida and Janelle arrived on time. I'd hate for Dinah to have to pay for unused legal time.

"Since Dinah hasn't joined us yet," Ted said, "how about if you tell me your take on what's been going on? You told me before about Dinah's birthday party. Anything more to share with me about it and her interaction with Henry Schulzer, or things that have happened since then?"

"Can we leave that for later?" I asked as a customer walked through the Barkery door.

"Okay." But Ted didn't look thrilled. He wanted me to talk outside Dinah's presence, but since he apparently was now her lawyer, I didn't think that was a great idea. Besides, I was in fact busy.

But I'd do as Ted asked eventually, when we went out for coffee with Dinah. The information he wanted sounded easy and innocent enough. I would only report what I saw—and nothing about what I thought.

For now, though, I left him alone while I continued working.

About ten minutes later, Frida arrived, and Janelle shortly after that. Both Dinah and I had been busy waiting on customers, and Ted had sat at one of the small tables in Icing with a scone and a cup of coffee from the pot we kept brewed for when customers wanted a drink to go with their pastries. I'd given him both, no charge. I hoped he wouldn't charge Dinah for this down time, especially since he'd admitted that he came in earlier than she'd told him to. He spent the time on his cell phone, and I wondered if he was conducting any legal research, the way Dinah sometimes conducted writing research on her phone.

Once both my other assistants were there and had begun working, I let them know that Dinah and I would be going out for a while. No issues there, fortunately, so I grabbed Dinah from the Barkery and we told Ted we were ready to go.

Where? To Cuppa's, of course. I knew we'd be able to find a table that was at least somewhat secluded, whether outside on the patio or in the main coffee house. Either way, I leashed up Biscuit so she could join us.

We walked there fairly quickly and decided to sit at a table in the corner of the patio. Our server was Kit, as it often was. I was interested to see that Ted ordered a muffin with his coffee. The scone I'd given him apparently hadn't been enough. I couldn't tell, due to his suit, but he didn't appear overweight to me despite his apparent affinity for sweets.

Irma was the one to serve our drinks and Ted's muffin rather than Kit. She looked good, as always. Today she wore a frilly blouse and pink slacks over tennis shoes. I hoped I would appear as attractive as she did as I got older.

"Joe's with some other customers," Irma told us as she bent over to pat Biscuit and place a bowl of water in front of her. "But he'll come say hi later. Good to see all of you." She did aim a curious glance in Ted's direction. I figured she knew who—and what—he was.

Only when we began to sip our coffees—Dinah's was a latte—did our conversation begin. At least, it was somewhat of a conversation. I was the only one doing the talking after Ted got us started.

"As mentioned, I want to know your take so far on what happened with Henry Schulzer," Ted said, looking solemnly across the table at me. "I'd like to hear what you recall of Schulzer's behavior at Dinah's birthday party, as well as any opinions you have about who might have killed him, and why."

"Sure," I said, and gave him a detailed rundown of who'd been at the party, how Henry had been invited to join us but wound up giving Dinah a hard time, the arrival of Mike Holpurn and his brothers, and how the rest of the party had gone after those men had left.

"And all of you at the party had words with Mr. Schulzer?" Ted asked.

"None of us were happy with him, at least not as far as I could tell. We all argued with him a bit. But the only people angry enough with him to consider doing him harm were the Holpurns—and I really don't know all of that story, other than that Mike Holpurn apparently believes that the crime he went to prison for, killing Flora Schulzer long ago, was committed by Henry himself. A motive for murder? Certainly that's more likely than Dinah's surprise about Schulzer's empty threats that he could hurt her career."

"Right," Ted said. He asked me a few more questions about that night—including what I knew of Dinah's second conversation with Henry and what I'd done afterwards—as well as where I believed the others who were at Dinah's party had ended up that night.

He also asked outright who I thought was guilty of this murder.

"Still checking into it," I said.

"Do you think it could be Dinah?"

I aimed a glance at her. She appeared tense as she waited for my answer. This was her lawyer, who would be defending her, asking the question.

I responded with a chuckle. "You know my reputation, Ted. I've taken on cases when friends, or myself, were potentially the main suspect. You're aware that Dinah's my friend as well as my employee, and that's the reason I've gotten involved with this one, too—although I have to admit that the police have questioned everyone who was at Dinah's party, so many people I know could be considered suspects, I suppose."

"I'm aware of that, yes," Ted said, aiming a puzzled gaze toward me.

"Well, the point is that I've cleared everyone who I've tried to, so far. And I fully intend to do the same for Dinah."

But I was sure it didn't escape Ted's notice, or Dinah's either, that I didn't come out with a resounding note of confidence that yes, I absolutely believed Dinah was innocent.

TWENTY-ONE

But Ted was her lawyer. And I was her friend. So, even though Dinah was sitting there with us, looking from one to the other, I asked Ted, "How are you going to make sure she's not arrested? Do you have a plan? Will you be speaking with the detectives to find out who they really suspect, or to try to point them on the right pathway if they're mostly focusing on Dinah? Or—"

"Interesting questions," Ted interrupted. "And I'll keep them in mind. But as I said already, I can't talk about my intended course of action or anything else. Attorney-client privilege is involved, for one thing."

I didn't think attorney-client privilege would prevent him from answering much of what I asked, though I wasn't familiar with its parameters. In any event, I wasn't surprised that he used it to basically tell me to get lost, even though I'd answered his questions.

"I understand," I said. And I did. Ted was in charge, or at least he wanted to be. And since it was for Dinah's benefit, I wasn't about to argue with him.

"But you can be sure," he added, "everything I'll do will be in my client's best interests. I hope you'll continue to cooperate and let us know if you see or hear anything, or something comes to mind, that could help exonerate her."

"Absolutely," I said, meaning it. Only… "But does this mean that if you come up with some idea that would clear Dinah but pin the murder on me, you'll run with it?"

Ted smiled. "Could be. You're not my client now, after all."

I wanted to kick him under the table, but that wouldn't resolve anything. "Well," I said, "my understanding is that you're an officer of the court, so attempting to frame someone else to help your client isn't a good idea either."

He laughed. "No, but I'd suggest, Carrie, that you do what you did with the other cases you were involved with and just find the real killer. That way, I'll still have done my lawyerly duty, and you won't be charged with the crime, right?"

"Right," I said, also smiling. When I looked at Dinah, she was the only solemn one at the table.

"I just want this to be over," she said. "And with me remaining free and absolved from any liability." She looked me straight in the eye. "No matter what you might think, Carrie, I didn't do it."

"Have I accused you?" I asked.

"No, and you've been great about trying to help me. But you haven't come right out and said that you're sure I'm innocent."

"I'm sure you're innocent." I looked her straight in her glum blue eyes while saying it. Did I mean it?

Well, it was what I was trying to convince myself of. And since it didn't make sense for her to have committed the murder, my statement was true.

I hoped.

"You look serious," she said, and her expression changed. Her glum eyes teared up and she smiled. "I think you mean it."

"Of course. Now, what's next?" I asked Ted, not wanting to get into any details about my statement, like why I felt so certain. Not now, at least.

At Ted's instigation, we talked for a while in generalities about Henry—who he'd been, what he'd done. The possibility of his guilt in his wife's murder. Where he'd lived since then, the members of his family who had come to Knobcone Heights for his memorial—all in the interest of bringing Ted up to date and sharing with him all I knew and thought. Including the upcoming adoption event involving Prince and Duke, Henry's dogs.

After a while, our coffee togetherness was over. Was I convinced Ted would ensure that Dinah was cleared?

He was a good lawyer, as far as I knew, so I hoped so.

Still assuming, of course, that Dinah was innocent. And she had to be. I'd already told her I believed in her innocence, after all.

Before we got up to leave, Joe and Irma came over to see us, with Irma holding Sweetie's leash. Their dog traded nose sniffs with Biscuit, and they both lay down near each other under the table.

Joe looked tired, but he grinned at all of us in greeting as he took a seat. Irma sat down, too. "Good to have you all here," Joe said. "So who's your client here, Ted? Is Carrie in trouble again?"

I felt sure Joe was aware of the suspicions about Dinah so I knew he was kidding. I said, "Absolutely. Don't you know that the police have come to suspect me for all the murders committed around here? It's almost like a game—a very nasty one—to be able to point them in other directions."

"Well, she's darned good at that, isn't she?" Joe said to Ted. "That means you don't have to take her on as a client. Now, our buddy Dinah, here—she'd make a better client, don't you think?" He winked one of his wrinkle-surrounded eyes at her, and everyone at the table laughed, even Dinah.

"Good idea," Ted said. "I think I will take Dinah on as a client."

We all talked for a little longer, and then the Joes excused themselves again, taking Sweetie with them. That was the cue for the rest of us to leave, too, since Kit had come over and I'd paid our tab. I figured that Dinah couldn't afford it since she had her lawyer to pay, and if Ted paid he would just add it onto Dinah's bill, plus a percentage or two.

Besides, on the salary I paid Dinah, I wasn't sure how she would keep up with her attorney bills. I'd already decided to give her a raise, as well as a loan that I'd never accept any repayment on.

Not that I was wealthy, but with my businesses and my part-time job, I was doing a lot better than she was.

We all walked back to my shops, since Ted had parked behind them. He said goodbye and headed toward his car.

Dinah and I went to the front doors so I could put Biscuit into her enclosure in the Barkery. "Thanks so much for everything, Carrie," Dinah said. "And I don't just mean the coffee."

I shrugged one shoulder—the one on the arm that held Biscuit's leash, and Biscuit looked up at me as if awaiting a doggy command. I just smiled at her and continued forward. "You're welcome, but thanks aren't necessary."

"But you at least said you believe in my innocence."

Then she'd seen through me. Not surprising. Dinah was an intuitive and smart person.

"I do," I said firmly, and realized I was meaning it more and more.

"And I know you'll continue helping me anyway," she said. "I have a team now, with you and Ted. Surely the truth will somehow come out and I'll be fully vindicated."

"That's definitely what I'm hoping for," I said, and meant it. And realized I had to do more to help, now that I really had started to accept my wonderful employee's innocence.

Which was a really good thing, I thought many times during the rest of the day. I didn't have a shift at the vet clinic that afternoon, so I stayed at my stores, alternating between them. Dinah primarily worked in the Barkery, and I stayed in her presence as much as made sense. I watched her work, interacting with customers and the dogs they brought with them. She even spent some time teasing Biscuit with treats—rewarding her often, so I think my sweet pup enjoyed it.

Dinah didn't act at all like a murderer.

Neither did she moan or cringe or act like the murder suspect she was.

There wasn't any time for her to engage in any research that day, either. Even so, I did manage to ask her, just before closing time, if she was going to do any research that night—and if so, what kind of story was she working on.

Frida and Janelle had joined us near the counter in the Barkery since the doors to both shops were now locked. They both looked at Dinah with apparent interest.

My dedicated full-time employee regarded all of us. "Hey, guys. You know what I'm working on when I'm not here. I hope to turn all of this into one great bestselling novel someday, and I'll probably write it in the first person, as if I'm a genuine murder suspect." She shot each of us a big smile, although the look in her large blue eyes wasn't entirely amused. "But for now, I'm continuing with my research about what happened to Mayor Schulzer ten years ago, why they were certain that Mike Holpurn did it, and any suspicions that Henry was, in fact, the killer . . . I can check a lot of that history online. Plus, I'm researching all current-day news articles to see how

Henry's murder has been reported and who the focus seems to be on as far as suspects, cop interviews, whatever."

I opened my mouth. "Does that include—"

Dinah raised her hand, to stop me from speaking, I supposed. "And before you say anything else, I mean suspects besides myself. Next time I have a day off, if I've got any better ideas, I may even go talk to some of those other suspects, show that I'm upset that anyone thinks I could have done it—and, oh, by the way, how do they feel about being in this position? Maybe someone will let something drop."

"Something like your head," Janelle said. She was shaking her own head and I could tell she felt concerned, as I did. "If you happen to talk to the real killer that way, what makes you think he or she will be nicer to you than to Henry?"

"I'll just try to make sure I'm not all alone in the dark or in my house when I prod them." Dinah's grin seemed genuine this time.

"Well, please be careful." This time Frida was the one to show concern. "It's one thing to write a story, true or not. But this situation involves two murders, maybe committed by the same person and maybe not. Like Janelle suggested, whoever is responsible may not be concerned at all about adding a third corpse to the list."

On that unhappy note, we closed both shops and headed home. At least I did. Janelle had indicated she was coming to my place, too, to spend the evening with Neal. Which was fine—Reed had some clinic matters to attend to, so we weren't getting together that night either.

I did see Neal and Janelle when they returned from dinner, but only long enough for me to take Biscuit and head to our bedroom. I figured I'd let them enjoy their time together without worrying about my presence.

I saw Reed the next day, at my afternoon shift at the clinic. In fact, I wound up assisting him most of the time, from matters ranging from preparing a Manx cat for her regular exam to bathing a small dog who'd injured his butt while playing in mud. A normal day of sorts at the clinic.

And now and then, when the patients left the room, I got in a few words with Reed, letting him know about my recent conversation with Dinah and my other assistants. Then I briefly wondered if I should have kept the plans I was developing to myself.

"So you're really thinking of doing some actual interrogations on your own?" he asked after a Dobie and her owner exited into the hallway and I began using a sterilizer on the exam table.

"I just don't get a sense that the police are doing much to find out who actually killed Henry," I said with a shake of my head. "And that could mean they're just trying to pile together whatever evidence they can find against their favorite suspect this time, Dinah."

Reed came over to me and grasped my upper arms gently so I had to stop scrubbing and look at him. His great-looking face reflected his concern—and he bent to give me a quick kiss, then glanced toward the partly open door. "I understand, and I know better now than to tell you to back off, especially when you care about the prime suspect." His grin was wry. "And sometimes those prime suspects really appreciate what you do."

"Thank you," I said, and smiled back. "And you know I've learned to be careful."

"Depending on how you define 'careful,'" he responded. Then, hearing Kayle in the hall outside talking to someone, we both stepped back, a good thing since the vet tech was carrying a small cage with a rabbit in it as he led a woman into the room.

"Great, you're both here," Kayle said. "Poor Homer here has been throwing up and we need to check him out."

Kayle clearly adored little Homer, so I was the tech to leave the room at that time. That was fine, since my shift was nearly over and I had to head back to my shops.

But I did catch Reed's eye before turning to walk out. He made a gesture of holding a phone to his ear, and I nodded.

We'd talk—and possibly get together—later.

The room was too crowded for me to hint at throwing him a goodbye kiss, so I just left. I saw Arvie in the hallway. My boss, in his usual white jacket, greeted me warmly, which I returned. I felt his inspection, as if he was trying to figure out what I was up to in addition to working in his clinic and running my own businesses. Arvie knew I was involved with this current murder.

"You okay?" my senior mentor and friend said.

"Of course." True? Kind of, but I wasn't about to add any limitations to what I'd said. "Thanks, Arvie." I gave him a quick hug and headed to the day care area to retrieve Biscuit from Faye and her helpers. Then we walked back toward the stores.

When Biscuit and I entered the front door of the Barkery, I stopped in my tracks. Detective Bridget Morana stood in front of the glass display case, her cat Butterball in her arms.

And Dinah was behind the counter, glaring at the cop, whose expression appeared vaguely amused.

What was going on here? Of course I had to find out.

I loosened my grip on Biscuit's leash a little since my pup was pulling in Butterball's direction—which was a good excuse for me to join the discussion, if Bridget needed an excuse.

"Hi, Detective." I interrupted whatever Dinah and Bridget were talking about. "Welcome. I assume Butterball doesn't want a dog treat, does she?"

"Of course not," the middle-aged detective said. "I'm here to pick up treats for some of my colleagues' dogs, like Chief Jonas's Jellybean."

I shot a glance at Dinah, whose face was pale, but she didn't contradict the detective.

"So what would you like to buy today for sweet Jellybean and the rest?" I asked, putting a cool but friendly expression on my face and in my tone.

Before Bridget could answer, the door to Icing burst open and both Janelle and Vicky stormed in. And stopped when they saw me.

"Oh, you're back, Carrie," Janelle said. "That's good."

"I'll go back into Icing," Vicky immediately added and left the room.

"What's going on?" I asked, not bothering to move my curious scowl away from Detective Bridget.

"Butterball and I have been here for a little while deciding what I should buy. And since we encountered Ms. Greeley, I used the opportunity to ask her a few questions."

"You know she's represented by an attorney," I said.

"Oh, I wasn't attempting to get her to confess anything." Bridget's somewhat bushy eyebrows lifted as if she was attempting to convey absolute innocence.

I nodded. "Of course not. But until you police have enough evidence to arrest Henry Schulzer's killer—which isn't Dinah—I'm going to remind her not to talk to you at all except when her lawyer is present." I turned slightly to aim a look at Dinah, who, lips puckered in a frown, nodded back at me.

"Okay." Bridget's tone was curt. She started pointing out a few biscuits and other dog treats here and there within the glass-fronted display case, and Dinah interacted with her again—putting her chosen items in a white paper bag.

I was the one to deal with the detective's credit card when it was time for her to pay. "Thanks for your purchase," I told her. I wasn't about to thank her for coming in, especially since the purchase was undoubtedly secondary in her mind to her inquisition of Dinah.

"You're welcome," she said. Holding the bag under one arm and Butterball under the other, she turned to stalk out, weaving between other waiting customers. But at the door she spun back around, and though her glare was aimed at Dinah, she said, "Oh, Carrie, by the way. We're all waiting on tenterhooks for you to solve this latest murder."

Then she and her kitty were gone.

I looked at Dinah, then, who remained behind the counter. "Are you all right?"

"I've been better." Her voice choked a little. "Looks like I'd better put my research into overdrive."

"I was thinking the same thing," I replied.

TWENTY-TWO

BETWEEN CUSTOMERS AND ENSURING we had enough baked goods in each store, I warned Dinah once again not to do any new investigation or interviews of suspects in Henry Schulzer's murder, since anything she did might appear suspicious.

"But you got very involved when you were a murder suspect," she reminded me as we were about to close the shops for the day. As if she had to remind me.

"Yes, but I didn't have others around who were really trying to figure out the truth," I said. "Except maybe for the cops. But like I've said, you can be sure I'm going to help you."

"Thanks, Carrie." She gave me a hug and a sad smile as she left through the kitchen door.

Janelle was still there, standing behind me. "She can be sure you'll try to help her," she said as I turned around to face her, "but you can't be certain you'll figure it out this time."

"True, and I wish these murders would stop happening, for many reasons." I took the drawer out of the cash register so I could lock it up in my office. "But since this latest murder affects Dinah, I'll stay involved till it's solved. And hope it's the absolute last one."

Because if it wasn't … well, I wasn't going to reassure anyone, let alone myself, that I'd stay out of future investigations.

But fortunately, the murders I'd solved had happened one at a time. And I had a case now that I needed to figure out quickly.

I ducked into the kitchen and put the financial stuff away in my office. When I returned to the Barkery, Janelle wasn't there, but I heard voices in Icing and went through that door.

Vicky and Janelle sat at one of the tables talking, and both grew quiet as I joined them.

"I've been looking at this week's schedule, and we have everyone but Janelle signed up to work on Friday," Vicky, my chief scheduler, said. "Isn't that the day when the adoption event will be held?"

"Yes," I acknowledged, "and we'll be really busy. Janelle, I'd love for you to take a shift, too, if you can work it out."

"Count on me," she said.

"I always do. And on you, too," I said to the reliable Vicky. "Now both of you go home and have a great evening."

I certainly did, since Reed and Hugo joined me—and Neal and Janelle stayed the night at her place with Go.

Early on Thursday morning, after we'd walked Biscuit and Hugo and eaten a light breakfast, Reed and I headed for our respective cars with our dogs.

"So," he said, stopping beside my driver's door. "I assume I'll see you this afternoon at your shift at the clinic. Anything else on your agenda besides your shops?"

"A visit to Mountaintop Rescue to check out the residents there who might come to the adoption event tomorrow along with Prince and Duke."

"I'm not surprised to hear that." He leaned over to give me a final kiss of the morning. It was a nice, memorable one even after our togetherness the night before, and it made me feel even better that I'd see him again that afternoon.

We both drove off. I hadn't been totally honest with Reed, though, since I also intended to do something else, too, if I could fit it in that morning: visit some of the people I wanted to talk to about Henry's murder and invite them to the adoption event. Would I learn anything more from any of them at the event, like an admission by the killer? It was highly unlikely, but it still might be very interesting to see them interacting with others now, given that it had been a while since Henry Schulzer's memorial service and no one had been arrested yet.

I followed our usual routine, parking behind the shops and walking around to the front to bring Biscuit into the Barkery. I let her run loose since the shops weren't open yet. I smiled as I glanced toward the signs I'd printed up and placed on small easels here and there in the shop, advertising the adoption event tomorrow. I'd let our usual outspoken customers know about it too, plus the media, and would be sure to remind people by emails later. I went into the kitchen to bake.

Dinah was the first assistant scheduled to join me, and she came in around six forty-five—a bit on the late side, since we opened at seven.

"Sorry," she said as she entered through the back door, placed her purse on the appropriate shelf, and washed her hands.

"Everything okay?" I asked, wondering if she'd spent her evening in her house, doing research.

"As okay as it can be." She headed for the Icing side of the kitchen and looked it over. I'd already started baking the usual red velvet cupcakes and designer cookies, so there wasn't a lot for her to do but check the timer to know when to remove them from the oven. "But I don't like that I'm losing sleep over this horrible situation."

Of course she was still worried, and stewing, as I was. Although that wasn't why I hadn't gotten enough sleep last night. Reed was, but I chose not to mention that.

We made sure that both shops' cases contained the appropriate treats by seven, and I went in to open the Barkery.

Only to find that the first person to walk in was Detective Wayne Crunoll, with his dachshunds Blade and Magnum. "Good morning, Carrie," Wayne said with a nice, innocent-looking smile that I didn't trust at all.

"Welcome, Detective and dogs." I waved them in and immediately went behind the counter to get some sample treats.

"Is Dinah here yet?" Wayne asked, as his best friends chewed their biscuits and began to nose my Biscuit in her enclosure.

I wanted to say no, to tell him she wasn't expected today, but all he'd have to do to prove me wrong was open the door to Icing and look in. "She's next door, but—"

"Great." Wayne had the nerve to hand me his dogs' leashes as he opened the door between shops. He didn't go in, but he must have caught Dinah's attention because he waved—then turned back to me.

"I assume you're not here to arrest her," I said, still holding the leashes and having a very quick passing thought of choking him with them. I wouldn't want to hurt Wayne's dogs. Him? Well, I knew it wasn't a good idea.

"No, just wanted to say hi." And undoubtedly remind Dinah that he was keeping his eyes on her as his favorite suspect. Of course, he could be acting similarly toward other suspects, too, but I knew he wouldn't admit to it if I asked.

"Well, I assume she said hi back, but I'm guessing she's busy. And in any case, she knows better than to talk to cops without her attorney present." I hoped.

"I'll go check." He walked once more to the door, and this time I looped his dogs' leashes around the fencing of Biscuit's enclosure and followed as quickly as I could.

When I stepped into Icing, Wayne was standing near the counter staring at Dinah. She appeared flustered as she waited on some customers who were interested in breakfast scones. But as soon as they'd paid and left, she said quietly to Wayne, "Nice to see you, Detective. Have you solved the murder case yet? Is that what you came to tell me? I didn't do it, so if you came for a confession, bye."

"Guess I'm out of here for now," Wayne said. "But I'll see you again soon."

He left via the Barkery, retrieving his dogs. I stood in the Icing doorway watching him, then turned back to Dinah. "You okay?" I asked, just as more customers walked in.

"Sure," she said courageously and got back to work.

And I knew I had to do more to figure this out faster, starting with what I'd been thinking about for the past few days.

I had to wait for a short while till my other assistants arrived for the day—Vicky and Frida. Only then did I feel comfortable excusing myself and heading to my office.

There, I called Neal. It was mid-morning now, and he was at work staffing the reception desk at the Knobcone Heights Resort. He wouldn't have all the information I needed, but it was a start.

Sure enough, he told me that Henry Schulzer's children and sister were still staying there and weren't due to check out for a few days. He hadn't seen Mike Holpurn and his brothers recently, though. And yes, he'd just seen Mysha take a few guests' dogs out for a walk, maybe twenty minutes ago.

217

I quickly visited Dinah in Icing. "Yes," she told me, "I know where the Holpurns are staying." She'd memorized the location of their Airbnb home, which was just outside of downtown.

Armed with this information, I told my assistants I was heading out for part of the morning for coffee. I didn't tell them my destination wasn't my usual, Cuppa-Joe's, though.

I headed to the resort. There, I gulped as I took the ticket to enter the parking lot, doubting Neal would be able to comp me that day. But I wouldn't be long, and the expense was worth it.

After heading into the lobby, I turned right and had to wait a minute while Neal assisted some arriving guests, a middle-aged couple dressed appropriately for this elite place, as my brother was, unlike me in my slacks with a Barkery T-shirt on top. I was able to speak with Neal soon, and he directed me to join him behind his desk. There, he handed me a phone receiver and connected me with the room apparently containing the Schulzers. This way, he wouldn't get chastised for giving out private information like that room number—but I still got what I wanted, the connection.

Yes, we could have done this without going to the resort, but this way maybe I'd get to see the Schulzer family again. Plus run into Mysha.

"Hi," I said brightly to Mabel, who answered the phone. "I'm down in the lobby, if you'd like to say hi. I've got some news about Duke and Prince."

"Good news, I hope. Well, just tell me over the phone. I'm too busy to come down and see you."

If she was that busy, what was she doing in her room? On the other hand, maybe whatever she did for a living could be partly accomplished on a computer, so she might be telling the truth.

"I understand," I said. Kind of. "I mostly wanted to invite you to my shop, Barkery and Biscuits, tomorrow. Mountaintop Rescue is holding an adoption event there, and your dad's two dogs will be among those who'll be available. I understand that your family signed their release papers. I hope you'd like to come say goodbye and see how things go with them."

A pause. Was Mabel going to hang up on me? Tell me where to go—besides an adoption event at my shops?

"Thanks," she said. "I'll be there, and I'll try to bring my brother and aunt, too." I told her the event would start at eleven a.m., then said goodbye. After hanging up, I gave a happy pump of my fist, and Neal laughed.

"They're coming," I told him unnecessarily. "Now, where can I see Mysha?"

"Hang out here for a while. I'm not sure how long her walk will be, but I saw her and her current dog about forty-five minutes ago."

As it turned out, hanging out in that attractive lobby was enjoyable—especially sitting behind the desk with my brother, who fortunately wasn't very busy. And within about five minutes, Mysha Jorgens appeared with an Irish setter on a leash.

"Excuse me," I said to Neal, and I hurried out to say hi.

Mysha was dressed nattily for walking dogs, in a knee-length skirt and lacy top, but she looked appropriate for the resort. "Hi, Carrie," she said. "What are you doing here?"

"Waiting for you," I said truthfully, then told her that the Mountaintop Rescue adoption event would be happening at our shops tomorrow. "Can you come?"

"Absolutely. I want to see Prince and Duke again, just for the last time."

Good. I was doing well getting people to at least agree to come.

But what about my real suspects, Mike Holpurn and his brothers? I decided to call the Holpurns, so I found a spot in the lobby and called Dinah.

"Sure, I've got Mike's phone number," Dinah said right away. I didn't ask her how she got it. Once she gave it to me, I called Mike, expecting to get chewed out over the phone.

But the guy sounded surprisingly nice when I told him about the adoption event, saying he'd come and bring his brothers, too.

Why? I wondered as I hung up. I hadn't told Mike Holpurn that he wouldn't be the only murder suspect there.

But he knew that Dinah worked for me, so he would know of at least one other suspect in Henry's death who was likely to be present. Was that his reason for agreeing to come?

Or did Holpurn actually like dogs? Maybe now that he was out of prison, he wanted one himself.

And wouldn't it be an odd thing if he happened to adopt one or both of Henry's dogs?

I hoped Billi wouldn't allow it, if that was Holpurn's goal. If he or his brothers showed any interest, I'd talk to her about it.

Okay, I was ready for the adoption event tomorrow. I hurried back to my shops, but before I got to work, I had a couple more calls to make from my office. One was to Silas Perring, and the other was to Francine Metz of the *Knobcone News*.

I wanted media attention for this adoption event, for the dogs' sake … and for mine, in case anything interesting might come out with all those suspects hanging out in one spot.

TWENTY-THREE

I SPENT THAT NIGHT again with Reed. We talked about the adoption event, and he said he'd try to drop by. I enjoyed our time together, along with our dogs, but I also kept thinking, maybe too much, about what to expect the next day.

No resolution of Henry's murder was likely to occur. I knew that. But... well, maybe the adoption event would cause the killer to do something that would tweak my suspicions enough to check into him or her more.

Or not. There were no guarantees that the killer would show up at the event, or even know about it. Maybe the murderer was someone neither I nor the police had thought about. Someone who'd already fled town.

Still, if the killer was someone local, or someone I'd already been considering, there was at least a chance of something happening at the event that would provide a few clues. I hoped so—but still tried to tell myself not to count on it.

Well, if nothing else, hopefully Duke, Prince, and other wonderful pets from Mountaintop Rescue would find their forever homes.

I arrived with Biscuit at the shops at the usual time. The first assistant to join me that day was Vicky, by design. I wanted Dinah there later, of course, but my mind was already too focused on hoping for a break that would lead to Henry's killer. I didn't need her there early, distracting me even more with hopes for that day's event.

As always on days with special events, the early morning was busy and stressful, and not only with our usual activities of baking, running both shops, and selling goods. Janelle and Frida arrived a little before seven and helped to keep things moving.

Since the adoption event was scheduled for eleven, Billi and Mimi arrived with some of the shelter's volunteers around ten thirty, bringing the pets who would hopefully find homes that day. Unsurprisingly, the first ones they brought into the shops were Duke and Prince. Both adorable golden cockers were leashed and walked with their noses in the air—fascinated by the smells of the treats in the Barkery. I leashed Biscuit, too, so she could come out of her enclosure for now and join the fun, but I planned to put her back later when we actually began the event. That way, no one should confuse her with a rescue dog available to be adopted.

"So who's staffing Icing this morning?" Billi asked. She was dressed in nice but casual clothes, even though there was always a possibility her City Council colleagues would drop in to see our adoptables that day. But she wasn't on government duty. And she definitely was in charge of making sure all adoptions went well.

"Janelle and Frida," I said. Vicky was helping out in the Barkery. I wanted Dinah to be with me in the Barkery, too, and not just for her wonderful assistance in my shops—or her research. If anything triggered some kind of reaction that could assist in solving Henry's murder, it might involve her. She remained, after all, a major suspect, and visitors that day who were introduced to Henry's dogs might talk about the case—and cause others to discuss Henry and what had happened to him ... and *who* had happened to him.

A stretch? Maybe. But I remained hopeful.

A few shelter volunteers came in carrying small crates from which loud meows issued. "Good, we'll have cats for interested adopters, too," I said.

Mimi came back in with a basset hound mix and a dachshund, both on leashes. I helped her secure their leashes to the outer portion of Biscuit's enclosure.

"How many animals have you brought?" I asked Billi.

"Not a whole lot this time," she said. Her smile at me was knowing. "I knew you wanted to concentrate on Prince and Duke."

"You're right," I acknowledged.

I'd seen that Billi had purchased a small ad in the *Knobcone News* about our event, so word was out, and not just among my customers who'd seen my signs or people who visited Mountaintop Rescue ... or those I'd told about the event, like the media folks. And, of course, those whom I considered somehow involved with Henry Schulzer and potentially with his murder.

My nerves began feeling frayed around 10:45. Maybe this was exacerbated by the number of people I saw through the shops' front windows walking around on the sidewalk, glancing toward us. Were all of them going to stop in to see the rescues? They could just be regular people wanting Icing or Barkery treats, or even simply pedestrians passing by along Summit Avenue.

I did another check of Icing and confirmed that it was busy, but Janelle and Frida could handle it. When I returned to the Barkery, I watched as Silas Perring and his cameraman Wilbur the Wise entered through the front door, ignoring Vicky, who was standing outside requesting that visitors wait until things were less crowded. Two of their colleagues were with them—Honey Raykoff and Bobbi

Hanger, but only Honey came in. She walked around the Barkery and then headed into Icing, clearly not intending to do a story on the adoption event.

Silas was another matter.

Oh well. I'd have preferred for the event to have publicity ahead of time, and I didn't necessarily want a huge crowd—just one consisting of people who had an interest in Duke and Prince ... and possibly Henry. But having a news segment about the event and my shops could help business later—and hopefully lead to more participation in future adoption events.

As usual when he was on camera, Silas was dressed in a suit, with wide, attentive eyes and an expression that encouraged people to talk to him. Behind-the-scenes Wilbur was clad much more casually, in a short-sleeved blue T-shirt and jeans.

"Good morning, Carrie," Silas said in a jovial tone. This close to him, I couldn't help noticing that he smelled a bit sweet—as if he had donned some pretty fancy men's cologne. "And hi to all your animals here. Which ones belonged to Henry Schulzer? That's why you're doing this adoption, right? You want to find them a new home."

"That's right." At least, it was a major part of the reason. "Those two golden cocker spaniels over there were his." I pointed to where Prince and Duke were tethered to Biscuit's enclosure, as were the other dogs Billi had brought.

"Very nice. Well, I'm not much of a dog person myself so I don't think I'll adopt them, but I hope things work out well for them."

"Me too." Billi had joined us from where she had been talking to Mimi near the cat crates. "Do you like cats?"

The crates had been put on the floor beside a couple of tables near the large dog biscuit icon. The kitties inside them apparently wanted to be out of their cages, like the dogs were, since they kept meowing loudly. But they wouldn't do well on leashes, and it certainly wouldn't work to leave them loose.

"No, thanks. I'm more of a people person." Silas straightened his shoulders and held the microphone toward Billi. "So, tell our viewers about the animals you've brought here for adoption from Mountaintop Rescue, Councilwoman Matlock."

Wilbur stepped forward with the camera, but before Billi answered, she looked toward the door and raised her eyebrows.

I followed her gaze. Henry Schulzer's family members had just entered the Barkery. Tula was first, followed by HS and Mabe.

Tula, dressed as nicely as if she were attending another memorial service for Henry, glanced toward Billi and me but hurried over to where Prince and Duke lay on the floor. "There you are," she gushed in a tone that suggested she'd been hunting for them. "And you look just fine." She bent and patted them, then stood—with no problem despite her stiletto heels—and hurried toward Billi. "I'll take them back now." Her voice had grown hard, as if she expected an argument.

She wasn't wrong. "If you wanted them, why didn't you let your family know sooner? Your niece and nephew relinquished them to Mountaintop Rescue, and we're going to find them good homes."

Tula's middle-aged face reddened and she looked ready to explode.

HS stepped in front of her, possibly to defuse the situation. Clad in jeans and a hoodie, he looked even bulkier than he had at his dad's memorial. I wondered what he did for a living. Nothing that required workouts, I figured. "I guess there was a bit of confusion," he said, looking surprised. "All three of us discussed the dogs, but—"

"It doesn't matter what I said before," Tula all but shouted. "I want them."

"Because they're purebreds and our mother used to make some extra money breeding and selling their ancestors?" Mabe Schulzer appeared disgusted. She was dressed down for today's event, appearing nowhere near as formal as she did at her father's memorial.

"It's nothing like that," Tula screeched. "I like dogs."

"Then why haven't you ever owned any?" HS's round face was getting cross.

"You haven't ever owned dogs?" Billi took a step toward Tula. "That could make a difference. You see, since the dogs have been signed over to us by heirs of the person who owned them, Mountaintop Rescue has the legal right and obligation to check out the places where any pets adopted from us would live, and we need to feel assured that the adopter knows what it means to own this kind of pet and would take excellent care of them. And it doesn't seem like that's the situation here."

"They're my brother's dogs." Tula's voice was still raised but she looked a bit less sure of herself. She maneuvered away from Billi and the dogs. "They should be mine if his kids don't want them."

I'd wondered if she would want the dogs for that reason, but she'd waited too long to ask—and didn't sound like a good fit."

"That's not the way this is going to work, Tula." Mabe now faced her aunt. "Sorry, but—"

"Tell us about those poor dogs and how our former mayor, and maybe her husband, too, used to breed them." That was Silas. His microphone was thrust in front of Tula's mouth. "And tell us how Mr. Schulzer took care of them lately."

"None of your damned business!" Tula shoved the microphone away and stomped off.

The woman clearly had a temper. Could she have had something to do with her brother's murder? Might Henry's kids have been in on it, too?

Well, I hadn't ruled them out, but I also had no indication that they'd been in Knobcone Heights when Henry was still alive. His memorial service had even been delayed a week to accommodate their arrival.

That didn't absolutely mean they weren't involved, but it also didn't make me feel that I needed to follow up with them.

Apparently Wilbur was still filming. "That was Ms. Tula Schulzer," Silas said, facing the camera. "She was the first person we've spoken with here at the Mountaintop Rescue adoption event at Barkery and Biscuits. The event's primary purpose is to rehome the dogs previously owned by murder victim Henry Schulzer. We're here to watch—and to make sure those dogs get a good home."

Silas stopped talking, and Wilbur lowered the camera.

"Are you going to hang out here till Billi finds some promising adopters?" I had to ask. I liked the idea of publicizing that kind of good news—it would help Mountaintop Rescue and its residents ... and my shops.

"Probably, or at least for another hour or so, unless something else comes up." Silas lifted his dark eyebrows as if in amusement. I wasn't amused, but I figured that was true of all journalists. They'd always go off to another story if something better than what they were working on arose.

I noticed that all three of the Schulzers had gone into Icing and figured they were done with what was going on here. Fortunately, Tula didn't seem to be pressing the adoption issue any further. I had to agree with Billi's insinuation that the woman wouldn't be a good dog-mom, given that she had no prior experience nor apparent interest until it became too late to take the fur babies home with her.

"Very interesting," I whispered to Billi.

"Yeah, you could call it that." Her voice sounded full of irony. She walked over to the dogs who'd been the subject of all this. Quite a few other people had been permitted to come into the Barkery by Vicky. Most were down on the floor with Prince, Duke, and the other dogs, and I hurried to put Biscuit back into her enclosure.

Fortunately, Dinah had arrived at some point, and she was giving an ad-lib talk about the two cockers and the dachshund and the basset hound mix, describing their characters collectively as sweet and smart and loving, but also letting people know some standard differences in the breeds' backgrounds and personalities.

While she was doing that, Mysha slipped through the crowd near the door and into the Barkery. She was dressed as she'd been at Henry's memorial service, in a nice blouse, long skirt, and boots, and she didn't have any dogs with her.

Had she come to try to impress whoever adopted Prince and Duke, so she could become their dog walker again?

Mysha had seemed to mourn Henry more than anyone else I'd seen, so I didn't consider her the prime suspect in his killing either. Then again, mourning could have been part of her process to get over her emotions about murdering him.

She waved at me, but immediately moved through the crowd to where others were playing with the cockers and got down on the floor with them. I moved so that I could see her well. It was clear the dogs recognized her, considering how much they attempted to move around the other people and come over to her, tails wagging and tongues out.

Mysha seemed to settle down in that spot, engaging in a bit of doggy love. I didn't get the sense she wanted to adopt her buddies, just see them and play with them. I doubted I'd get any further indication of whether she was the murderer, at least not here.

And watching the lovefest she was having with those very sweet dogs, it was hard to think of her as a possible killer anyway.

More people came in and played with the dogs. Some of our visitors also spent time with the cats, removing them from the crates with Mimi's help, admiring them, hugging them, and laughing about them.

In fact, the first people to be directed toward Billi as possible adopters appeared to be a married couple who'd taken possession of a golden tabby, and then a twenty-something woman who kept laughing into the face of a black cat she'd been holding for quite a while.

I was glad there were some adoptions pending, although of course Billi and her people would be checking out living arrangements just as they would with those who wanted to add dogs to their households. And, sadly, so far the only person who'd expressed an interest in Prince and Duke, at least that I'd seen, was Tula Schulzer.

Dinah must have been aware of that, too, since she once again took a position near where Mysha was playing with the cute cockers and gave a talk about how wonderful they were, loud enough to be heard over the crowd.

That was when Mike Holpurn and brothers Bill and Johnny maneuvered their way into the Barkery. I wasn't surprised to see them. After all, Mike had actually said he would come when I'd spoken with him.

Good. Now I needed to get them close to the dogs to see everyone's reactions—both the Holpurns' and the pups'.

I wended my way through the crowd—and was glad to see that Dinah had now slipped behind the counter and was actually selling treats to some of the people who'd come in. I soon reached the spot where Mysha was on the floor with the cockers and bent down to pick one up.

"We're going to wander a bit," I told Mysha, "just in case some likely adopters haven't been able to get over here to meet these sweet guys."

Not that I imagined the Holpurns would want to actually adopt Prince and Duke, of course. But to my surprise, Mike seemed awed and adoring when I approached him with Prince in my arms.

"I don't need to tell you how long it's been since I owned a pet," he told me, sounding saner and nicer than any other time I'd talked to him. "Emotional support dogs are sometimes brought to prison to help settle inmates down, but—well, I got to play with some now and then, but not as much as I'd have liked."

Interesting, I thought. I handed Prince over to him, and the dog licked Mike's face as he began petting him. Holpurn's brothers gushed over the dog, too.

And this small episode made me doubt, at least for a moment, whether any of the Holpurns could have murdered a human.

But I shook off that thought quickly. Just because a person was a dog lover didn't mean he liked people enough not to kill them—especially when a particular person was giving him a hard time.

Still…

Mike soon gave Prince back to me and I hugged the dog close. "That one's great," he said. "And I do want to get a dog, but I need to get my life back together first."

"And how do you intend to do that?" Once more, Silas was near me, thrusting a microphone into the face of someone I wanted to know more about…but not necessarily through a news interview like this.

"It's nothing I want to talk about here," Mike muttered, going back to the stony, unfriendly personality I'd come to recognize since meeting him.

Okay, maybe I needed to keep him high on my suspect list.

Mike didn't move away, though, so neither did Silas. Prince was becoming restless in my arms and even making deep growling noises, and I wondered if he wanted to go outside.

Just in case, still carrying him, I headed over to where Mysha was still on the floor with Duke. "Care to help me take these two and my Biscuit for a short walk?" I asked.

"Absolutely," she said, smiling up at me.

TWENTY-FOUR

It wasn't a long walk, and when we got back to the Barkery I noticed that Silas was interviewing Dinah. Or at least trying to. She looked very unhappy and kept turning, trying to keep her face from being filmed by Wilbur.

What was Silas up to?

"I wonder if they're talking about Dinah's argument with Mr. Schulzer," Mysha said.

"At her birthday party? They've already talked about that." I know my tone was chilly, but I couldn't help recalling Silas's manipulative editing of that interview.

"But—okay." Mysha shot a strange glance at me, then got down on the floor to play with Duke and Prince again.

I noticed that Billi was with some people who had the dachshund on a leash and I believed that the pup had found a new home, assuming all went well in the vetting. But things looked potentially good, and I was always thrilled when pets from Mountaintop Rescue who'd been brought to our adoption events found new families.

I would have enjoyed going over to meet those folks, but I couldn't allow Silas to browbeat Dinah. I moved in that direction.

Dinah stood behind the glass-fronted display case, but there were openings on both sides and Silas had maneuvered his way behind the cash counter toward her. Despite how she kept moving her head away, he stuck his microphone toward her mouth.

"Why don't you leave her alone?" I demanded as I reached them. "You've already interviewed her—and from what I've been told, you did some editing that was harmful to her."

"What, made her look like she'd killed Henry Schulzer?" Now Silas stuck the microphone toward me, and I saw that Wilbur was filming me as well. I again noticed Silas's sweet smell.

"I invited you here to memorialize the adoption event," I told him through gritted teeth. "Not to annoy my assistant or make her look bad. Maybe it's time for you to leave."

"Maybe," Silas agreed. "But you wanted me to publicize how those dogs that belonged to Mr. Schulzer found a wonderful new home, and I gather that hasn't happened yet."

"No," I said, "as far as I know, it hasn't." Which saddened me. Maybe it wouldn't take place this day. "And just in case it doesn't," I went on, "it would be a great thing if you filmed them and showed the world what great little dogs they are, so the right people will come to Mountaintop Rescue to adopt them. Okay?"

Silas didn't look thrilled. I gathered he'd rather harass people than do a human interest story about cute dogs. But Wilbur was heading in their direction with his camera. I saw that Francine Metz was near the adorable cockers, too.

"If you don't do it," I said, "the *Knobcone News* will do it and get all the credit when the dogs get new human parents."

Silas scowled at me but began to follow Wilbur in that direction. Francine was now holding one of the dogs—Duke, I believed. Silas shook his head and didn't get up close and personal, but he did nod to Wilbur to film what was happening, even with a reporter from another news organization in the shot. Arm outstretched, Silas stuck his microphone nearly in the dog's mouth.

Duke looked startled, growled, then wriggled to get down, and Francine obeyed.

"They're both so cute," she said. "I wouldn't mind adopting one of them, but I know they need to be kept together. That wouldn't work in my apartment building. Oh well."

Oh well, indeed, I thought, but I said, "Mountaintop Rescue has lots of other dogs needing new homes who can be adopted individually." I grinned.

"I just might do that one of these days," Francine said.

"Great!" I responded. But would she? Who knew? If she did, she could always do an article about how it all worked out.

We'd said the event would go until one o'clock, and it was approaching that time already. Silas and Wilbur had walked off to interview others in the Barkery about why they were here and what dog treats they liked—nothing controversial, but it might please their audience.

I saw the Banners, Henry's former neighbors, walk through the door with their little Chihuahua, Marshmallow. Kris and Paul had seemed very nice, but I doubted they'd be up for adopting Henry's dogs any more than anyone else. Even so, they stood at the entry and looked around, taking in the view of all the people, the few animals available for adoption, and all the love and sweetness and good wishes going on.

Or so I assumed. I didn't really know what their thoughts were, but the pleasure in their gazes suggested I'd figured them out.

I headed in their direction. They'd known Henry a little bit, and Duke and Prince, too. I had no reason to think they had anything against Henry, but neither could I completely exonerate them, at least not yet. What if they'd had some kind of dispute that no one else knew about…?

"Hi, you three," I said. "Here to adopt a sister or brother for Marshmallow?"

Kris sent me a sad smile. "I wish we could. But our little girl is a handful—literally. And we'll only be in town for another week or so. We live in a rented condo in Portland that has limits on pets."

"Besides, if we were going to take in another dog, we'd most likely check out a local shelter near our home and adopt there," Paul said. "Be supportive of the local facilities and all."

"I understand," I said. And I did. I certainly wanted to ensure that Mountaintop Rescue remained successful in both taking in and rehoming needy animals, and that was at least partly because it was here in Knobcone Heights. Plus, it helped that Billi was a friend of mine. "So," I said, deciding to change the subject slightly, "do you think Marshmallow would like a sample treat?"

Kris stooped to pick up the tiny dog. "What do you think, girl?"

Marshmallow presumably didn't know what her mom was asking, but she licked the human's nose anyway. I laughed along with Paul and Kris. "Come over here," I commanded with a smile and gestured for them to follow me to the display case. I scurried behind it and came out holding a couple of small peanut and cheese dog biscuits. I told Marshmallow's owners what they were, and they approved my giving them to her.

Marshmallow downed them with no hesitation, then looked up at me as if asking for more. I smiled at her perky little face. "Maybe one more, if your mom and dad agree."

"No more for now," Kris said, "but we want to buy a couple dozen to take with us."

"Great." I asked Dinah, who was again behind the counter, to get them ready. I glanced back at the area crowded with customers and potential adopters where Silas remained, his microphone up to the mouth of someone I recognized well but hadn't seen arrive: our current mayor, Sybill Gabbon.

At least he wasn't annoying Dinah at the moment.

But what were Silas and the mayor talking about—pet adoptions? Henry's murder? Something embarrassing to the mayor? She appeared uncomfortable. She seemed to tell Silas to get lost, then made her way toward the door—where some of the others I'd expected to see today were just coming in: Detectives Wayne and Bridget. Interesting. Was I not the only one who was hoping something would happen here at the adoption event to root out who'd killed Henry?

Or were the detectives simply interested in what pets were looking for new homes?

As the mayor reached them, they all seemed to grow particularly serious, and not for the first time I wished I had a dog's keen hearing so I could know what they were talking about.

Then, almost as if they'd heard my thoughts, the three made their way through the crowd together toward me.

"Nice event," Mayor Sybill said. Of the three of them, she'd always struck me as the kindest and most down-to-earth, not necessarily having an agenda when she spoke with anyone—although I assumed she wanted to make a good impression on the town's citizens so she would continue to be elected.

"Thanks," I told her.

"You've got Henry Schulzer's dogs here from Mountaintop Rescue, right?" asked Bridget. Since she was looking toward the area of the room where they were leashed near Biscuit, I felt sure she knew the answer even if she couldn't see them in the crowd.

"That's right," I acknowledged.

"Who seems to be interested in them?" Wayne asked.

"No one at the moment, so apparently whoever killed Mr. Schulzer didn't do it with the motive of adopting his dogs when they were available." I was half serious about that, although Tula's actions earlier still made me wonder ... but not enough to point a finger at her. Not now, at least. And no rational motive had occurred to me regarding any of the people I considered suspects.

Did the cops feel the same way?

I sort of asked, bending toward them but keeping my voice low. "I know you're not keen on my butting into your investigations, but in case you're wondering, my main intention today was finding those two a good new home—and my secondary one was getting as many people as possible who knew Henry to come in and check out the dogs and talk to me and others, including you, if you were here ... and hopefully say something to lead us to the actual killer."

"I figured." Wayne didn't sound thrilled, despite the nasty grin he aimed at me.

"And have you had any luck?" the mayor asked.

"No," I admitted. "And it's almost one o'clock, when the event's scheduled to end. I've had little success in anything I hoped for." I shook my head sadly as I looked once more toward where Billi now knelt on the floor with the two golden spaniels.

As usual, she wasn't alone there. But this time she appeared to have a family around her: a mom and dad and two daughters.

Two twin daughters.

Prince and Duke were twins of sorts—brothers from the same litter, and they certainly looked alike, as did the two girls, who appeared to be maybe ten years old.

Was I wrong about my lack of success, at least in finding Duke and Prince a home? Would that family adopt the orphaned pups?

Would a household like theirs suit Billi's stringent vetting of new homes for the pets she placed?

"I think I'll go talk to Billi," I said.

"Looks like maybe she found those dogs a new family," the mayor observed.

"Maybe," I agreed.

"Hey, before you go over there, I want to know one thing," Wayne said.

"What's that?"

He moved sideways and bent toward me. Bridget did the same, though not Mayor Sybill. Uh-oh. This might be a cop thing.

"We do think you ought to keep your nose out of police business," Wayne said quietly so only the three of us could hear. "But are you zeroing in on a suspect in the Schulzer murder?"

"I've got some ideas," I said, which was true. "And I'm still sure it wasn't Dinah Greeley." Which was also true...mostly. "But no, I don't know yet who did it, nor can I point you to any possible evidence you haven't already unearthed."

"Sorry to hear that," Wayne said.

"Keep us informed," said Bridget.

After nodding sadly, I hurried over to Billi.

By then, Dinah was leaning over the spaniels, too. So was Janelle, rather than taking care of customers. And when Billi confirmed that this family, the Lesiters, with their twin daughters Cate and Candy, were putting in an application for Prince and Duke, we all cheered.

"The other pets we brought also all have applications," Billi said, standing up to talk to me. "And so far the situations seem to be acceptable, although we still have to check into them. But it appears that this adoption event was a big success."

"I'm so glad," I said, giving her a hug.

And I was.

But I wished I'd learned something more today, something to resolve the other matter that was battering my brain.

Who killed Henry Schulzer?

TWENTY-FIVE

The closing time for the adoption event finally arrived. Not the closing time for my stores, though.

Once more, diligent Dinah was the one to talk to the members of the crowd who were left. She thanked them for coming, told them that treats of both the canine and human variety were still available for purchase, and reminded them to watch for the next Mountaintop Rescue event to be held here at Barkery and Biscuits.

"Of course, you don't have to wait for one of our special events," she concluded. "Mountaintop Rescue is open regular hours during the week and weekends, and they're always taking in wonderful animals who need new homes—as well as finding new families for those under their care. Like you, maybe."

I grinned as the remaining folks there applauded her, and I joined in, too. So did Billi and Janelle, the other staff member who remained in the Barkery.

I hadn't seen Silas and Wilbur leave, but I no longer saw them anywhere. Francine Metz was still in the Barkery, though. "This was wonderful," she said. "Check the *Knobcone News* for a feature about it that we'll be publishing soon." The pretty and dog-loving editor gave a curt nod that indicated she was serious, then she smiled. "Like I said earlier, maybe one of these days I'll head to Mountaintop Rescue myself. I think a pup is in my future."

This time when I applauded, it was for Francine. "Wonderful!" I said. "Just let Billi know when you're ready, and she'll introduce you to some of the most wonderful rescue dogs ever. A lot of great ones wind up at Mountaintop Rescue."

"I'm counting on it. In fact, I'm starting to take notes to write an article about my entire process once I've adopted someone."

"What a wonderful idea." I'd assumed she would do this, and it could certainly be helpful to Mountaintop Rescue. "And you can always come to the Barkery for healthy treats, and take your new darling to the Knobcone Vet Clinic for exams and shots, and—"

"Enough!" Francine waved her hand that held her tablet. "I'll want all your ideas eventually, but it's too soon now."

"Got it."

She left, then, and for the next half hour Billi and her Mountaintop Rescue crew got the animals and their supplies back in the van to take back to the shelter—for now. Each of the people who'd filled out an application had promised to visit the shelter over the weekend and give Billi any further information she needed to determine if the proposed adoption was a good match.

My fingers were crossed that every one of them would work out.

I purposely hadn't scheduled a shift at the vet clinic that day, since I'd already taken a lot of time from my stores—but the event had been absolutely worth it, particularly since there was a good chance that all the rescues had found new forever homes.

Including, hopefully, Prince and Duke.

The shops remained busy until closing time, and I had to send a couple of my assistants into the kitchen to do a little more baking, primarily for the Barkery. But no one minded. And we all shared our impressions and stories about the adoption event and our excitement about how successful it had been.

"Billi needs to bring more dogs next time," Dinah said as we got ready to close the shops. "More pups can find new homes."

"Right," I said. "This time the focus was on—"

"Prince and Duke." Dinah had removed the apron and now stood there in her casual clothes, including a *Dogs Rule* T-shirt. "Anyway, I'm happy for the pets. And I can't wait to see how the stories on TV and in the newspaper portray them and our event."

I was looking forward to it, too. That was my intended plan for that evening, at least concerning the TV news. I would look online to see if Francine had posted a story on the *Knobcone News* website, but I figured it was more likely to appear tomorrow in the paper— and I intended to buy a hard copy, or several, to save.

I wasn't the only one who wanted to see what Silas said, as it turned out. I told Reed about everything, and he was happy to watch the news segment with me. Janelle had already told Neal that she intended to watch it and that he was welcome to join her.

And so we all headed to my house. Neal picked up some pizza on the way home, while Janelle went to retrieve Go. Reed and Hugo arrived a little after the others, but that was fine. I set my television's DVR to record the local news, both the early and late versions.

We walked our dogs. They got along well. They'd seen a lot of each other, after all, and none was particularly aggressive.

Then I got the dogs treats from the kitchen, and all the humans went in to pick out their pizza and drinks—wine, beer, or water. Next we adjourned into the living room, where I turned on the TV.

It was late enough that there'd already been a half-hour segment of the news, but since I'd set it to record before we walked the dogs, we could watch it from the beginning. Soon we were all sitting on my living room's fluffy old beige couch, or on the matching chairs beside it, with the dogs lying on the floor near us.

I used the remote to tune in, then to speed through the beginning till I got to the part about the adoption event. Sure enough, Silas dominated the screen. He was shown interviewing my customers and other people who'd just come in to see what the event was about. He talked to the cops and to Mayor Sybill and to the Holpurns—which was interesting, but nothing particularly stood out as useful.

Silas also talked to the Banners, and to the Lesiter family who'd put an application in to adopt Henry's dogs. He sat down on the floor where the cat crates were and meowed at them. He held out his arms for the other dogs Billi had brought in, including the basset hound mix. I wished I'd gotten their names. Maybe I still would.

The dachshund snuggled onto Silas's lap, and the newsman said nice things as he petted the friendly dog.

Which somehow set my mind reeling as I recalled something.

Something that hadn't seemed important at the time, and yet ...

The segment was soon over and I let the news continue so everyone could still watch it.

But my mind wasn't there—not entirely. I probably was just creating a mountain out of a molehill ... but I needed to ponder it, at least overnight.

And maybe I'd figure out what to do about it.

The next day, I still hadn't determined the best way to handle it—to do my research, as Dinah would put it.

But I had to do something, as quickly and safely as possible. If I was right, the results could be far-reaching. But my idea was just too bizarre to have a basis in reality ... right?

Well, I had to follow up on it to at least be able to eliminate it from my thoughts.

I didn't let Reed know, though. We went through our usual regimen of his getting up early with me and walking our dogs, then he left for home while I got ready to head to my shops. We went out to our cars together with Biscuit and Hugo. Neal, Janelle, and Go were presumably still sleeping.

"So—I know you don't have a shift at the clinic today," Reed said, standing near my driver's door with me. "Interested in getting together this evening?"

"I'm always interested," I said with a smile, and the long, sweet kiss we shared only underscored why I wanted to get together with him that night.

"Are you okay?" he asked, staring with what looked like puzzlement into my eyes. "You seem—well, stressed."

"I'm fine," I assured him, glad in some ways that we were close enough that he could read my moods, but I didn't want to discuss anything about what I was thinking. Not yet, at least.

He gave me another kiss, still appearing concerned, and I gave him another hug. Soon Biscuit and I were on the road, driving to the shops.

With my mind continuing to swirl.

As I started the baking, I considered the best approach to take. I'd keep it casual, and just observe the reactions of the person I'd zoomed in on.

We opened the shops at seven, as usual. Since it was Saturday, my assistants were Dinah and Frida. Dinah kept shooting me strange glances as I worked with her in the kitchen and then the Barkery, as if she could tell something was going on in my mind.

Reed had noticed too, of course. I directed myself to remain calm and normal, and hoped that I was succeeding.

At just as little after nine, I went into my office and called Billi. "When is that wonderful family who's adopting Prince and Duke coming in?" I asked.

"The Lesiters? They're really eager. I told them they could come in at eleven. I've got a few more questions for them but nothing momentous. I've got a feeling this one will work out."

"Wonderful," I said. "I'll try to be there. And I'm hoping to get Mountaintop Rescue some additional publicity about this amazing situation."

"Great!" Billi said. "See you then."

Hopefully she would continue to consider it great. I made my next call to Silas Perring. It apparently wasn't too early for the news anchor to be at work today, since he answered right away. "Yes, Carrie?" He apparently had my number programmed into his phone, though I'd had to look his up.

I told him that the wonderful result of yesterday's adoption event was most likely coming to its conclusion today. "I saw your story on TV last night and thought you might like to do a follow-up. You spoke with the Lesiters and maybe already know they've put in an application to adopt Prince and Duke. The adoption will be finalized at eleven this morning, at Mountaintop Rescue, and I'm going to be there. Not sure about Francine Metz. I've talked to her but haven't let her know this timing yet."

"I'll be there," Silas said. "No need to tell Francine. She'll do her own follow-up later."

"Maybe." I planned to stay in touch with Francine about the autobiographical story she was thinking of writing, about adopting a pet. If she wanted to get in touch with the family adopting Prince and Duke, for a story on them, she could always check with Billi.

I had one more call to make, a different kind of follow-up with my detective friends. And then I hurried through the kitchen to my shops to keep busy till it was time to go.

I left for Mountaintop Rescue about ten thirty. I had every intention of getting there early. I left Biscuit in the Barkery in the care of my assistants.

"My fingers are crossed that all goes well in Prince and Duke's adoption," Dinah said as I left.

"Me too," I responded, not mentioning the other, related matter that was making me head to the shelter.

I drove, since I wanted to get there quickly. Mimi let Billi know of my arrival, then sent me up to her boss's office.

"I'm delighted you're here," Billi said. She wore one of her frilly tops over jeans and, as always, looked very pretty despite not being dressed formally. "I know you care about what happens with Prince and Duke. I think the adoption will work out fine."

"I hope so." I paused. "Have you heard any more from Tula Schulzer? Is she still trying to get her brother's dogs?"

"No. I'm not sure what that little squabble was about in your store, but I think I made it clear that she'd have to qualify like anyone else to adopt them—and that it was doubtful I'd approve her. And with this wonderful family so interested, I know where those dogs should go."

"I agree," I said. "I'm looking forward to the pups going home with their new owners—especially those cute twin girls."

We chatted for a little while longer, then headed downstairs. This time, Billi wouldn't take the cockers into one of the usual adoption rooms decorated like nice, though small, living rooms. I'd been in some before, but not often. They were good locations for potential adopters to get to know their new family members a bit better. But too many people were going to be present for this.

"Would you like to wait in there anyway?" Billi asked me once we were on the ground floor.

"No, I'll wait in the reception area." I'd already told her I had invited Silas to film the situation—and also the detectives because I had some questions for them.

Billi seemed puzzled about the latter, but I didn't explain. I could tell her more later, depending on how things worked out.

I'd asked Silas to arrive a little early so he could film when the Lesiters arrived and their likely cute emotions when they saw Prince and Duke again. Sure enough, he soon walked into the reception area with Wilbur close behind him.

"Hiya, Carrie," Silas said, standing next to the tall reception counter where Mimi watched us. As always, the nice-looking news anchor was impeccably dressed. But once more, he had overdone his cologne. "So this is supposed to be an emotional human interest story I'm here for, right?"

"That's right. The family who was at my stores yesterday is hopefully getting approval to adopt the two dogs owned by Henry Schulzer. Their kids are cute, and so are the dogs."

"I prefer real news, but the story on your adoption get-together yesterday got a lot of views and comments, so this should, too."

"Great." I hoped it would have another result, as well—assuming I wasn't trying too hard to solve the murder by making up odd scenarios in my mind.

Well, I'd see.

I saw the door open behind Wilbur and heard some excited kid squeals. They'd arrived! I moved around Silas to greet the Lesiters, all four of them.

Little Cate and Candy's matching brown hair was pulled back into ponytails, and they wore T-shirts that said *Dog Love* over their denim capri pants. Cute—of course.

Their parents appeared somewhat frazzled. Because of the girls' behavior—or because they worried about whether this adoption would go through? Maybe both.

Billi came into the waiting room then. "Hi," she said to the Lesiters. "Please come upstairs to my office so we can go over a few things, and then we'll bring the dogs out for you. I think everything's looking good."

"We certainly hope so," said Mrs. Lesiter.

"And once we bring them out and this gang gets together with them, that'll be a great time to film it," Billi said to Silas, who just nodded.

Billi directed the Lesiters to precede her up the stairs. At the top, she turned to look down at me, her expression somewhat quizzical. I still hadn't told her all that was on my mind. Well, she'd find out soon, one way or another.

I just smiled and nodded at her. Then, hearing a noise, I turned to see Detective Bridget enter the reception area door. "Good morning," she said to Mimi first, then to the rest of us. Her face, too, appeared quizzical—and not particularly happy. She didn't know what I was anticipating here, either.

But at least one of the detectives had come.

"Hi, Detective Morana," Silas said, holding his microphone out to her, Wilbur filming beside him. "What brings you here today?"

"Just a short visit to the area's only pet rescue facility. We check things out here often." That was what Bridget said into the camera, but the next look she aimed at me, once the camera pointed downward, was less pleased.

If I was wrong, I'd have to apologize for wasting her time. But if I was right ... well, we'd just have to see.

We chatted a bit about nothing. Well, not entirely nothing, since the topic was mostly rescue animals. All of us seemed to support the adoption, even Bridget and Wilbur the Wise. Or at least it appeared that way, as the news crew and detective seemed eager to find something to talk about while we waited.

Soon, Billi came down the steps with the Lesiters behind her. One parent held the hand of each of the girls, which was a good thing on that somewhat steep stairway.

"So how are we doing?" I asked Billi, meeting her at the bottom.

"We have a go, here." Pleasure radiated from her smile, and I grinned back.

"Fantastic. Are we going into a meeting room then after all?"

"No, let's go outside to the patio."

I let the others follow Billi more closely, observing everyone's attitude. The Lesiters all appeared thrilled. Silas looked determined, and Wilbur amused. Detective Bridget's face was unreadable, but I still didn't get the sense she was particularly happy.

The patio area was just outside the back door, near the enclosures where the residents were housed. The ground was an easily cleanable cement, and someone had brought out a few folding chairs.

I remained standing, and so did the others with me. Billi hurried to the other side of the patio and into the kennel area. Soon she returned with Prince and Duke, and the little girls squealed and hugged them. Their parents, arms around each other, just watched with huge grins on their faces.

"Are you filming this?" I asked Silas.

"Sure. I'll interview them in a minute."

I watched as Wilbur maneuvered in a circle around the clearly thrilled family, keeping his camera aimed at them. Silas remained a short distance away, just watching.

"Everything looks great," Billi said, joining me.

"I'm so glad to hear that." I waited for a few minutes, then approached Silas, who still hadn't begun his interview. "Why don't you get down on the ground with those kids and their new dogs?" I asked. "That would be a really moving scene on the news."

"That's okay. I'm not dressed for getting on the ground. I can dub in some background info later."

Interesting. And maybe a bit corroborative of what I was thinking. But it wasn't enough. I doubted Silas would hold back from getting on the ground, no matter what he was wearing, if the story was titillating enough. He'd gotten on the ground for the dachshund, after all.

Of course, this story was a cute human interest one, nothing dark and dirty, or real news. Silas could actually hold that attitude—no particular taste for the fun stuff, but anything for a hard-tuned story.

Still … I couldn't let this end there.

"I understand," I said, then hurried over to where the two little girls were hugging their new pets. "May I borrow Prince for just a minute?" I asked. "I want to make sure he gets his picture taken."

"Okay," said the child holding Prince—Cate?—as she released him from her hug. I immediately picked the small golden dog up and carried him directly to Silas. I held him out toward the reporter, noting that Wilbur was filming this.

Immediately, as Prince neared Silas and came within sniffing range, he growled, then barked.

"Oh my," I said. "It'll be hard to interview him this way."

"Get him away," Silas spat. "I don't like dogs, and they don't like me."

I glanced over his shoulder. Good. Bridget stood there, observing. An expression of interest lit her face. Did she understand what I was doing? I figured she did. She was one smart detective.

"But you were holding the other dogs up for adoption at the Barkery on your film segment last night. That little dachshund and the basset hound mix and you seemed to get along just fine. You were even hugging them."

I glanced up again to make sure Bridget was listening to this. Did she get what I was attempting to point out?

Both of Henry's dogs had growled when they were near Silas during the adoption event, although I hadn't attributed it to Silas at the time. But now ... now Prince was doing it again.

Did that prove Silas was the killer? No, but it was something to check out.

People at the resort had said they'd heard Henry's dogs barking. At the killer?

At Silas?

"Some dogs and I get along okay," Silas amended. "But not all. And I was trying to get good footage before. I definitely don't like dogs."

Especially when they identified you as a killer?

At least the groundwork had been laid for an investigation into Silas.

TWENTY-SIX

CLAIMING HE HAD ANOTHER story brewing that he needed to follow up on, Silas left soon thereafter, Wilbur trailing behind him.

That was okay. I'd made my point—sort of. Bridget had seen it.

"We've already checked out the Lesiters' home," Billi told me, coming over to stand by my side. "It's great for dogs. So are the family, with their attitude and lovingness. They're good to go."

"Great!" I said. "If you do any follow-ups, let me know. I'd love to see them again, particularly in their new environment. And hopefully to make sure I see them again—" I reached into my purse and pulled out a plastic bag full of Barkery treats. I approached Mrs. Lesiter with them. "These are for your new family members," I said. "And please bring them often to my Barkery for more." Visits to my shop could be part of their new environment, after all.

"That's wonderful. Thanks so much." The beaming woman gave me a hug, then knelt on the pavement and handed her daughters each a treat from the bag. "Now, you give Prince and Duke a treat," she told them, and they did.

The dogs both appeared delighted, wagging their tails, and they both begged a bit on Mr. Lesiter's command.

So maybe Henry had trained his dogs. It would be interesting for the Lesiters to see how much they knew.

But I'd stay out of that. All that was important to me was that they were getting a good home.

They soon left—the humans and their new canine family members. I couldn't help smiling a lot as they walked off the patio and through the reception area, dogs leashed beside the adults, who also each held a daughter's hand. I then gave Billi a big hug.

"Good job, Councilwoman."

"Thanks. I think we both deserve some kudos here."

"Yay, us," I said. "And yay adoption events at the Barkery."

We hugged again—but I saw Detective Bridget over Billi's shoulder.

She caught my gaze as well. "All right, what was this all about—although I think I can guess why you invited me here."

I stepped back from Billi and faced Bridget. "Have you considered Silas Perring as a possible suspect in Henry Schulzer's murder?" I hadn't ... before.

"No, and I still see no reason to. What would his motive be?"

"That I don't know—yet. But you saw how the dog growled at him. Both of Henry's dogs growled a bit at Silas during the adoption event—nothing really nasty, so it might mean nothing. But I've spent a little time with Prince and Duke, and I haven't heard them growl at anyone else. And you're aware that Henry's body was discovered because his dogs were barking."

"Yes, I am. So ... well, I suppose if you stretch things, there could be a little connection. Or not. But I'll have someone in our office do a little research." She glared at me. "And you keep Dinah away from it. Yourself, too."

Okay, I'd try—as long as I believed they were actually looking into the possibility that Silas was involved.

Although … well, I might not physically place myself in any situation of nosiness, but I could certainly do a bit of online searching about Silas's background, any stories he might have done about Henry, whatever made sense. But I wouldn't tell Bridget that.

"Of course," I said. "I would appreciate it if you'd keep me informed about your progress. Nothing that's confidential to the police, of course, but just general updates on what you're doing and if you're finding anything helpful."

"We'll see," she said, not sounding helpful at all.

Which indicated I'd have to follow up with her. Nicely, of course. And not be too assertive when asking for status information.

I'd figured Bridget wouldn't be too forthcoming. Maybe I could ask for Wayne when I called in. He seemed more friendly, at least a little bit. Or maybe, in the interest of not seeming too pushy, I could alternate between them—although I figured they'd trade that kind of information.

Well, I'd just have to do whatever seemed appropriate to make sure they were at least looking into Silas as a possible suspect, like they'd done with so many people who knew Henry.

And I had to admit to myself that the possibility did seem remote. What would Silas's motive have been?

"Okay, I'm leaving," Bridget said to Billi. "I have to say that the adoption you just did was really cute. I didn't adopt my Butterball cat from Mountaintop Rescue, but if I were ever going to take in another pet, I'd definitely start at your facility." We followed Bridget to the reception area. "Keep it up, Billi," she said near the door.

"You can be sure I will," Billi responded.

"And you, Carrie…"

She stopped talking, so I encouraged her. "Yes?"

"Just because you figured some things out in past situations doesn't mean you're now a walking, talking, skilled investigator. Leave it to those who really are."

"I'd love to," I said. "But you've zeroed in a lot on people who were completely innocent, and I suspect that's what's been happening recently." Like with poor Dinah. "I never promise that my ideas are helpful—but they've proven so in the past, so it really won't hurt for you to check my latest hunch out."

I didn't try to contact either Bridget or Wayne for the next couple of days. Not that I figured they'd get in touch with me, but I didn't want to seem too forward about my idea. Still, Bridget had seen Silas's reaction to Prince. But everything on TV and otherwise appeared normal, with Silas on a lot of news stories but with only one other brief segment about the adoption event, and nothing else particularly interesting.

I did try calling Bridget on the third day after our meeting, but didn't reach her. Nor did she return my call.

And so I waited some more, still watching the TV news—and Silas still seemed to be the same outspoken news announcer he'd always been.

Okay. I might have been barking up the wrong tree, so to speak. Apparently the cops had either checked him out and didn't find any evidence against him—or they were ignoring the situation that I'd brought to their attention.

I did research Silas online, but mostly found his newscasts. There were a couple of bios, too, but nothing that indicated he was anything but a dedicated reporter. On some stories, he'd been the first to report on them, so he was apparently good at his job.

I couldn't find anything that would get the detectives interested in him.

Nearly a week had passed. Francine Metz ran a cute article about the adoption event in the *Knobcone News*, as she'd promised. Was she still looking for a new pet of her own? Her article hinted at the possibility, at least.

I didn't think about the situation with Silas all the time, but I was frustrated when I did. I tried calling Bridget again, and when she didn't return my calls yet again, I finally called Wayne while sitting in my office with no one else around. He, at least, answered.

"Hi," I said. And then I got right to the point. "Has anyone checked Silas Perring yet as a possible suspect in Henry Schulzer's murder?"

"Yeah, Bridget told me about that little episode you staged last week. Seemed a bit of a stretch, don't you think?"

"If I thought there was no possibility of it being a reality, then I wouldn't have brought it up. Did she tell you that when one of Henry's dogs got close to Silas, the dog growled?" I reminded Wayne that Henry's body had been discovered thanks to the barking of his dogs. They'd apparently been present for the murder—and just might still be angry with the killer.

"Yes, she told us about that—and not just me, but also the chief. I won't tell you what we did to look into it, but I can tell you we didn't completely ignore you."

I didn't like the word "completely." It suggested they hadn't behaved too seriously, whatever they'd done.

I leaned forward, elbows on my desk, and closed my eyes. "Look, Wayne. You've obviously been having trouble figuring this one out, since you haven't arrested anybody—and you can be sure that in saying this, I'm not encouraging you to go after Dinah. I know I'm not one of you. I don't have the training and knowledge that you all have. But you've seen me have a little success in these kinds of cases, and you've even sort of acknowledged that I've been of help. Am I certain Silas is the killer? No. I have no idea what his motive would be or if he knew Henry as anything but a possible interesting news subject since he was married to the former, murdered mayor. But—"

"Okay, Carrie." It came out as a sigh into my ear. "I do hear you. And maybe we haven't checked enough. No promises, but I'll suggest we follow up some more on Silas as a possible suspect."

I felt myself grin—in relief? In pride that Wayne was actually sort of listening to me? It didn't matter. "Very good," I said. "And—well, to the extent you can keep me informed about what you do and anything you find, I'd really appreciate it."

"We'll see," he said. Well, at least it wasn't a "bug off, already." I'd have to live with that.

We said our goodbyes. It was Friday afternoon, and I was scheduled for a shift at the clinic, so I quickly went through the kitchen into the Barkery to get Biscuit, and we were soon on our way.

I continued smiling, at least a little, the whole way there. Okay, I knew that the agreement I'd gotten from Wayne wasn't much, nor could I be sure I'd actually set him looking for a genuine suspect. But at least he'd listened.

That smile got Reed's attention. He was the first vet I was scheduled to assist.

Our first patient was a somewhat belligerent pit bull mix—but his aggressiveness turned out not to be surprising because he had a large cyst on his belly that must have been painful. The owner was shocked and upset—and grateful when Reed told him to leave the pitty for surgery the next morning. Then Reed helped me get the poor dog into our kennel area in the back and into a crate to wait for what was to come. I hugged the poor dog and patted him for a few minutes. At least he seemed calm and appeared to enjoy my attention.

"You're not looking very cheerful now," Reed said, looking into my eyes as we left that room. "But when I first saw you, you appeared pretty happy. Some break in the Schulzer murder case?"

I laughed. "You know me so well. The answer is ... maybe. At least I've gotten a verbal commitment from Wayne Crunoll to do more checking into Silas as a possible suspect." Yes, I'd hinted to Reed about my suspicions, partly because I just couldn't keep it inside, and I knew I could trust Reed.

"I know you were getting frustrated about that," he said, "so I guess that's good news."

"Guess so," I said.

I wasn't surprised when I didn't hear anything from Wayne for the rest of that day, even when I returned to my shops. At least Reed and I spent the night together, which helped get my mind off it—a bit.

Nor did I hear from Wayne the next day. Nothing unusual about that, I told myself. On Sunday, I nearly called him. At least I had his number on my phone now, so all I'd need to do was press the button. But I didn't. Surely Wayne would call that day ... but he didn't.

Same thing on Monday. And Tuesday. I was getting frustrated again, deciding when would be the best time to call him.

Wednesday morning, I figured that day had come. I'd wait till later and try to prime myself not to nag—much.

Reed had spent the night at my house, and Neal had stayed with Janelle at her place. As always, the sweet veterinarian got up early with me and we left my house together to start each of our days. At the Barkery, I began my baking as usual—dog treats first, of course. They always came first.

Dinah had, as usual, been off on Monday and Tuesday, but she was scheduled to be my first assistant of the day. I expected her to arrive around six.

But almost immediately after I'd started baking, I heard my phone make the noise that indicated a text. My hands were covered in biscuit dough by then, but I figured that a text at this hour might be important. So I washed up and pulled my phone from my pocket.

It was a local grocery store letting me know they'd received some ingredients we'd ordered for Icing's baked goods, and they were about to deliver it to the kitchen door. I was glad to hear it. I mostly just went to pick stuff up at the store but had begun recently to receive a delivery once or twice a week. So one scheduled for today? I supposed so. But it was a lot earlier than they'd ever delivered anything before.

Shaking my head, I turned off the sound on my phone so I wouldn't hear it ring or text again. I'd check on it later, especially if it vibrated in my pocket. More importantly, I'd follow up again with Wayne just to bug him a bit, if necessary. I even thought through things to make that call … maybe.

Then I went to the back door of the kitchen and opened it, in case the delivery had already arrived.

And was shocked to see not a delivery person or a carton of ingredients, but Silas Perring—alone, without Wilbur along.

"Good morning, Carrie. We have some things to discuss." Without waiting for me to reply, he shoved me out of the way and stalked through the door.

"I don't think so," I said.

But then I noticed he wasn't wearing one of his usual on-camera suits, but jeans and a T-shirt—and rubber gloves.

And in his right hand he held a nasty-looking knife. After he slammed the door shut and locked it, he raised the knife toward me.

TWENTY-SEVEN

UH-OH. I'D EXPECTED SOMETHING... but not this. I ignored how my heart began doing flip flops and my mind started screaming at me to run. That wouldn't work.

No, I had to stay calm. Or at least as calm as possible. Otherwise—well, I didn't want to think about *otherwise*.

Well, the good thing, I told myself as I willed myself not to shake, was that Silas's appearance, in this manner, suggested that the cops had in fact been checking into him as the potential murderer.

The bad thing was that no matter what I might have anticipated from him due to my recent pushiness, it didn't include this kind of reaction—at my shops, at this hour.

Well, Silas had certainly figured out a way to get my attention. Maybe he'd even been watching me and my shops and figured out the grocery delivery situation. So what now?

Yes, I'd solved murders before, and the killers generally seemed inclined to attempt to do away with the person—me—pointing at them as the major suspect. But I'd been resourceful enough to find ways to save myself.

This time?

That knife looked pretty lethal.

And I was thinking too much, without coming up with answers.

We were standing near the back of the counter where I'd been preparing Barkery treats. I had knives around, too. This was a kitchen, after all.

But I seldom sliced meat for our treats, though I did occasionally for liver biscuits. My knives were smaller than his.

And facing off against Silas with my own knife just sounded foolish.

"How did you get the idea to text me to say you had a grocery delivery?" I asked, forcing myself to sound calm.

"Your assistant Dinah isn't the only one around here who does research." Silas's grin was nasty. "That's part of a reporter's job."

Okay, I'd already figured that one out. But … what now? "You said you wanted to discuss something," I said. "What do you want to talk about?"

"Oh, I think you know. You have one hell of an imagination, and also a very dishonest mouth."

I'd considered Silas to be good-looking, or at least attractive enough to be a reporter who people would pay attention to, with his dark hair and interested eyes. But right now those eyes looked smug. They seemed to challenge me to move, to do something that would give him a reason to stab me right then.

"But if it was all my imagination and lying, why are you here?"

Okay, he could consider that a bit of a challenge, I guessed— since he took a step toward me, arm raised. I heard Biscuit barking in the Barkery and was glad she was safe, at least for now. But if Silas killed me, what would keep him from harming my dog, too?

"Because you pushed those detectives to intrude into my life and ask some nasty questions. And now you're going to pay for it."

"But if you're totally innocent, and you gave them truthful answers, why not just let it all go?" Right. Once again, though, what could I do…?

Then I got an idea. It was partly thanks to Silas's earlier actions. I'd muted my phone, but I'd already programmed it so it was ready to place a call to Detective Wayne as soon as it was an acceptable hour of the morning.

For something like this, I didn't need to wait for an acceptable hour.

"You're really scaring me, and my legs are shaking," I told Silas. "I'm going to lean against this counter now, for balance. I'm not going to pick up something or anything like that." Not yet, at least.

When he didn't object, I moved a little bit, which allowed me to swivel my hips—and reach into my pocket to press the front of my phone.

Was it calling Wayne? I couldn't check to find out. But if it did, Wayne would be able to hear us without us being able to hear him. And that was thanks to Silas's grocery delivery text, which had gotten me to turn the sound off. Thanks, I thought wryly.

If nothing else, I was slightly farther away from Silas now, since he remained at the end of the counter. I could smell my latest batch of carob dog treats, which were close to being fully baked, but at least I'd used the timer on the oven. Nevertheless, I turned to glance toward that oven.

"Okay, that's enough." Silas took a step toward me. "You're against the counter now. Don't wriggle around. And you want to hear the truth?" His tone now sounded furious. "I'll tell you the truth, since you're not going to survive to make any more allegations to your cop buddies." He lifted the knife and began shifting it back and forth between his hands.

"Okay," I said softly. "Please tell me."

And please be listening, Wayne.

"Yes," Silas said with an entirely evil smile on his face. "I'm the one who killed Henry—and his damned dogs were there, so that's why they don't like me."

"I gather that your attempt to change your scent didn't put them off in the slightest." I tried to keep my tone somewhat sympathetic but doubted it came across that way.

"You noticed. I assumed a dog lady like you might, but I had to give it a try."

Uncomfortable, I shifted slightly against the counter, but moved as little as possible and tried not to shake. "So why did you kill him?"

"Ah, I figured you'd want to know that. It goes back a long way."

Silas then proceeded to tell me a story that addressed a lot of the questions currently hovering around Knobcone Heights. It turned out that he had been the one to murder Henry's wife, Mayor Flora Schulzer, ten years ago. "See, I was a renowned reporter back then, too," he explained. "But our dear mayor learned of some instances where I exaggerated negative facts about her and some fellow politicians to make a better story. She promised she would shout it to the world—and to my employers. Not a great reason to kill someone? Well, I thought it was, since it was my career on the line."

And so Silas had been delighted, of course, when Mike Holpurn wound up confessing to Flora's murder.

I had to ask. "Why would Holpurn confess to killing Flora when he didn't do it?"

"I wondered about that too, so I looked into it a bit, and it seems the guy actually did have an affair with our mayor, though I've no idea why she would have gotten into bed with that stupid construction worker. But Holpurn had a girlfriend back then, and I think he was convinced that she was the one who did it, because of his affair. So, to protect his girlfriend, he took the fall and confessed. And before you ask, I have no idea what happened to the girlfriend, but she moved away as soon as Holpurn went to prison. So, when I learned that Holpurn was being paroled, I tried to research the situation again, including about the girlfriend, but whatever went on in court is apparently subject to a gag order. So if that's in fact why Holpurn was paroled, I couldn't find any details. I tried. Boy, did I try."

"Okay," I said. "I understand ... I think. But all this time later, why did you kill Henry?"

That knife trick returned—left hand. Right hand. Left hand.

I tried to be unobtrusive as I looked around the kitchen again, trying to figure out how to run away, or what to grab to protect myself with ... and knew I had very little hope.

What time was it? Nearing six o'clock? Dinah would arrive at six—but I didn't want her in danger, too.

"Because," Silas responded, "from the little I was able to learn, it seems that Henry was the source who put authorities onto the idea that Holpurn was protecting his girlfriend. Maybe he felt guilty about Holpurn's incarceration. Maybe he was curious about the man and did some research into his possible motive, and when he found out about the girlfriend—whoever and wherever she is—he learned something that made him suspect Holpurn had confessed to a murder he didn't commit."

"I still don't understand how the police had enough to parole him," I said.

"With a gag order involved, who knows what went on in the courtroom?" Silas said. "But whatever happened, Henry still seemed hostile toward Holpurn—or at least Holpurn was hostile toward him. And now Henry was back in Knobcone Heights. To try to figure out what had actually happened, if Holpurn wasn't the killer? Or maybe he had another reason, like nostalgia or whatever, and wanted to make sure his wife was never forgotten. Whatever his motive, just his being here, asking questions now that Mike Holpurn was free, reminding people … it would have opened up all those old questions again. I couldn't have that going on."

"I see."

I supposed I did see. And I still pondered how I'd get out of this.

I couldn't count on Wayne hearing us. And now, most of Silas's story had been told. How much longer would he keep me alive?

I wasn't about to ask, but I did address a related question. "You know," I said, "if you kill me, the police will look at you as the prime suspect since I've been pointing fingers at you as Henry's killer. You'd be the logical one for them to go after. But if you just let me go, I promise I'll keep quiet about this, and if I'm asked, I'll just tell the police I changed my mind about you, that I have no reason to believe you've harmed anyone."

"Good idea," Silas said, sticking his face closer to me and baring his teeth. "But we both know that wouldn't work. So here's what's going to happen. Right now, I'm appearing on a TV newscast that's supposedly live, and my good buddy Wilbur will ensure that no one finds out otherwise. Wilbur has been my backup in all this from the beginning—and has been generously compensated, by the way."

"I see." I tried not to sound despondent that he had an alibi set up. I needed to keep my fear to myself. "But the police will want another logical suspect, and who would want me dead besides you?"

"Well, your dear assistant Dinah may hate you for allowing her to remain a suspect in Henry's murder—which of course isn't a surprise, because in my scenario, she's the killer. And now she wants revenge for your betrayal. So she's going to kill you when she arrives in a few minutes, or so it will appear. Yes, I know her schedule, and everyone's at your shops. Just like with your grocery delivery. I've done my *research*." Silas drew the word out, clearly making fun of

Dinah. "And then Dinah's going to flee—courtesy of me. Of course, she won't survive much longer."

Oh heavens. I knew Silas was evil, mentally deranged, and even worse. I couldn't really protect myself. How was I going to save Dinah?

A buzzing startled me. Silas, too. "What the hell's that?" he demanded.

"The oven, saying that the biscuits inside are done. I can go turn it off, or it'll turn itself off in a minute."

"No, go do it. But don't try anything stupid."

I just walked the few steps to the oven and turned the timer off. I opened the door just a little to let the heat out, so that, hopefully, the biscuits wouldn't burn. But even if they did, who'd notice now?

After I'd closed the oven door, I turned back toward Silas and just stood there.

Was it time? Was I somehow going to have to find a way to ward off lethal knife stabs?

How?

"Look," I said, "you might not like the scenario I suggested, but what would satisfy you enough to not kill me, or Dinah either?"

If he did kill us, would the police accept his alibi—or realize what had really happened? And would Wilbur go along with this murder, too, and continue to cover for his boss? I had no reason, unfortunately, to assume otherwise, especially if Wilbur got paid for it.

What time was it now? I assumed it was almost six. I wished there was some way I could warn Dinah to stay away.

I hadn't forgotten my attempted call to Wayne. With any luck, he'd heard some or all of what was going on. But even if he had, would I survive until he got here, even if he was on his way now?

At least maybe he would tell Dinah not to come in …

The back door began to open. "Stay out of here, Dinah!" I screamed, even as Silas leaped toward me, his right hand, holding the knife, extended.

"Drop it!" came a very welcome, well-known male voice.

I glanced that way and saw not only Wayne but Bridget and a couple of uniformed cops, too, entering the kitchen, guns drawn and aimed at Silas.

At least Dinah would be safe, I thought as Silas continued toward me. "Bitch!" he yelled, raising his arm to stab me.

A couple of guns were fired. Blood spurted from Silas's arm and the knife clattered to the floor.

I had never imagined I'd feel glad about having to clean blood out of my kitchen—but remaining alive was a wonderful trade-off. There might also be holes in the wall to deal with.

Yes, worth it.

Silas was shouting and moaning, but I paid no attention to what he said.

I simply stood there, still breathing, as I watched the uniformed cops take him into custody.

Then I was joined by both Wayne and Bridget. "Thank you, thank you," I said.

"We heard it all, thanks to you," Bridget said.

I thanked the heavens that my phone idea had worked. And, in some ways, I thanked Silas for bringing it all to a head.

"Yep, you've done it again—solved another murder," Wayne said. "Maybe we should consider hiring you."

"No, thank you," I responded emotionally. Then—"Is Dinah all right?"

"She's outside. We told her to stay there till we got things resolved in here, which I think they are now."

The cops walked Silas out the door. I assumed they'd deal with his wounds as they should, taking him to the hospital before throwing him in jail.

I wanted him to survive, after all, to be tried for Henry and Flora's murders—and his murder attempt on me.

The next moment, Dinah ran inside and came right over to me. She glanced at the blood-streaked wall, then gave me a hug. "Are you okay, Carrie?"

"I am now," I said.

TWENTY-EIGHT

OR AT LEAST I thought I was. Turning my back on what the cops were doing, I dashed into the Barkery to check on Biscuit. She was fine, thank heavens. I gave her a big hug, even though it would mean an intense hand-washing session before I began baking again, assuming the cops would let us use our kitchen today. I placed her in her enclosure and returned to the kitchen, shutting the door behind me.

It appeared that Wayne and Bridget were free for the moment. Or, as it turned out, they were waiting for me. "We'll need a statement from you, Carrie," Bridget said.

"Which needs to include how you called me so efficiently," added Wayne. "I gathered that good old Silas couldn't hear me when I answered and kept saying 'Carrie, Carrie' before I shut up and listened. And recorded, by the way."

"That's all great," I said. "But before we continue with this, there's something else I want to do." I turned the volume back up on my phone, then located the KnobTV website. "Maybe you've already handled this, but I just want to see..." I focused in on the site so I could look at excerpts from the morning news. Sure enough, the site showed a clip of Silas apparently somewhere around the resort, talking about how the lake was sparkling today as the early morning sun rose. The clip that had been shown on TV as if in real time. "Or maybe you haven't handled it yet," I added.

"We've got a team on our way to the studio and another going to the lake," Wayne said defensively. "It takes a little time to—"

Almost as if someone at the TV station had heard us, another clip popped up, featuring Bobbi Hanger. The young reporter looked wild-eyed and even frightened. "Er …" she began, not very professionally. "Good morning, ladies and gentlemen. Sorry for the interruption, but there were a few errors on our broadcast this morning, and … Anyway, I believe we're about to have some breaking news about some of our own staff. Please stay tuned." She disappeared as a commercial began.

"Well, at least they can use this to their station's advantage," I said. "They'll certainly have more information about this interesting bit of news, at least at first, than any other TV station."

"That's for certain," Bridget said.

"Now, can we take your statement?" Wayne held his phone toward me, clearly ready to record what I said.

"This may take a little while," I said. "Why don't we go sit down in the Barkery?"

I left Dinah in the kitchen, where, after the cops took photos and gave her the okay, she promised to do a preliminary scrubbing of the walls to remove the blood. That would also involve tossing any of our baked goods that happened to be out on any kitchen counter. Only then would she remove anything new from the oven and finish preparing our initial goods for both stores. I got the detectives and myself some scones from the glass-fronted case in Icing. Then, seated around one of the Barkery tables, I answered

271

their intense questions—even while recognizing that they already had most of the answers, thanks to Wayne's eavesdropping on my frightening conversation with Silas.

And when we were done, Wayne rose first, then Bridget.

"Okay, Carrie," Wayne said. "Thank you for helping to solve not just one but two murders here in Knobcone Heights."

"Two *more* murders," Bridget clarified, aiming an apparently amused smile toward me.

"Yeah, two more murders," Wayne echoed. His expression appeared more amazed than amused.

"You're very welcome," I told them, also smiling, but only for a second. Then I said to both of them, "And thank you for saving my life."

"You're welcome, too," said Bridget as Wayne gave a formal, detective-like nod.

They left, then, making it clear they might have more questions. Well, whether I'd have more answers wasn't clear to me, but I'd cooperate as much as I could.

It was time to open both shops, and Janelle was my next assistant to arrive. She burst into the Barkery from the kitchen and flung herself at me, arms out. "Oh, Carrie." She hugged me. "I'm so glad you're all right. Neal is, too. We saw the breaking news about the capture of Silas Perring—the newscaster, of all people—just before I left this morning, and your involvement in it all, and ... well, we tried calling, but you didn't answer."

"The detectives hijacked my phone before they took my statement," I said. "It has evidence on it. Looks like they'll keep it for at least the rest of the day."

I opened the door to the Barkery and had to step out of the way as a flood of people entered, all congratulating me, wishing me well, and expressing happiness that I was okay. A lot of those kind people had their dogs along and bought treats for them. I gave out almost no free samples today, but we did have enough items available in the Barkery thanks to my early baking.

Dinah apparently had opened Icing on time, for when I headed in there, it was as full as the Barkery. Its patrons, too, were full of best wishes, and we had enough fresh leftovers to at least start the day.

I appreciated the business and the good wishes—but I'd had enough for now. Both Vicky and Frida soon came in, even though Vicky wasn't scheduled till the next day. I took advantage of their presence, grabbed Biscuit, and headed to Cuppa-Joe's. No respite there. Lots of people at the coffee shop knew who I was and also made a fuss over me. The Joes insisted that Biscuit and I spend some down time at a table with them and Sweetie. And they hugged and congratulated me a lot.

Things weren't much different when, after returning to my shops, I headed for my late-day shift at the vet clinic. Arvie, the other vets and my fellow vet techs, doggy daycare manager Faye and her staff, and even pet owners waiting for appointments all expressed concern and amazement. I was becoming exhausted from all the good wishes and worries.

When Reed broke away from his latest patient and grabbed and kissed me in the hallway, I clung to him.

"I know you were getting frustrated that the detectives seemed to ignore your suspicions, but I'd rather it was that than ... Well, at least you seem okay. Are you?"

"Now I am," I told him with a smile, then nestled back into his arms despite the traffic in the clinic hallway. I needed that hug.

I didn't do much vet tech work that day, and I popped over to see Billi at Mountaintop Rescue without leftover treats. "Next time," I promised. "And tell me when you're ready to do another adoption event at the Barkery."

My friend shook her head as she smiled. "You never quit, do you, Carrie?"

"Not if I can help it."

But things were quieter as I returned to the shops. The only unusual thing was the appearance of Neal, since he hadn't been able to reach me. "Just wanted to see for myself that you're all right, sis," he said, giving me a big brotherly hug.

"I'm okay," I assured him as I hugged him back.

So ... it was over.

Things remained somewhat quiet over the next few days, too. Oh, a lot of people asked what had happened, how I'd figured out that Silas was the killer, and how I'd helped to bring him in, but the interest fortunately began to wane. The news commentators seemed to be having fun with the idea that one of their own getting arrested was the biggest story. Silas was booked and incarcerated, and so was Wilbur. Their trials would occur sometime in the future. But their colleagues in the news industry seemed to have no doubt they'd be found guilty.

I hired a local crew to finish fixing and scrubbing the kitchen wall. The cost was worth it.

And my life got back to normal ... mostly.

At least until that Friday night, when Reed and Hugo joined Biscuit and me at my house, and Neal and Janelle and Go were there, too. We were all in the living room watching—what else?—TV news, and there was a story about the ongoing investigation into the Schulzer murders and the current suspect.

When it was over, Neal used the remote to turn off the sound and walked over to look down at me where I sat on the sofa.

"Your presence is requested at the resort restaurant tomorrow evening, Ms. Kennersly. The town is throwing you a thank you celebration for getting to the bottom of this situation that had so many unanswered questions over the years, not to mention its most recent developments. Will we see you there around seven tomorrow night?"

I glanced at Reed, who nodded. There was a strange smile on his face that I couldn't quite read, but that was okay.

"You can count on my presence, Mr. Kennersly," I told Neal.

We all spent the night at our house, each couple giving the other one space.

When I eventually slid into my bed beside Reed, both of us in our pajamas with our dogs near us on the floor, I said, "The party idea is really sweet, but I think I've had enough attention over solving those murders. I just want to get fully back to my normal life."

Reed pulled me close. "I don't imagine you'll ever get back to the way things were before," he said. But before I could ask what he meant he began kissing me and using his hands in a highly enjoyable way . . . and so the subject was dropped.

I was full of anticipation the next day, like it or not. Dinah, at the shops, seemed so jazzed about my party that night. "It'll be even better than the birthday party you threw for me," she said. We were once again in the kitchen, baking, before the shops opened. "And you know how awesome that was."

"Yeah, and it also kind of led to a murder. Is that what this is all about? Who'll be the victim this time?"

Dinah laughed. "No victims," she said. "But I bet it'll be a lot of fun."

I hoped she was right—and I fretted for part of the day over what to wear. I decided on an outfit that was far from casual, but not formal, either—a pretty blue lacy blouse over a navy skirt, and short-heeled beige pumps. I wore a blue ribbon in my hair and tied a matching one around Biscuit's neck.

Neal told me he would drive Biscuit and me there and we'd meet everyone else in the restaurant. He parked in the employee lot and the three of us headed inside.

Reed had said he would meet us there too. He had some last minute things to finish at the clinic.

Neal, Biscuit, and I strolled through the resort lobby, which was busy as usual, and headed straight to the restaurant. We walked through the arched doorway. As when I'd thrown the party for Dinah, the area to the right was filled with people, and on the left side of the room a lot of tables had been pushed together to make one long one, with the restaurant's pristine white tablecloths gleaming on top of it.

But when I'd arrived for Dinah's gala, the party area had still been empty. Tonight, it seemed my entire world of people was there!

Near an empty spot at the head of the table sat Reed, with Janelle guarding another empty seat that was clearly for Neal. Hugo and Go were with them, too.

Then there were Arvie and the gang from my vet clinic. Joe and Irma Nash from Cuppa-Joe's. My assistants from my shops. Billi and Mimi from Mountaintop Rescue. Les Ethman and a couple of other City Council members.

And not far from where I would be sitting were Mayor Sybill Gabbon, Chief Loretta Jonas, and the two detectives. Wayne even handed me back my phone.

I cringed when I spotted Francine Metz from the *Knobcone News*, but at least I didn't see anyone try to step into Silas's role from KnobTV, at least not here.

"This is quite a celebration," I said to Neal.

"It's meant to be."

I was soon seated beside Reed, who looked very handsome in a suit. He handed me a glass of champagne. I gratefully took a sip. "Did you know things were going to be so … big?"

He smiled, and his eyes captured mine. He still seemed to be hiding his thoughts, but oh well. "I had a hunch they would be."

Our orders were soon taken—chicken, fish, or salad, and I chose fish. Then Neal rose and said, "Thank you all for coming. I always want to celebrate what a great person my sister is, but it's nice to see I'm not the only one. We'll talk more later."

He sat back down again. I was a little surprised he hadn't made a toast, but maybe that would come later, too.

Reed touched my arm. "It's a bit crowded in here. Let's go out to the balcony overlooking the lake." He shrugged his shoulder in the direction of the window. "Okay?"

"Sure."

We stood, and after we got Janelle to hold Biscuit's and Hugo's leashes with Go's, Reed took my hand. A few of the others looked in our direction but most kept up their conversations—although I saw a couple of smiles that hadn't been there before and wondered what they were talking about.

Reed led me out the door, then past the few people who were outside to the end of the balcony, where it was mostly dark. Lights from boats and the shoreline reflected on the lake. It was a pretty night. A pretty place. And—

Oh my. Suddenly Reed got down on one knee on the concrete pavement, still holding my hand.

"I thought we still had some talking to do," I choked.

"I think we've talked enough." Reed smiled and opened his other hand, which held a box. He let go of me and opened it—displaying a ring with a diamond. "Carrie Kennersly, I love you. Would you do me the honor of marrying me?"

"Oh, yes, Reed," I said. "I love you too."

He rose and put the ring on my finger—and I wasn't surprised when the lovely thing fit perfectly. Then we kissed.

And kissed again.

"We'd better go back inside." Reed sounded regretful.

"Does everyone know what we're doing out here?"

"Some do, and I'm sure the others suspect it."

"Maybe I should solve multiple murders, both historic and current, more often," I said as I clasped his hand—and as other people on the patio grinned at us.

"Maybe you shouldn't," he said, again looking down at me. I stopped, stood on my toes, and we kissed again.

"We'll see," I said. "Now, let's go have some more of that champagne."

I now knew why Reed had indicated last night that my life might never get back to normal.

And I was glad.

THE END

BARKERY AND BISCUITS DOG TREAT RECIPE

Grand-Dog Treats
½ cup water
¼ cup vegetable or canola oil
1 egg
2 tbsp crunchy peanut butter
¾ cup white whole wheat flour
¼ cup unbleached all purpose flour
¼ cup quick oats
¼ cup cornmeal

Preheat oven to 350°F. Line baking sheet with parchment paper.

Combine water, oil, egg, and peanut butter
in food processor (or mixer).

Stir together dry ingredients (flour through cornmeal) and add to
peanut butter batter. Mix until well combined. (Add more water if
dough is too crumbly.)

On a lightly floured surface, roll dough to about ¼" thick.
Cut dough into shapes using your favorite cookie cutters
and place on baking sheet.

Bake for 10 minutes. Remove from oven and turn treats over.
Return to oven and bake for another 10 minutes. Turn oven off
and leave treats in oven for another 20 minutes.

Remove from oven and allow to cool completely.

ICING ON THE CAKE PEOPLE TREAT RECIPE

Please be aware that because this recipe contains chocolate, it is *only* for people, not dogs! Chocolate can be poisonous to dogs.

Choco-Cranberry Drops
½ cup butter, softened
½ cup margarine, softened
1¼ cups firmly packed brown sugar
½ cup granulated sugar
2 eggs
2 tsps vanilla
1¾ cup flour
1 tsp baking soda
2¼ cups quick oats
1 cup semi-sweet chocolate morsels
1 cup dried cranberries

Heat oven to 375°F.

Beat butter, margarine, and sugars until creamy.

Add eggs and vanilla; beat well.

Combine flour and baking soda. Add to batter and mix well.

Stir in oats, chocolate morsels, and dried cranberries.

Drop by rounded tablespoonfuls onto
cookie sheet lined with parchment paper.

Bake 4 minutes on lower oven rack. Turn and bake
approximately 4 minutes on upper rack until golden brown.

Cool 1 minute on cookie sheet, then remove
to wire rack to cool completely.

Makes about 6 dozen cookies.

ACKNOWLEDGMENTS

Once again, I thank my wonderful agent Paige Wheeler. I also thank the great people at Midnight Ink who have worked with me, including editor Terri Bischoff and production editor Sandy Sullivan. I have enjoyed being a Midnight Ink author and will miss that wonderful mystery publisher when it is gone.

And again, I thank my friend Paula Riggin, who enjoys cooking and developing recipes. Once more, I owe the recipes included here to her: Grand-Dog Treats for dogs and Choco-Cranberry Drops for people.

© Christine Rose Elle

ABOUT THE AUTHOR

Linda O. Johnston (Los Angeles, CA) has published fifty romance and mystery novels, including the Pet Rescue Mystery series and the Kendra Ballantyne, Pet-Sitter Mystery series for Berkley Prime Crime. With Midnight Ink, she's published *Lost Under a Ladder, Knock on Wood,* and *Unlucky Charms* in the Superstition Mystery series, along with the first four Barkery & Biscuits Mysteries: *Bite the Biscuit, To Catch a Treat, Bad to the Bone*, and *Pick and Chews.*